The wings that came with the smoke were wide and white, and they carried the scent of burning leaves. With Te-kia, Dara soared above mountains frosted with ice and forests so green they shimmered in the clean, hard sunlight.

"We are risen again," Te-kia sang silently. "We are made of new blood and bone but the old love is in us and we are vigilant and clear-eyed. Let them do what they will across the sea. They will not kill our land again, not so long as one of us lives."

FEATHER STROKE

The Soaring New Fantasy by

SYDNEY J. VAN SCYOC

Author of
CLOUDCRY · BLUESONG · STARSILK · DARKCHILD

FEATHER STROKE

SYDNEY J. VAN SCYOC

AVON BOOKS 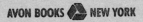 NEW YORK

FEATHER STROKE is an original publication of Avon Books. This work has never before appeared in book form. This work is a novel. Any similarity to actual persons or events is purely coincidental.

AVON BOOKS
A division of
The Hearst Corporation
105 Madison Avenue
New York, New York 10016

First Avon Books Printing: March 1989

AVON TRADEMARK REG. U.S. PAT. OFF. AND IN OTHER COUNTRIES, MARCA REGISTRADA, HECHO EN U.S.A.

Printed in the U.S.A.

K-R 10 9 8 7 6 5 4 3 2 1

CHAPTER ONE

It was afternoon and the sun beat hard at Wahonin, stinging Dara's bare forearms and drawing strong perfume from the turned earth. Straightening, she settled back on her heels to gaze at the tree-cloaked mountainside that rose above the field where she worked. She had never gone there, where the Ilijhari lived, nor to her knowledge had any of the simple folk. But she could guess how cool it must be among the shadows on a warm spring day. Blotting sweat from her forehead, she looked back over her shoulder at the sun, and for a moment it seemed to blaze even more brightly against the blue of the sky.

Brushing her forehead again, Dara glanced back at the seedlings she had just planted. She frowned. Pila's row was straight and careful. So was Tarnin's. But the seedlings Dara had planted wandered along the furrow, straggling from the soil at untidy angles. And her carrier was empty, although she did not remember setting the last flat of young plants into the ground.

"Dara, have you forgotten your turn with the pails?"

Dara started, flushing. How long had Chigar been standing behind her, watching as she went through the distracted motions of planting while caught in one of her absent spells? And when had the others finished their turns with the pails? She did not remember seeing them come and go.

Flustered, Dara jumped up, startling the yellow-beaks that poked at the freshly turned furrow. "I was just about to go."

"Were you now?" Chigar bared square white teeth in a smile that was half humorous, half challenging. A man could be persuaded, after all, to give a forgetful librarian work on his crew, but he did not have to expect much of her. "Then do it."

Dara shrank. "Yes. Of course."

Brushing the dirt from her hands, she hurried to the end of the field and took the yoke. The pails banged at her legs as she scrambled across the furrows toward the trees that lined the stream. She was intensely conscious of others looking up as she passed.

The streamside trees offered welcome shelter from their curious glances. The afternoon perfume was different there, brisker, lighter. The air was speckled and spattered with sunlight, and it was quiet except for the voice of the stream and the quarreling of the grey-duns in the treetops. Pausing, Dara glanced up into the dappled sunlight and felt her shoulders ease.

She knew she should not linger in the cool shade. Chigar was waiting. But to fill the pails and meet his mocking gaze again so soon . . . Sighing, Dara lowered the pails, lifted the hair off her neck, and drew a long slow breath.

She did not recognize her mistake until it was too late. Because by the time she drew the second slow breath, the weightlessness was upon her. Her thoughts drifted, rising and floating away like leaves, like feathers. She tried to retrieve them, but they evaded her. It almost seemed, as her consciousness scattered, that she was being buoyed away to some unnamed place, prisoner of the wind. She was briefly aware of the touch of mist against her cheek, of faint colors passing somewhere below. Then there was only absence: of thought, of awareness, of sensation.

And all it took to conduct her into the void was two long, slow breaths. Sometimes she was not even aware of drawing them.

"How long must we wait for the water, Dara?"

Dara shuddered, her eyes flying open. Dismayed, she looked up at Chigar, then down at the empty pails. The quarreling of the grey-duns suddenly seemed very loud. "A—a moment," she stammered, confused. How long had she been standing here, lost?

Long enough that Chigar had come himself to fetch her. And she hadn't even heard the sound of his boots on the soil. "Only a moment," she repeated. "I—I stopped to wash my feet. I—"

His sandy brows rose. He was a fair man, brawny, his face seamed by the sun. "They dried very quickly."

So quickly there was no sign of moisture anywhere. Dara stared down. "They did. And now I will fill the buckets. I'll—"

But Chigar had already bent for the pails, his broad face amused. "No. I will fill the buckets—and you will go to your father and tell him you're going back to your library table. I promised Norna a place on my crew when her youngest was ready to return to dayschool. She will join us tomorrow."

Norna was taking her place? In the middle of planting season? "Chigar—"

"Just tell your father I promised Norna a place and she's ready to begin. He'll understand."

Dara stared up at him in dismay. Of course her father would understand. She had worked with the spring planting crews before and had done little better than this time. In fact, her father had been reluctant to offer her another chance.

She had been just as reluctant to insist and chance failing again. But how could she accept nomination to Second Council if she could not share in the real work of the valley? If she could only sit behind library walls while everyone else worked in the sun?

Why had Fiorina and Rili even nominated her?

"Chigar, if I try harder—"

But he only shook his head, and this time he didn't smile. "There are only so many places on a crew, Dara, and my crew is filled."

"I'll tell my father," she said dully. Best to go directly

to his offices and tell him now. If she waited until the dinner hour, he would already have heard.

Still she hesitated at the edge of the trees before plunging across the field, her face burning.

She walked blindly until the halls lay ahead, a collection of long stone buildings erected at the center of the valley floor almost two centuries before. As simple as the simple folk themselves, built without flourish or ornamentation, they were grouped in squares of four, joined by flagged courtyards and walkways. Reaching them, Dara made her way down clean-swept walkways to the hall where her father had his offices.

It was dim and cool within the tall, beamed corridors. It was quiet too. Every person who could be spared was in the fields. Dara found Harmin sitting alone in his office, a single crop report open on the long table before him. Headsman not just of Wahonin but of all the five valleys where the simple folk lived on the new shore, he was made like the halls he governed, solid, square, and uncompromising. He wore his iron-grey hair clipped short, his shirt snugly belted. He glanced up and motioned Dara to a chair. If he was surprised to see her in the middle of a workday, he gave no sign. "You'll be reporting back to the library in the morning?"

Dara shrank. "Chigar spoke to you already."

"No, but why would you be here in the middle of a workday if you hadn't been discharged?"

So he had not appeared surprised to see her because he was not. Because he had fully expected that Chigar would discharge her sometime before the season was done.

At least he wasn't amused. She stared down at her hands. "I'll ask Fiorina and Rili to withdraw their nomination," she said in a low voice.

Harmin's eyes narrowed. "There is no reason for you to do that."

"Isn't there?" Dara looked up, stung by his tone. "How can I sit on Second Council when I can't even plant a row of seedlings? How can I vote on work projects when I can't work?"

Carefully Harmin closed the report and pushed it away. "You can't work? What is it you do in the library then?"

"I dust books. I copy reports. I help the teachers and planners find references," she said in exasperation.

"Is there anyone else who can do the work as well as you do it?"

"No one else spends all her time in the library." She had finished her schooling two years before. Yet she scarcely felt like an adult member of the community, locked up behind library walls each day. "I think I'm wind-touched. I think Chanona has set a sprite in my mind," she said bitterly.

Certainly that made as much sense as any other explanation. Sometimes her thoughts deserted her even when she was safely at her worktable. They deserted her— and she didn't know where they went. She didn't know where *she* went, except that she drifted. Like a leaf. Like a feather. Like a wind priestess from one of her grandmother's tales of the old land.

Harmin's face darkened. "Your grandmother was a foolish woman. Had she spent her last years weaving linen instead of tales—

"And you know very well that we don't speak by name of the Four here. Nor do we build temples to them or make them offerings or pay tithes to their priests and priestesses. We fled the old shore to be done with those things. And the stories your grandmother told you—"

"I never believed them," Dara said defensively, although at times she had. At times she had believed that the earth lived and bore the name Nod, that the waters answered to the name Serinona, that the sun called itself Tith, that—

"Oh, the Four are real, but they have no life. They have no will. They don't hear and speak. Certainly they don't reward those who offer at their altars and punish those who hold back. The men and women who use their names do that.

"But no longer do the priests of the Four live off us. Not on this shore. And remember, their powers aren't a gift of the Four. They're inborn, as accidental as the wind—and little more useful most of the time.''

Embarrassed, Dara stared down at her hands.

''And you have abilities we need, even if you insist upon deprecating them. Fiorina and Rili would never have submitted your name—and I would never have approved it—if we didn't think you had something to offer.''

Dara met his eyes and glanced quickly away. ''Please let me think about it,'' she pleaded, slipping from the chair.

''There is responsibility as well as honor in this nomination,'' Harmin reminded her.

''Yes.'' Didn't he understand? It was precisely that that frightened her. Mirina had accepted nomination to Second Council without qualm, but Mirina had inherited all Harmin's authority, all his certainty. Mirina would be headsman one day, if she chose. Dara knew very well that she would never be.

Harmin sighed, dissatisfied with her response. ''It will be afternoon bell soon. Go to your room. Wash and change for dinner.''

''Yes,'' she said.

But when she reached her room, she neither washed nor changed. She threw herself across the down-stuffed quilt that covered her bed and fell asleep, suddenly too tired to think.

She woke just before afternoon bell and lay quietly, holding to the uncluttered stillness of the room. Freshly whitened stone walls, unornamented bureau and worktable, deep-silled windows— She had put no mark upon the room. That would have been vanity. Yet it was very much her own, just as it once had been very much her mother's and very much her grandmother's.

Stiffly, Dara rose and went to the window. The sun was low in the sky. It cast long rays across the courtyard below. Swords of Tith her grandmother had called those last, long blades of light. Workers streamed among them, returning from the fields to dress for dinner.

Dara turned back to her bed, then spun to the window

again at the sound of hooves clattering up the track from the woodland road.

A rider emerged from an elongated cloud of dust and pulled his horse to a halt in the courtyard. He slid down, a young man dressed in a tailored uniform, red trimmed with gold. When his boots struck the pavement, his horse snorted and tried to back away. The young man jerked roughly at its reins, and the horse screamed and raised fine-boned legs to dash its hooves against the stone flagging.

"Messenger from Master Rinari!"

Dara stared at the animal in the courtyard. It was like a creature from her grandmother's tales of the old shore, like a horse bred to bear aristocrats or their armed guard. She had seen nothing like it when she visited Port Calibe with her father two years before. Certainly it was a different breed from the heavy-boned, phlegmatic animals her own people kept. And the gold-trimmed coat and trousers the messenger wore— No one dressed that way in Port Calibe.

But they had dressed that way in her grandmother's tales of Hemnistora and Khanistra.

She studied the animal a moment longer, disturbed by its very grace, then turned to her door. By the time she reached the courtyard, her father was striding across the pavement.

"Are you Harmin? Headsman here?" Seen more closely, the messenger was a hatchet-faced young man with a crooked nose and challenging eyes.

"I am."

The young man shrank slightly from Harmin's narrow-eyed frown, then squared his shoulders. "Well, the master's coming tomorrow. He'll be here with morning to meet with you. So hold yourself ready." Without waiting for a response, the messenger jerked again at the horse's reins and swung himself back into the saddle. Kicking the animal, he made it dance a restless circle before he spurred it away.

Dara stared after him as he disappeared into the evening, wondering what it meant: a horse and guard from her grandmother's tales appearing in their courtyard at dusk—and just as abruptly disappearing.

But no, they hadn't come from a tale. They had come from Kels Rinari, whose trading company took grain and linen from Wahonin in exchange for manufactured goods from the old shore.

And he was coming tomorrow? To speak with Harmin?

Frowning, puzzled, Dara turned to find Mirina looking after the horse and messenger with a troubled frown. Dara glanced down, ashamed of the quick, familiar flutter of inadequacy. If she could be so poised as her sister, so competent, if she could be so tall and fair and blue-eyed—

But Dara was none of those things. Instead she was slight and dark-haired, with eyes the grey of slate. No one, seeing them together, would guess that they were sisters. "Why is he coming now?" Dara wondered aloud. "We signed the trade contracts two months ago." There was no reason for Rinari to return to Wahonin again until fall, when the grain was ready.

And why was Mirina so pale? She met Dara's anxious gaze and said absently, "Aren't you going to dress for dinner, Dara?"

Dara glanced down at her clothes, stained from the field. "I'm not hungry."

Mirina sighed, frowning toward the track where the messenger had vanished. Finally, with an effort, she met Dara's glance again. "Nor am I, and the dining hall will be full of talk. I'll bring a tray to your room for us both. Soup—and cheese pastry if you want it."

Dara frowned. Didn't Mirina want to join in the speculation about the messenger and his message?

Dara shrugged. Certainly she did not. Rinari had come to Wahonin four times since his arrival on this shore, and he had never given her more than a disinterested glance. Yet even that brief intersection of gazes had made her start and flush. He was a man of the old world, and while he had always traded fairly with them, she had heard stories of how he had acquired his share of Fidler, Wasson and Rinari.

Meeting his glance, she had believed the stories, all of them. "I'd like the pastry," she said. "If you want me to go for it—"

"No, I must talk to Father. We have a meeting after dinner." But she stood for a while longer gazing into the dusk before she went.

It was dark and the fuel lamp threw shadows on the walls before Mirina appeared with the tray. They placed it between them on the bed, as they had done many times before when they wanted to talk over a meal. But this time Mirina ate silently, her head bowed, a distracted frown contracting her brows.

When the tray was bare, Dara set it on the bureau and turned back to the bed. Mirina frowned over a torn nail now, although clearly it was not the nail that disturbed her. Dara sat carefully on the puffy coverlet. "Mirina, does Father know why Rinari is coming?"

Mirina glanced up, then quickly down again. "I'm sure he has his reasons."

Dara frowned, disturbed by the faint bitterness of the words, more disturbed by the mood underlying them. She stared down at her own hands. They were slender and unblemished, with smoothly tapering fingers. Impulsively she counterposed them against Mirina's hands, strong and callused and stained. Hands that worked, hands that did not. "I wish mine were like yours."

Mirina laughed softly, casting aside her distraction for the first time since the messenger had come. "Then let us trade, because I like yours better." She caught Dara's fingers before Dara could pull them away and her face became serious again. "Dara, you must not yield to your uncertainty. Father wants you to accept more responsibility, and you're afraid. But you can bear it. You won't fail on Second Council. You'll see. A year from now you'll feel far more sure of yourself than you do today."

Dara drew back. How did Mirina always know what she

was thinking? "You never felt the way I feel now." Anxious. Unsure. Inadequate.

"Of course I did. And one day you'll feel as I feel now. I'm certain of it. But until then, you must not yield to your uncertainty. You must not let it limit you. You must step beyond it. Will you promise me that? No matter what happens, will you promise me that?"

Dara caught her breath. "What—what is going to happen?"

Mirina glanced quickly down, her lips tightening. She folded Dara's fingers over her own and pressed them. "Anything can happen at any time. You know that. I want your promise, Dara."

Dara licked her lips, uneasy with the evasion. "You know why Kels Rinari is coming."

"No. I don't. And even if I did, you owe me a promise."

Dara stared at her. If she didn't know, why had she just used those words? *No matter what happens.* Why did she refuse to meet Dara's eyes now?

And why refuse to tell her what she guessed? Or what she knew?

"I promise," Dara said reluctantly. "But Mirina—I'll go to the tower to watch for him tomorrow." If no one would confide in her, at least she could do that much.

Mirina squeezed Dara's hands again, sliding off the bed. "I'll be in the field. If you would run to Father's office as soon as you see Rinari—"

"I will. And if you want to stay tonight, or if you want me to stay with you—" Because it was clear that Mirina was troubled.

"No, no, the meeting will run late. I would only wake you coming in." Briefly she took Dara's hands again. "But thank you. Thank you for thinking of it." She smiled, lingering for a moment. "We're so different, Dara. Do you know, I think sometimes I know the reason for it—so that each of us can help the other when she needs it."

But when had Mirina ever needed it? She wouldn't even

admit now that she needed help, for whatever reason. Impulsively Dara embraced her, then went to the window to watch her cross the courtyard below. Her grey gown quickly merged into the shadows, but her fair hair was visible for moments longer.

Dara sat on the sill until the moon rose. Then she extinguished her lamp and went to bed.

CHAPTER TWO

Dara woke before sunrise and slipped quietly down the stairs to the courtyard. The morning was grey and still. Animals called from their pens and domestic fowl complained sleepily to one another. Glancing up, she saw a single catch-fly watching her from its nest beneath the eaves, its eyes half-lidded. Dara passed around the side of the hall and down a sheltered walkway to the library. There she packed pen and ink and clean linen pages into a case. At least she could do copywork while she listened for the sound of hooves.

The tower stood at Wahonin's eastern extremity, ivy-webbed and square, built of quarried stone. It had seven broad-balconied floors constructed around an interior staircase. Two hours later Dara paced the top floor, still too tense to open the writing case. She paused at each broad window in turn, watching.

To her east, the narrow road that emerged from the woodland and led up the slope to Wahonin was deserted. To her west, the halls of the settlement itself were clustered sturdy and square at the heart of the valley. Planting crews worked in the fields, undisturbed. Barely an hour earlier, an Ilijhari had descended the lower slope of the mountain, his hunter gliding after him, the smaller birds of the valley sweeping around him in noisy celebration.

Their cries were lost over the distance, but some shrill echo had touched Dara anyway. Because the stillness, the peace below meant nothing today. There was no good reason for Kels Rinari to ride to Wahonin.

Another hour passed. Restless, Dara stepped into the morning sunlight and paced around the balcony, looking down over the orchards and grazing fields. Strangely, the sun seemed to brighten as she watched, growing briefly more intense.

Some trick of the eyes, Dara decided, and leaned against the warm stone wall. Almost immediately the familiar lightness gripped her and the colors of land and sky began to shift and bend.

She started erect at the sound of hooves and peered down the woodland road, her heart racing at the quickly rising volume of the sound.

Kels Rinari had not come alone. Twenty riders emerged from the trees below, riding in a double column. They were dressed in uniforms of red and gold, as Rinari's messenger had been. Long blades glinted at their sides. Kels Rinari rode at their head, caped in black, astride the only white horse. He was unmistakable even from this distance, his brows like black wings, his jaws broad and tightly held. His blade was bright, his boots so highly burnished that they glinted. Behind him rolled a horse-drawn cart, a small carved chest lashed to its bed.

It took Dara a moment to understand what she saw. Then she drew a shivering breath, stricken with cold. If Rinari thought he could ride here out of one of her grandmother's tales, bringing a *damen-kest* with him—

The twenty uniformed men who rode with him had not come from a tale. They had come from the docks at Port Calibe. Their salt-burned faces told her that. But Rinari— Rinari had come to Port Calibe from the old shore, where aristocrats still rode into the valleys of the simple folk, bearing the *damen-kest*.

He had come for Mirina.

Dara had never guessed she could run so fast. She descended six flights of stairs without a second breath. She didn't even feel the ground beneath her boots as she raced through the orchards and across the grazing fields. She stumbled once, picked herself up, and then she was pounding across the paved courtyard toward the hall where her father had his offices.

Kels Rinari was coming for Mirina, and both Mirina and their father had guessed it.

The sound of her boots preceded her down the long, beamed corridors. A crew of sweepers turned and gaped after her. Ebin, her father's assistant, was already on his feet when she reached the office. His mouth gaped with alarm.

Dara had just enough breath to speak. "My father—"

"He's gone to the pharmacy. The Ilijhari—"

Of course. The Ilijhari she had seen earlier had come from the mountain to trade. Quickly Dara ran down the corridor to the pharmacy where her mother had once worked.

She found the pharmacist and her assistants gathered warily at one side of the anteroom. At the far side of the room, the Ilijhari had unloaded bundles of dried herbs on a long table. Their tang mingled with the other scents of the pharmacy: sweet, musty, sharp.

The Ilijhari turned at the sound of Dara's boots, his glance grey, unsurprised. Lithe, slightly built, he wore his dark hair pulled back in a single braid decked with bright feathers. His quirri perched on his shoulder, studying Dara with piercing yellow eyes. The lobe of the Ilijhari's left ear was mutilated, as if the bird had torn it.

Meeting his gaze, Dara took an involuntary step back, her breath catching painfully. Although why she should be afraid of the Ilijhari, why anyone should be afraid of an Ilijhari—

There was no reason, yet everyone was wary when savages came from the mountainside to trade. Dara forced herself to speak. "My father—has my father been here?"

The pharmacist glanced uneasily at the Ilijhari. "He went to the meeting hall. Someone—" She hesitated, confused. "Someone said there were horsemen coming. A company of them."

So that moment of absence, her face turned to the sun,

had delayed her long enough that someone had already reported Rinari's approach. Dara turned away.

She had only to cross the courtyard to reach the meeting hall. She found her father there, sitting alone at the long council table, his hands knotted on the white-scrubbed tabletop.

"Father—" Dara drew a steadying breath. "May I stay? He's bringing— Kels Rinari is bringing a chest. It looks—"

Harmin directed her to a chair. "Te-kia told me what Rinari is bringing. I've sent for Mirina."

Dara hesitated, frowning uncertainly. Te-kia had told him? How could the Ilijhari have told her father about the *damen-kest* when she had seen him enter the hall almost an hour before Kels Rinari had emerged from the woodland? Unless what she had heard was true, that the Ilijhari could see through the eyes of their quirri. Frowning, Dara took a chair.

Mirina came a few minutes later, her face tightening as her eyes flickered between them. She wore her field clothes, and her hair was drawn back in a careless knot. "Tell me," she said in a low voice, slipping into a chair.

Harmin's voice was as hard as his eyes. "Kels Rinari is riding up the woodland road with a uniformed escort and a *damen-kest*."

Mirina's features drew still more taut. "So it isn't an offer he intends. It's a demand." Carefully banked anger flashed in her eyes. "And what makes him think he's entitled to bring a *damen-kest* here? Has he found someone to sell him a title? And what does it mean on this shore if he has?"

Harmin shook his head. "I doubt he's bought himself a name. I don't think he can prove the blood for that. But the men who hold the ports to the south have granted themselves titles on their own authority. Why not Rinari?"

"And he expects us to honor that? Two hundred years after our people left Hemnistora, he expects us to honor a title with nothing behind it?"

Harmin's brows drew hard together. "Make no mistake,

Mirina. He's better than some we've dealt with in Port Calibe, but he's a looter and he has a looter's mentality. He expects us to honor whatever he can force us to honor.''

Mirina drew a long breath, staring down at the tabletop. "How do you want me to answer him?"

Harmin frowned at the bitterness of the question. "Have I ever asked you to speak any way but from your own conviction?''

Mirina released a long breath and stared down at her clasped hands. "No. Of course not.''

Tensely, Dara glanced from one to the other of them, waiting for them to go on. Waiting for them to name the solution to the problem. Because surely they knew what to do.

But neither of them spoke again until hooves clattered in the courtyard. Then, deliberately, Harmin leaned back in his chair. "We will not rise when he enters," he said. "Dara, you will say nothing while he is in the room. I will say as little as possible. We know the place they give women in Port Calibe. It will put him off his stride when he finds he must speak directly with you, Mirina.''

Mirina nodded grimly. "I will put him as much off his stride as I know how.''

The strike of hooves on flagging, the clatter of boots, and Kels Rinari was at the door, taking possession of the long, plainly furnished room with a glance. He was a man little older than Mirina, yet he was tall and stark in his black cape. And his presence, the force and tension of his character, were even larger than his person. His boots struck the stone floor sharply as he approached the table. Dara recoiled as he unsheathed his long blade and struck the tabletop with the flat of it.

Two uniformed men hurried to place the small carved chest where he indicated. The other men of his troop stamped into the room and arrayed themselves stiffly against the rear wall. Distractedly, Dara noticed that all were young and that none was as trim as his uniform, nor as clean.

When Rinari had every eye, he opened the chest. The

satins he unfurled were white, scarlet and a purple so dark it was almost black. "Headsman, you recognize what you see here." With his blade, he touched each color in turn. He spoke ceremonially, but with a hard undertone of purpose. "Here is your daughter's purity, which I have come to claim. Here is my strength, which I offer in your protection. And here—" He tapped the purple-black fabric. "Here is the blood of our enemies, as soiled and dark as it will be when my sword spills it on the stones of your dooryard. Answer my petition with your consent, and of these three things will our pact be constituted." Hard-eyed, unsmiling, he sheathed his blade.

So the demand had been formally made. Dara's heart pounded at her ribs, whether from anger or fear she didn't know. Tensely she glanced at Mirina.

Mirina sat easily in her chair, her hands clasped loosely in her lap, as if she considered Rinari's demand no more than casual conversation. Only her paleness betrayed her—that and the faltering timbre of her voice when she first spoke. "Mr. Rinari, I believe you have mistaken the century and the continent."

Rinari's eyes flickered briefly to Harmin, then settled on Mirina. He squared his shoulders, his features rigid and impatient at once. "I know very well when and where I am."

"Do you?" Mirina's voice was light, almost disinterested. "When my grandmother lived, she told me romances of the old land. At least, she considered them romances. I suppose even now in Hemnistora and Khanistra, nobles come riding into the valleys where my distant relations make their homes and demand the headsmen's daughters as their wives. Because even in the old land, even now, the simple folk hold to their principles and their ways. And where else can a nobleman find a wife who will never intrigue with his enemies or bear a lover's child instead of his own? Where else can he find a wife who cannot be turned against him with the promise of possessions or privileges? Those things mean nothing to us. We don't adorn our persons and we don't adorn our homes.

We have no taste for vanity or excess—and no stomach for deceit.

"But my own family left Hemnistora two centuries ago. We came to this shore decades before the first trading port was established. And we are well pleased with the life we have made for ourselves in these five valleys. We pay tithes to no temple—because there are no temples. We aren't obliged to send children to serve the priests. There are no priests. And I am not required to marry any noble-man who comes riding into my valley and demands me—because there are no noblemen here.

"I understand that you began as a looter, in fact. A looter of ships belonging to the men you now call your colleagues."

Rinari's face darkened. His brows drew together in a hard line. "Fidler and Wasson are my partners. And yes, I bought into partnership with their own goods. I had nothing of my own. Nor had they before they went looting the shipping lanes twenty years before me." One hand bunched on the skein of scarlet satin. Incongruously the broad nails were so clean, so well trimmed that they appeared sculpted. "But I have something now. I have a third interest in the largest trading company that runs from Port Calibe, and I have a house and barracks and men to guard my grounds. And with it all, it is time I had a wife I can trust and allies with some substance to them."

His dark eyes darted back to Harmin. "Headsman, we are men who see clearly, both of us. We see the future we want for this land. Yet neither of us is proof alone against the future others may try to force upon us instead. So I tell you this: I will have a wife from your house, and thereafter I will protect your house as I protect my own. In return, you will supply my household as if it were a part of your own and you will give me and my men retreat here should we require it. The customs that serve in the old land will serve us both here."

Harmin's brows drew together in a brief frown. But he only inclined his head, acknowledging Rinari's words without responding to them.

Mirina's hands tightened in her lap, but when she spoke, her voice was as light, as unconcerned as before. "Whom do you propose to protect us against, Master Rinari? To my knowledge, we have no enemies here."

Rinari's gaze flicked back to her in irritation. "You will have," he said impatiently. He turned back to Harmin and bared teeth as clean and unflawed as his nails. "Headsman—"

"Yourself, for instance, if I choose not to come to your house in Port Calibe?" Mirina suggested.

This time the face Rinari turned to Mirina was openly threatening. "If you insist upon asking a man's questions, then I'll give you a man's answer. Yes, I will be your enemy. So will my two partners—and any other associate I call upon. You have a fine home here, in its plain way. What is this rich land for, if not for taking? What are these solid buildings for? What are these people for? They're good workers. They will farm this land as well for me as they do for you, if you insist that it be so."

Spots of color appeared in Mirina's cheeks. "I see. And with everything else, what am I for?" she suggested.

Rinari's eyes narrowed, then gleamed. Suddenly he seemed to find pleasure in the exchange. "Exactly! What are you for, if not for the taking? And you need not remind me that I have no traceable bloodline. I learned I was no aristocrat the first time I had my face scrubbed in the mud as a child. No, I have no standing on the old shore. But here we begin with a fresh slate. Here the nobleman is the man who chooses to call himself that. I choose so, and the children you give me will have whatever advantage and whatever protection a title can be made to yield.

"And if you choose not to give me children, then the children you do bear will know how mud stings the nostrils. Your father will know how it feels to be headsman of a ruined valley. Your people will know what it is to starve. And I don't say any of this emptily." His gaze passed from Mirina to Harmin, from Harmin to Dara. Then he turned sharply and strode to the door. When he turned back, he tapped one bootheel against the stone floor. "Your answer, Headsman?"

Strangely, Dara heard tension as well as arrogance in the question. She saw the same thing in his eyes, in the set of his lips.

Harmin cleared his throat. "The answer, of course, is for my daughter to make."

Rinari's black brows rose steeply, like angrily arching wings. He turned to Mirina. "Your answer then?"

Dara glanced at her sister and felt her throat tighten. There were isolated spots of color in Mirina's cheeks, and her eyes had a hard sparkle. "I am so pleased you came, Mr. Rinari. We've met before, of course, but so briefly. I didn't understand until today that in your way you are as principled as I am."

"I have one principle: strength."

"Exactly. I have one principle too: responsibility. I believe that whatever I say, whatever I do, whatever decision I make is my responsibility and only mine. I can blame no one else for what I do, and no one can absolve me if I choose the wrong course. So I must consider every alternative very carefully. That is my principle.

"Now I see that whatever you do, you do with an equally clear-cut principle."

"Then you see me clearly. My principle is to be strong, not weak," Rinari said, pacing nearer, his gaze holding hers. "And that means I intend to be rich, not poor. I intend to take and to hold, not to yield. However great the force brought against me, I will not bend. I will give up everything at once rather than give myself away in pieces. Whoever wants what I have must kill me or die."

For a moment Mirina was very still, very alert. Then, slowly, the tension left her body. At the same time, the glitter left her eyes and the color deserted her cheeks. "Yes. The lines of your character are as firmly drawn as my own," she said almost indifferently. "You will have my answer tomorrow evening. My father will bring it to you at your home in Port Calibe."

Rinari frowned, disconcerted. "You have no more argument about my blood?"

"I will treat you as the person you declare yourself. I will send my answer." Carefully Mirina stood. "Now if you will excuse me? I have work." Stepping around the table, she moved past him, past his men, out the door.

Her footsteps sounded firmly on the stones of the courtyard, then were gone. Rinari turned to watch her, then turned back to Harmin. Much of the force had gone from his face. Tension and strain remained. He nodded at Dara. "Headsman, if we can speak alone—"

Harmin stood. "There is no point in speaking until we can discuss my daughter's answer."

Rinari scowled. "There may be more point than you realize. There may be—"

Harmin shook his head. "Mr. Rinari, if I'm to spend tomorrow traveling to Port Calibe, there is work I must attend to today. Whatever you wish to discuss will wait."

Rinari drew himself up and for a moment it seemed he would argue. Then he shook his head. "I will station men at the posthouses along the road to ensure your safety," he said. "We've had a break from the port prison. There are thieves and deserters in the woodland, trying to find their way from the area."

"I'll be alert for their presence," Harmin said with flat disinterest. "And now I must excuse myself."

Rinari hesitated, obviously reluctant to be so casually dismissed. "Tell your daughter I will receive her on the date she designates."

"I will tell her you said it," Harmin said with as little interest as before.

Flushing, Rinari turned away. His boots struck the floor sharply as he withdrew. His men followed.

Dara ran to the courtyard to watch the troop depart. Their horses threw their heads and squealed shrilly as they skittered across the flaggings. Then they pounded down the road, raising plumes of dust. Dara turned. Her father stood behind her, his face set, unbetraying. People had left their work and stood at the margins of the courtyard. Others watched from the windows.

For a moment Dara was grimly pleased. If Rinari had come expecting them to bow tamely to him, then he had been mistaken. And he had gone away with his face burning.

But he had not withdrawn his demand. "She can't go," Dara said.

Harmin shook his head, gazing narrowly down the road. "No. No matter what Rinari's situation, no matter what has driven him to this demand, if she goes, there will be no end to it. Any looter who can put together a personal guard will think he's entitled to present the *damen-kest*. Soon they'll conscript our sons to work on their piers and in their counting rooms. And eventually they'll let the priests in to build temples and collect their tithes from us all. It will be just as it was on the other shore. And it will be that way because we permitted it."

Dara frowned. She had not considered Rinari's demand in those terms. She had thought only of Mirina. "But if she doesn't go— Do you think he means it? Do you think he means what he said?"

"That he will ruin us?" Harmin's eyes were cold blue stone. "Why shouldn't he ruin us? What are we to him if we refuse to be used?"

"But can he do it?"

Harmin shrugged. "We are a few thousand people scattered among five valleys. We have no weapons beyond our implements and tools, and no tradition in the use of weapons if we had them. Nor do we have friends or allies anywhere on this shore. Rinari has only to come with rabble from the port and destroy our crops and we'll starve."

And Kels Rinari would do that to have Mirina, Dara realized with sinking heart. But no, not to have Mirina. To have what he had decided to have. There was a difference.

Could Mirina permit that? Could she permit Wahonin to be destroyed? "We could set guards on the fields. We—"

Harmin had turned to the people who stood at the margins of the courtyard. "Go back to your work. We will discuss this later."

"Father, if we kept people in the tower to watch for him— If we posted sentries—"

"Daughter, even if we found weapons and taught ourselves to use them—overnight—Rinari and his friends could turn more evil loose on us than we'd ever be able to ward off. We don't take our living from the ground easily, and he can hurt us in a hundred ways. Perhaps no one of them would be fatal alone. But together?"

Reluctantly Dara nodded. She knew how hard it was to fill the granaries and the storehouses when the ground thawed late, when insects swarmed, when a summer sickness passed through the field crews. If Rinari set his hand against them, it would be impossible to bring the crops to harvest. She stared down at her own hands, slender, tapering, unmarked, and was suddenly ashamed of them. "Father, if you would assign me to a planting crew again—" Surely if she tried harder—

"You have work in the library. You should be there now."

Work? How could he call it work, sitting in a cool room, copying faded texts onto fresh cloth? Dara bowed her head, desperately choking back argument. "Yes. But, Father, what will she do? Can she refuse him if—" If it meant Wahonin must be destroyed?

A vein jumped in Harmin's temple. "That is for Mirina to decide. She will tell us when she has done so." He turned and strode back toward his offices.

Helplessly Dara watched him go. Then, just as helplessly, she stepped to the edge of the courtyard. It was barely an hour since she had looked out over the valley from the watchtower. The morning was as warm, as still as it had been then. Crews worked in the fields, fowl quarreled in their pens, and somewhere the children of the dayschool laughed.

Everything was the same, yet everything had changed. Kels Rinari had cast his shadow over Wahonin. Dara felt the chill in the air.

CHAPTER THREE

The afternoon was longer than any Dara remembered. She sat at the library table and ruined every page she touched pen to. Low voices in the corridor, children laughing, the call of the yellow-beaks who nested outside the window— Was she the only one who realized the calm was false? Fear came in cold waves. Her thoughts ran in circles.

Mirina could not go to Kels Rinari.

Mirina could not refuse him and let Wahonin be destroyed.

Occasionally people stepped into the room and spoke to her. Afterward she could not even remember what they had said. When afternoon bell sounded, she deserted her table, leaving the pen unwashed and the ink bottle open, and ran to the hall where Mirina had quarters. There she perched at the foot of Mirina's bed, her hands twisting the fabric of her trousers.

The worst of it was that when Mirina came, Dara didn't know what to say. She stood, wordless, searching her sister's face for some sign that she was welcome.

Mirina was as pale as she had been when she left the meeting hall. Her hair had strayed from its knot and her face was smudged. She carried a small bunch of dried wildflowers in one hand. She laid them on the bureau after a blank moment and inclined her head, touching her hair. "Have you come to braid my hair for dinner?"

"Yes. Yes, that's why I came," Dara agreed quickly,

24

although neither of them had worn braids since their mother's death.

"Then let me wash and change first. It was so warm this afternoon."

So warm in the sun, where she had worked while Dara sat in the cool of the library. Dara bit her lip. "Will you wear the clips Mother left you?"

Mirina stepped to the bureau and poured water from pitcher to basin. "Yes, and the linen shirt Grandmother made for her first stitchery lesson. Will you get it for me?"

Dara lingered for a moment, uncertainly, then hurried down the corridor and brought the fragile, awkwardly stitched shirt from storage. It smelled of the herbal sachets the hall keepers used to sweeten the closets against winter damp. She pressed the fabric to her face and thought of her mother and her grandmother.

She found the clips in the top drawer of the bureau. They were plain, unornamented. There was no vanity to them. Yet they gleamed richly in her hand.

When Mirina had washed, she stood silently while Dara worked with her hair, making thick white-gold braids, coiling them around her head and clipping them carefully into place. Dara's hands shook as she worked. They must be thinking the same thing. Why couldn't they speak of it?

Dara tried to begin, but no words came. When she was done with Mirina's braids, Mirina stepped away and turned to look searchingly back at her. "Tell me what you're thinking."

Dara's shoulders sagged with relief. At least they were going to speak of it. And what *could* she be thinking? "Have you decided what you will do?"

Mirina's eyes met hers. They were the color of the summer sky, but there was no brightness in them. She glanced down at the bundle of dried flowers she had laid so carelessly on her bureau. "I decided before I left the hall."

Dara frowned, remembering the hard sparkle she had seen in Mirina's eyes, remembering the moment when it had vanished. "He's scum," she said fiercely. "He's exactly what you called him: a looter. He's—'' Dismayed, she checked herself. Mirina's expression had not changed, yet she had somehow withdrawn. "You—you don't intend to go to him?" How could she? How could she ever let him touch her?

How could she refuse him, knowing the consequences?

"You felt nothing for the fact that he knows what it is to be oppressed and that he refuses to be oppressed again? That he began with nothing and now has a house and a mounted guard and a trading company?"

"He has those things, but how did he get them?" Dara demanded.

Mirina raised her shoulders in a light shrug. She seemed detached, as if she stood at a distance from her own argument. "The only way he could. The only way any man in their world can. But of course if we once let them introduce the old customs on this shore, we've lost the very things we came here for."

Freedom from the *damen-kest*. Freedom from work conscription. Freedom from the tithes and a dozen other forms of oppression. "So you won't go," Dara said—and immediately felt not relief but the cold sting of fear. When would Kels Rinari come with his men? Would they come at harvesttime, with torches? Or sooner? Perhaps as soon as Harmin delivered Mirina's answer.

Mirina crossed the room and gazed out the window, staring into the distant sky for so long that Dara grew uneasy. Then, silently, she turned and extended her hands.

Dara took them. The fingers were cold. "Mirina, if you want me to tell Father what you've decided—'' Surely she could do that much, although he had probably already guessed what her decision would be.

Mirina shook her head. "No, you needn't. He'll know it from me. Shouldn't you wash and dress for dinner, too?"

Did she want to be alone? She already seemed far away. "Yes. I should," Dara agreed quickly.

"Good. Come back to me later then, at last bell, and

hold my hands again. Warm them for me a little. Will you do that, Dara?''

Dara stepped back, confused. "Yes, if you want."

"I want. And remember you made me a promise last night."

A promise not to yield to her uncertainty, not to let it hold her back. Dara dropped Mirina's hands and kissed her lightly, quickly on the cheek. Then she fled, carrying with her a strange, frozen image of Mirina's face, so pale it seemed carved from whitestone, a single tear poised at the corner of one eye.

Tith cast his swords across the courtyard below her window when she reached her room. Dara stared at them, remembering the flash of Kels Rinari's blade against satin, reviewing her disturbingly unresolved conversation with Mirina. Then, hardly aware of what she did, she slipped into fresh trousers and shirt and pulled her hair into a knot at the nape of her neck.

By the time she reached the dining hall, the tables were crowded. She guessed, from the way the talk quieted as she made her way to her place, that people were discussing Kels Rinari's visit, that they didn't want her to hear. She took her seat and glanced around the room. She met questioning eyes on every side. Neither Mirina nor her father had come yet.

The meal was half-done before she glanced up again and saw the Ilijhari sitting nearby, alone except for his quirri. The hunting bird crouched on the tabletop, tearing at a chunk of raw meat. Dara watched, grimly fascinated, until she realized that the Ilijhari watched her in turn.

She frowned down at her platter, confused. Why should the Ilijhari study her? He seldom spoke to anyone but the pharmacist and her father when he came to trade. Certainly she had not known him to come to the dining hall before.

How much did he understand of their language? Of their customs? He was dressed like a man of Wahonin, in clothes taken in trade, and he was as carefully groomed as any other in the room. Dara glanced covertly at the

Ilijhari again, then saw her father making his way across the dining hall. His face had the same carved pallor she had seen on Mirina's face earlier. He spoke to no one until he reached the table. "Your sister will eat in her room."

The taut set of his jaw did not encourage questions. "Does she want me to bring her something?" Dara asked quickly, half rising.

"No, Fiorina has already sent up a tray. She wants us both to come to her at last bell," he said and did not speak again before leaving the table a few minutes later, his dinner untouched.

When he did not return, Dara cleared his platter with hers and made her way from the dining hall. Groups of people parted around her, their glances questioning, concerned. Those who greeted her did so in low voices, telling her more with the quick squeeze of hands than with words.

She hesitated in the corridor, reluctant to return to her room and listen to the normal sounds of evening: the tread of boots in the corridor, low voices from the courtyard, the occasional protest from the stock pens. Because this was no normal evening. There might not be a normal evening again.

Yet it was too early to knock at Mirina's door. Dara turned and slipped down the corridor toward the little-used rear door of the hall.

The air was cool now, the sky clear. Dara paused for a moment, listening to the catch-flies that nested beneath the eaves. Then she slipped around the back of the hall and down a sheltered walkway.

A forgotten calf wandered in the grazing field, trailing a misshapen shadow. In the orchard, the trees exuded night-perfume. The watchtower cast a rugged silhouette against the starlit sky. Dara paused at the foot of the first flight of stairs, gazing up into the shadows. It didn't seem so many years since she and Mirina had slipped away to the tower on summer nights and picked their way up the vines that laddered the tower walls, laughing as they scrambled through the broad-silled windows. It was hard tonight to believe they had ever been so young. Quickly she ran up the stairs.

She paused on the fourth landing, peering out the east-ward window toward the woodland. Once, on a clear night, she and Mirina had seen the lights of Port Calibe winking a tawdry yellow in the distance. Or so they had told each other. Dara had not realized how far the port city lay from Wahonin until she had gone there with her father a year later. The journey had taken most of a day by wagon.

Kels Rinari would not take so long, riding his white horse, his mounted guard clattering behind him. Dara's hands tightened on the stone sill.

A moment later she started at a small sound behind her. Turning, she saw a grey-dun huddling down on the op-posite sill. The bird regarded her drowsily, then tucked its beak into its feathers.

Shrugging, she turned back to the window. Where in the city had Rinari built his house? she wondered. She didn't know Port Calibe well. It sprawled along the sea-ward plain, raw and unswept, Its streets choked with sail-ors in faded sea clothes and women offering themselves for the night. Only the masted ships that stood in the har-bor offered any fascination. She had watched them rock with the tide and had wondered what the men who crewed them felt when the land fell away over the horizon and they were surrounded by sea.

Abruptly a piece of the night swept free of the sky and dropped directly at her. Dara jumped back, and at the last moment the winged shadow rustled upward and vanished. Startled, Dara pressed herself against the stone wall, then held her breath at the soft sound of footsteps on the stairs.

Te-kia stepped from the shadows of the stairwell, the quirri poised on his shoulder. He studied Dara silently for a moment. "Have I given you some reason to be afraid?" He seemed neither annoyed nor apologetic.

"No," Dara said, although her heart still pounded er-ratically. She had never heard him speak before, she realized. His voice was low-pitched, the words carefully shaped.

He stepped to the landing and studied her again from there, his grey eyes shadowed. Finally he turned to the window opposite and scooped something from the sill. "Give me your hand."

Dara's lips trembled. "What—" The Ilijhari was not imposing. He was smaller and slighter than most of the men she knew. The hand he extended was not square and work-hardened but slender and smooth, with tapering fingers. But there was authority in his low-pitched voice.

"Give me your hand," he repeated, and when she complied, he placed the grey-dun she had seen on the sill earlier in her palm and closed her fingers around it.

Surprised, Dara looked down at the bird. It nestled in her hand, winking at her sleepily, without fear. "How—"

"Have you never held one of these small-songs before?"

"No," she said. Sometimes, though, the small birds of the valley came so near she thought she might touch them.

"Then hold this one. Keep him with you as long as you need. You'll feel calmer when you stroke his feathers. Later, if you want, you can teach him far more than you might expect, although he will never feed you or steal for you."

Keep the tiny bird? She would feel calmer if she stroked it? Dara glanced involuntarily at the hunter hunched on the Ilijhari's shoulder. Was it true that the Ilijhari could see through the bird's eyes when it flew? "He steals for you? What does he steal?"

"Sometimes he brings me a knife or a kitchen implement or even a piece of clothing—anything he thinks I might like. Tonight he brought me this from one of the halls." From his shirt, the Ilijhari drew a withered flower.

Dara touched it hesitantly and wondered why he looked at her so closely as she did so. Its color was faded, its fragrance slight. It might have come from the bunch of dried wildflowers Mirina had carried earlier.

"There are difficult times ahead, small-song."

Dara looked up sharply. His low-pitched voice lent the words an authority that made her shiver. "Kels Rinari—"

"There will be trouble. It is inevitable, and it is far graver than your father imagines. If you must leave Wahonin—I have spoken with Harmin of this—you are to follow the stream up the flank of the mountain and cry in voice with those who come with you. Do you understand?"

She stared at him blankly. "No." She didn't understand at all. He had spoken to her father? Why did either of them think she would desert Wahonin? Her people were here. Her home was here, whatever happened after Mirina announced her decision. "My sister—" she began. But something in Te-kia's eyes stopped her.

"You don't recognize this, do you, small-song?" He touched the petals of the dried flower almost tenderly.

Disconcerted, Dara said, "It's a flower. Mirina—Mirina was carrying some like it this afternoon."

He nodded, watching her closely. "We call it the cup of peace. When one of our people is suffering beyond hope of recovery, we brew it into a tea. Peace comes quickly. Your people sometimes use it in the same way, although your pharmacists don't speak of it openly."

"He sleeps? The person you give it to sleeps?" Why discuss medicinals now?

"He sleeps for a few minutes. Then he passes to a more permanent peace."

Somehow Dara's body understood what he said before she did. Her fingers became ice. Her head rushed with blood. Her heart ballooned; she couldn't draw air past it to her lungs.

The bundle of flowers in Mirina's hand.

Her remoteness as they talked, as if she were already far away.

The cold of her fingers when they parted.

"No!" Dara had thought Mirina must choose between accepting Kels Rinari or refusing him. Yet in her grandmother's tales, women had sometimes taken a third course when presented with the *damen-kest*. She stared wildly at Te-kia. "It isn't true," she said.

But she knew it was. She knew what course Mirina had chosen even before the deep-bell began to toll from the heart of the valley. She stared blindly toward the halls, where rows of windows sprang bright with lamplight. Even her lips seemed to be ice. Only death rang the deep-bell.

The sound went on forever, shivering deep in her bones. "They're calling me," she said when finally the clangor died. "My father—my father will need me." But there was no feeling behind the words. She spoke from the icy depth of shock. She turned, faltering, to the stairs.

The Ilijhari detained her, placing one hand on her arm. "Small-song, it is my obligation to be certain that you understand. Your haven is with me. Follow the stream and cry. I will find you and do what must be done."

His words meant nothing. She shook off his hand and stumbled down the stairs. Her fingers, her lips—she must reach Mirina before her legs turned to ice, too. Before they refused to support her, to carry her.

She didn't taste the fragrance of the orchard as she ran through the trees. She didn't feel the lash of grass at her boots in the grazing field. Nor did she hear the voices of the people already gathered in the courtyard outside Mirina's hall, but that was because they were silent—silent and pale.

Harmin stood at the foot of Mirina's bed, his hands clenched at his sides. Dara halted short of the bed, staring down at her sister. There was faint color in her face, more than there had been earlier, and her lashes lay against her cheeks as if she were sleeping. Her hands were clasped loosely over her breast. For a moment Dara was convinced that if she spoke, Mirina would wake. Wildly she wondered why her father hadn't thought to waken her himself.

But how could Mirina wake when she was caught in a cold web of immobility? "It isn't true," Dara said again. Perhaps it would become true later, in the middle of the night—or tomorrow at breakfast, when she and her father sat alone. She could not accept it now. Why had Mirina chosen this course?

But was it any worse than either of the others? Rinari had offered her death in three forms. This was the swiftest, but no more final than the others.

Harmin paced across the room and stood for a long time at the window. "There is a note," he said finally. "On the bureau."

Numbly Dara crossed the room. There were two notes on the bureau top. One was inscribed with her name. She unfolded it.

> *Sister, I have not left you. I am in the stones, in the soil, in the smoke that rises from the hearth. When you need me, call, and I will touch you with fingers of love and sunlight.*

Dara threw the note down angrily. She didn't want poetry. She wanted her sister. Without thinking, she unfolded the second note, the one addressed to Kels Rinari.

> *Here is my decision. It contains a lesson, if you are prepared to learn. Study it and think more carefully of what you demand in the future, because some things can be given but never taken.*

There was no signature.

Dara stared at the carefully formed words and felt rage build like a distant storm. He had killed her. Kels Rinari had killed Mirina as surely as if he had driven his blade into her. Dara bit hard at her lip, containing an angry sob, then turned back to her father. "Did you know she would do this?"

"I guessed it."

"And you—you let her?"

"She was the only one who could answer him." His face held no expression, his eyes no life. "Tomorrow we will go to Rinari with her response. Pack clothes enough for several days. It may be that long before we return."

Dara drew a hissing breath. "You're going there? You're going to Kels Rinari?"

"I will deliver Mirina's answer, as I promised."

"And—what will you do when you meet him? What will you do to him?" Could he match Rinari's strength? They were of a size, but her father was twenty years the elder and he had none of Rinari's stark grace. Nor had he ever wielded a weapon.

"I will do nothing to him. You know that."

"But he's killed her. He's—"

"He placed a demand upon Mirina. She refused him. Now I will deliver her decision to him and he must decide what to do next. Certainly I will not step down to his level."

Dara's shoulders sagged. Of course he would not. He would be as strong in his principles as he was in everything. And violence had never been the way of the simple folk.

Tonight she wished it were. She stared down at the floor, realizing suddenly that her eyes were dry. Angry and dry. "Did you say that I'm to go with you?"

"Yes. We will leave at daybreak."

"But there must be observances for Mirina. Where—where is she to be buried?"

"The new orchard. There is a tree there she planted herself. And the observances will go ahead without us. Neither of us needs a public formality."

No. Mirina's death had already seared them as deeply as it could. The scars would be forever. "I want to stay with her tonight," she said. How could she leave before she found tears?

Harmin nodded. "Do you want me to send someone to sit with you? I'll be in my office most of the night, writing instructions for my absence."

"I want to be alone." She could not accept consolation for her grief when all she felt was anger.

Harmin studied her. "I feel the same things you feel," he said finally. Then he turned and left, his boots silent on the flagged floor.

Dara stared after him, wondering if his feelings could possibly be as savage as her own. Wondering why she had seen no spark in his eye if they were. Impatiently she jammed her hands into her trouser pockets—and in one, found a small warmth.

When had she thrust the grey-dun into her pocket? She drew it out and it nestled in the palm of her hand. Frowning, she touched its feathers, wondering if it was sick. Otherwise why hadn't it struggled when she pushed it into the dark hollow of her pocket? Why didn't it fly away now? The eye it opened at her touch was clear. The tiny bird studied her calmly.

Frowning, she set the bird on the windowsill and clapped her hands. The bird only shuddered delicately, then huddled down. She stared at it. It was like an omen, one she could not read.

Shaking her head, she turned back and drew a chair next to the bed. Dry-eyed, she took Mirina's hands in her own. The fingers were still supple, but they were cold—as cold as they had been last time she touched them. And no matter how tightly Dara pressed them, no matter how closely she held them to her face, she could not warm them.

She did not cry until much later. She sat stiff and alone beside the bed. People came softly to the door and looked in, then left her. She heard their voices in the hall, whispering. Finally she slumped forward, no longer able to keep her eyes open, and dreamed of a snowy white bird fluttering into the dawn mist, where she could not follow. She woke shortly before dawn to find Mirina's hands still clutched in her own, wet with her tears. The grey-dun was gone from the sill.

CHAPTER FOUR

Morning was an ache. Stock woke and muttered irritably as Harmin urged the team past the pens toward the road. A cock sprang to a high wall and cried loudly at the wagon. Behind them, indistinct faces watched from every window. Occasionally a hand rose in a silent gesture. Dara huddled on the wagon seat and pulled her cape nearer, too dispirited to respond. Harmin did not glance back at all. His jaw was set and white, his hands clenched on the reins.

Shock was gone. The loss was real. When they reached the road, Dara turned and watched the tower grow slowly smaller at the top of the rise and knew Wahonin would not be the same when they returned. There would always be a misty paleness lingering somewhere, in the orchards, in the corridors, a jeweled tear at the corner of one eye.

Dara pressed her own eyes shut against tears again and hardly noticed when the wagon entered the woodland, wheels rattling on the rutted road.

The trees of the woodland brooded in the slow dawn. Moss grew in heavy patches on their dark trunks and in places undergrowth choked the soil. Whenever Dara glanced at her father, she found him concentrated and grim, and she felt fresh pain in the pit of her stomach. Even the small flock of grey-duns that followed the wagon had no song today.

They approached the first posthouse an hour after entering the woodland and found the guard sitting impatiently on his mount, his bright uniform carelessly buttoned, his gold-trimmed hat pressed down hard on his head. His horse tossed its head restlessly and rolled its eyes as he urged it down the road to meet them.

The guard was young, with red hair, a hard, narrow face and ruddy brows that met at the bridge of his nose. Dara had seen him standing stiffly at attention at the back of the meeting hall yesterday, a hard sparkle in his eyes. This morning there was suppressed excitement in his sharp features. "How long will it take this trap to make the road to Calibe?" he demanded, flicking a careless hand at the wagon.

Harmin pulled the team to a halt. "We'll be in Port Calibe by dusk. Has there been any sign of the men you were to watch for?"

"Them? They'd be fools to come near the road. They know they'll be hauled back if we see them."

"How many are there?"

The guard laughed, a sharp, incredulous bark. "That toe-fingered jailer dropped a ring of keys and an entire wing of the prison emptied out—twenty-seven men in all."

Dara shivered. She had forgotten the men who had escaped the port prison. "Are you to escort us to Port Calibe?"

The guard laughed again. "Me? I've stood my duty here. There's no one going to molest you between this posthouse and the next. Now I'm to ride direct to the master's house and tell him the hour you made my station. Then I'm off to the festivals. And we'll see what we see, now the holidays have come," he added obliquely.

He touched his forehead in a mock salute and kicked his horse's flanks. The animal screamed and reared and bolted down the road. The guard's intemperate laughter rang back at them.

Dara stared after him, puzzled. "The festivals?"

"This is the first day of festival month."

"They permit the festivals of the Four in Port Calibe?" Her grandmother had told her of festival month. Today, if it was the first day of celebration, would be Tith's. In the old land, his priests would convene in the great temple plazas and chant until their eyes glowed like hundreds of lesser suns. Then, when Tith himself stood directly overhead, the people who had gathered to see would cover their heads, and pyres would burst into flame throughout the city.

Sometimes homes and shops burst into flame, too. Occasionally people who had failed to tithe became pillars of fire wherever they stood. There was no hiding when Tith's priests gathered in their numbers.

But that was on the old shore, not here.

"The traders bar the priests from touching land here," Harmin said, "but the ports are choked with sailing men and there's no keeping them from their celebrations. Especially not when it brings so much profit to the local dust merchants and brawlhouse keepers. It appears to me Rinari's man has begun celebrating early—and overdosed his horse." He raised his brows at her startled expression. "Doesn't that seem like sport to you, drugged and drunken men riding crazed horses through crowded streets? One day of festival and you'd understand why your mother and I never wanted to hear the names of the Four from your lips."

Dara drew back, understanding dimly that he used bitterness as a shield. She settled back on the wagon seat, wishing she could find some remnant of bitterness to dilute her own grief with. But anger had deserted her sometime in the night. This morning she felt only the hard ache of loss.

Today even the lightness, the absence did not touch her. Rattling, bouncing, the wagon carried them deeper into the woodland. The clouds thinned briefly and the sun cast a few wan rays among the trees. They found the second posthouse standing empty, its door swinging.

"Bolted with his friend," Harmin said. Strangely, he seemed grimly pleased. With a sharp lash of the whip, he sent the team forward again.

They found the third posthouse deserted as well, but at the fourth a sullen guard scowled back at them as he emerged from the trees and led his horse to the road. Harmin slowed the team as the animal pounded away.

By then it was midday and Dara ached from holding herself erect against the jolt of the wagon. "Father, if we could stop for just a few minutes?"

His expression as he pulled the wagon to a halt made her breath come short. "You must walk for more than a few minutes."

"What do you mean?"

"I mean that you must leave me now and go to Te-kia. He told me he would speak to you before he left Wahonin last night."

She stared at him blankly. "He spoke to me. I met him in the tower. He said—" He said, *Your haven is with me.* She frowned and drew a ragged breath, trying to understand. "But why would I go to him?" And why get down from the wagon in the middle of the woodland to do it?

"Because Rinari has resolved to have a wife from my house, Dara. And Mirina was not my only daughter."

Dara gripped the side of the wagon. Why hadn't she seen that? When, in her grandmother's tales, had an aristocrat come bearing a *damen-kest* intended for anyone but a headsman's daughter? And with Mirina's death, she was the ranking daughter in the five valleys. "But I can't leave you now. I can't—I can't hide with the Ilijhari. They're savages." A strange, irrational protest delivered in a voice that hardly seemed her own.

"You must leave me. And who has ever said the Ilijhari are savages? They don't permit strangers to wander in the mountains, but certainly you'll be safe there. Te-kia—" Harmin hesitated, frowning, then shook his head. "You're to follow the stream up the mountainside. Te-kia will find you and he'll look after you until you can come back to us."

Until she could come back? But when would that be? "What will you tell Kels Rinari?"

The familiar grim smile touched Harmin's face. "I'll tell him we were attacked shortly after we passed the fourth posthouse. I'll tell him a group of escaped prisoners took you. And I'll tell him the condition of the men he set to guard the road."

A sharp breath hissed between Dara's teeth. "And then?"

"Then the next move is his. He can believe me or he can disbelieve me. And he can do whatever he wishes, under either circumstance. Perhaps he'll ask for a daughter from one of the junior headsmen. But of course only Amin and Pardina have daughters. And Amin's daughters are children and Pardina's already have children of their own."

"He could try to have you removed from office," Dara said slowly, trying to think as Kels Rinari might. "Janne would probably be elected in your place, and Karina is my age." In fact, Janne's daughter had been Dara's schoolmate. "But the Council confirmed your life appointment last spring."

"And I don't intend to surrender it. But we mustn't sit here. I must go on to the next posthouse and report your abduction—if there's anyone there to report it to. Take one change of clothes from your case, no more. And your cape. I slipped your heavy boots out of the storage room. I've packed bread and meat enough to last you several days and a jug of water.

"It would be best to hide yourself this afternoon and walk tonight. Because you must not be seen. Not by any of the escaped prisoners who will be trying to find their way out of the area. Not by Kels Rinari's guards, if he sends them to search. And not by anyone from Wahonin. When you reach the valley, make your way toward the mountainside by dark. Only you and I must know where you've gone."

"No one will see me," Dara promised. She jumped from the wagon. "The guards saw me in these clothes. Take the shirt. Tear it. If you want to cut me to make it bloody—"

"I'll draw blood from one of the horses." Stepping down, he pulled her case and a bulging pack from the bed of the wagon. "Here, I brought your holster and knife too. You must watch carefully for the prisoners. They're thieves

and brawlers—sailing men and ship's deserters, most of
them. They'll be little better than animals.''

"I'll watch," she promised, wondering why she felt no
fear as she stepped behind a tree to change her shirt.

Then they faced each other, Harmin holding her at arm's
length, studying her with a long frown.

"Father," she said impulsively, "I'm sorry I was never
more like Mirina. I'm sorry I was never—" Tall. Fair.
Poised. Calm.

He put a finger to her lips. "Daughter, I'm sorry you
think of it. Go and be safe. And tell Te-kia that we tried.
Your mother and I tried. I hope you will never look back
and feel that we did wrong."

Then, before she could ask what he meant, he boarded
the wagon and took up the reins. He snapped the whip
sharply.

Dara looked down the road until he was gone. Only
then did fear tighten on her heart, driving her breath away.
"Father—" she said weakly. If she ran after him, if she
cried for him to stop . . .

Quickly she stepped into the trees, removing herself
from temptation.

She hesitated for a while in the shadows. Then she
picked her way to the north, toward the deeper trees. In
places the brush was dense, so tangled she could not pass.
In other places, vines and fallen trees blocked her path.
Moss grew heavily on the tree trunks. The air was musty
and thick. Overhead the sun still had not found its way
through the clouds.

She had walked for almost an hour, so tense, so alert
that the smallest sound made her heart pound, when she
reached a place where several tall trees had fallen. They
slept like giants, their trunks covered in moss and lichen,
their exposed roots overgrown with vines. The clouds had
parted. The sun threw a wide shaft of sunlight down the
circular well where the fallen trees had once stood.

The birds had fallen into nervous silence at her approach. Dara stood at the edge of the well of sunlight until
they began to call again. Then, too tired to walk farther,

she spread her cape in a hollow beneath the largest of the fallen giants and curled up, half-hidden, to wait for dusk.

She stirred occasionally, aware of the afternoon slowly passing, of the sky alternately darkening and brightening as clouds passed over the sun. Once the familiar lightness touched her and she felt mist against her face. The absence seemed brief, no more than a few seconds. After a while she slept.

She woke abruptly and sat, her heart hammering—for no reason she could name, except that the sun was gone and the breeze had died, leaving the woods silent and empty. Even the birds were still in the sullen dusk. Uneasily she reached for the water jug.

Then she understood why she had wakened, why the birds were still. Slowly, numbly, she lowered the jug and stared into the shadows.

The intruder was a man in his mid-twenties, tall but spare, as if he had not eaten well for a very long time. His hair was drawn back from his pallid face and tucked under a cap. His clothes were strangely cut, soiled and torn. He stood silently, studying her. His eyes . . .

But Dara had no time to fully register the color of his eyes. He was an escaped prisoner. Who else would wander the woodlands alone, ragged and pale? Her heart leaped once against her ribs and began to flutter. Stunned, terrified—how long had he been standing there? how long had he watched her?—it was a moment before she could push herself to her feet.

She did not stop to note which direction she took. She flung her pack over her back, snatched up her cape and ran. Her pack slapped against her spine. Her cape tangled between her knees, tripping her. Sobbing, she pushed herself up and ran again, never looking back.

She ran until she could run no more. Then she collapsed into a tangle of brush, drawing her trembling knees against her chest to make herself small. At first she heard only the painful gulp of her own breath. When that quieted, she heard nothing. Nothing at all. Nor did she see any sign of the fugitive.

She pulled off her boots and set off again, as silently as she could.

Once, stopping to listen, she thought she heard the scuff of feet nearby. She waited and heard nothing else. A second time she heard the rattle of foliage. Again the sound was not repeated. If the fugitive still followed her, he gave no sign.

She picked her way through the deepening dusk until she could no longer find her way. Then she sat down to wait for the moon.

The sky did not clear with night. The moon, when it came, threw only a diffuse glow through the dark-bellied clouds. Setting out again, Dara picked her way as much by feel as by sight. Massive trunks loomed out of the gloom. Low-reaching branches touched her hair. Occasionally her foot caught on a root or vine and she stumbled. Once a small animal darted in front of her, scolding. She caught a startled breath, remembering there were larger animals in the woodlands, too.

She met none of them. She walked until the clouds grew so thick, so dark, no moonlight seeped through. Thunder had begun to grumble in the distance. There was a feeling of storm in the air, like a silent expectation among the trees. Uneasily she sat and huddled in her cape, waiting.

Thunder grew nearer, sharper. Wind began to tug at the trees. And then the rain began its long walk through the woodlands. She heard it in the distance, moving softly, rattling carelessly at the leaves. By the time it reached her, it swirled in stinging sheets. She pulled her cape over her head and pressed herself against the trunk of a tree.

Suddenly the storm was rushing and furious. Rain stung, soaking through Dara's cape, wetting her to the skin.

Stillness, when it finally came, seemed quivering and unreal. Dara shivered, hugging herself tight, afraid that if she raised her head, it might all begin again.

Later it did begin again, and after the second storm, rain continued to fall from a black sky. Finally, wrapped in her cape, Dara fell into an exhausted sleep.

She was marginally aware of the dark hours passing.

Eventually the rain stopped and birds began to call in the half-dawn. Stirring, Dara looked up. An entire flock of grey-duns lined the branches of the tree where she sat. They talked softly among themselves, their feathers puffed, their eyes half-lidded. Briefly Dara listened to them. Then she slept again.

Slowly daylight grew brighter. The talk of the birds grew louder.

Then, abruptly, the grey-duns fell silent. Dara drew a shuddering breath and forced herself awake. She looked up.

Three men stared back at her: big, heavy-limbed, loosely made. Their beards were overgrown, their hair uncombed. They wore their clothes in sweat-stained layers. When she woke, the darkest of the three leaned over her. His hands were large, the nails stained brown, and there was a bitterness in his eyes that must have been born there.

Seamen, escaped from the port prison—and they didn't even have to speak. She saw their intention in their eyes. She was shocked motionless, trapped in the wet, heavy folds of her cape. Her knife, she realized numbly, was holstered at her waist. Nor did its small blade promise much in the way of defense. But if she could reach it—

"My father—my father has gone to fill the water jug," she said. "My brothers—"

The darkest seaman bared his teeth in a yellowed grin. "The same father who left all these tracks in the wet here? The same brothers?"

Dara glanced around. The only tracks in the damp litter beneath the trees were those of the three fugitives. Shifting, she moved one hand slowly, cautiously toward her knife.

They saw even that slight motion. Glowering, the darkest of the three snatched at her cape and whipped it away. With a second swift motion, he yanked Dara to her feet, twisting her arm back. Her knife was in his hand before she could cry out.

And so she didn't cry out. The seaman held her so close she could smell his breath, and she bit her lip and refused to utter any frightened sound. She met his dark stare. "If you leave me now, I will not tell my family."

The seaman laughed. "So—are you here in the woods alone because your family cares so much for you? Well, I can promise you, girl, that you will not tell them what happens here, even if they do care." He pressed her against the tree, bending to rub his beard hard against her bare cheek.

Dara closed her eyes, trying to shrink away. But the other two seamen had caught her arms. The first was working at the buttons of her shirt, dragging his beard across her neck, across her bared shoulder. She struggled uselessly as the seaman pressed himself against her.

"No. *No!*" A sobbing protest, followed by a long, ragged breath reflexively drawn, then by a second breath just as harsh, just as ragged.

With the second breath, her eyes snapped open and she stared at the grey-duns quivering in the trees. She stared at them as a familiar lightness lifted her and buoyed her. Distantly she realized that she no longer felt the seaman's hands. His companions' laughter was far away. It was as if the morning breeze had touched her and she floated away, leaving the struggle behind.

She left it, she abandoned it, she deserted it, glancing back distantly as if at someone else.

That was strange enough. She had abandoned herself entirely. She drifted in the air.

Stranger, as she watched, the grey-duns followed her. They swept up from the branches where they perched and gathered around her in a living cloud. She felt the beat of their wings in the air. She heard their cries as a single shrieking protest.

Or was it she herself—the other Dara, the one the seamen embraced—who uttered the cry she heard? She could not tell. But the cry came from some throat, and then the cloud of grey-duns began to swoop in agitation, swirling around the seamen, around the struggling, abandoned Dara, all but hiding them. The beat of their wings had grown loud, like the rushing of blood. And, Dara real-

ized, she no longer drifted in the air. She darted at the seamen with the grey-duns. She fluttered. She screamed. She
tore with tiny claws. She clutched at uncombed hair,
she tore at ragged clothing, she scratched unwashed flesh.

The seamen slapped hungrily at the screaming birds.
The darkest seaman crushed one against the trunk of the
tree and brushed another out of his hair. But there was
blood on his neck. It appeared in tiny pocks. And the
birds' frail claws drew scarlet streaks on the back of his
hands.

Dara was so lost in the clamor, in the confusion, that
at first she hardly heard the voice from the trees. The
syllables it chanted meant nothing. They barely touched
the perimeters of her consciousness.

But the seamen heard. The darkest stiffened and spun.
Just as abruptly his two companions grunted and released
Dara's arms. The three of them stared openmouthed at the
person who stood among the trees.

The grey-duns swirled for a moment longer, then swept
back to their perches. Dara shuddered and blinked in confusion, dropping weakly to her knees.

His head was thrown back, his arms raised, fists
clenched. His hair was bright, his eyes were golden. He
wore trousers but no shirt. An inhuman face was etched
upon his chest, round and angrily beaming, sharp rays
darting from it in every direction. Its puffy cheeks and its
rounded forehead were marked with intricate designs. Its
mouth was sharply downturned, its eyes glaring.

Dara stared in shock and confusion, recognizing the
fugitive she had run from the evening before—at the same
time recognizing the face of Tith drawn on his bare chest.
Recognizing instinctively that although the chant came
from the fugitive's throat, the words were Tith's.

And the sun was angry. His etched mouth worked as
the chant rose and fell. His eyes bulged. The fugitive made
fists of his hands and pulled his arms sharply down, and
Tith's fierce brow rippled. He arched his back and drew
in his stomach, and Tith grimaced.

The seamen turned ashen, the youngest uttering a low

moan of terror. Then the one who had pinned Dara to the tree shouted something unintelligible and the three of them bolted. Kneeling on the wet ground, Dara watched as the youngest slipped and fell in his panic. The other two snatched his arms and dragged him away. Cursing, the three of them disappeared into the trees.

Slowly, shaken, Dara pushed herself up. Two grey-duns lay at her feet, their necks broken. The rest of the flock was poised in nervous silence, feathers twitching. She stared at the fugitive, trying to understand what had happened. First she had been whisked out of her body. Then the grey-duns, who seldom even squabbled among themselves, had drawn blood from her attackers—and she had flown with them. Finally *he* had come and driven them away. And the face etched on his chest—

But priests were not allowed on this shore, not here in the north, nor to the south. Every port on the new shore was barred to them. She shook her head, trying to clear it. "You followed me. Last night."

The fugitive—the priest?—bent to retrieve his ragged shirt. "Yes," he said, pulling it on, covering Tith's face. His voice was low-pitched, not at all like the voice he had used in the chant.

Was that all he had to say? Just "yes," when his uncanny eyes studied her so closely, even as he pulled on his shirt?

"You followed me. You were near me in the storm. Why?" She pulled her clothes together, knowing she should not stare. But she had never seen eyes like his before. What could he be but Tith's priest, with hair that was red and gold blended to a subdued flame, with eyes the color of the sun at setting?

He disregarded her question. His eyes flickered to the grey-duns poised in the trees and narrowed. He turned back to her, studying her more closely still, studying every detail of her. "You're dressed as one of the simple folk," he said at last.

Why so subtly make it an accusation? "I'm dressed that way because I am one of the simple folk," she said, then hesitated, guessing his next question. "I—I was going to Port Calibe with my father. A group of men—like these—attacked the wagon and carried me away." Surely she must tell him the same story her father intended to tell Kels Rinari.

The priest's golden eyes narrowed fractionally. "I'm sorry to hear of it. Did this happen today?"

Dara frowned at the faint edge of skepticism she heard in the question. "Yesterday. Near midday." Uneasily she waited for him to ask how she had escaped the first group of fugitives, how she happened to be carrying food and water, how she had managed to bring her cape with her when she was snatched from the wagon.

He examined her silently for a moment, but instead of questioning her, he only shrugged and said, "My name is Kentith. I come from Chindora, at the northern border of Hemnistora, where it joins Khanistra. I crossed on a merchant ship as a deck worker. I've been on this shore since last autumn."

He had been on this shore, jailed, since last autumn. Surely. Why else was he in the woodlands now, pale and starved? But—a priest of Tith in the port prison? Dara touched her forehead, suddenly dizzy. "I'm—I'm Dara," she said. And her legs were weak again, as if shock had abruptly overtaken her. "I—I must sit down."

"Of course. There's a fallen tree just back there. You can sit there. You'll feel better in a moment."

Weakly she followed him to where a long trunk spanned a small clearing. He scraped the damp moss from the massive trunk and helped her climb up.

"Just sit quietly. Would you like me to find water?"

"I have water. The jug—in my pack." His concern seemed genuine despite the skepticism she had heard in his tone just a moment before. And she was cold—colder than she had been when she sat in the dark in the driving rain. She could not stop trembling.

He found the jug and put it to her lips. She sipped, choking at first. When she had taken what she could, he withdrew the jug. "It might help to eat if you're carrying supplies."

"Oh!" A quick twinge of guilt steadied her. How long had he been wandering in the woodland with nothing to eat? "Here—" Her fingers still shaking, she opened packets of meat, fruit and bread and portioned out food for them both, giving him the larger share.

He reapportioned everything, saying nothing.

Dara was surprised at her appetite—surprised afterward that she felt so much better for having eaten. She frowned, picking a stray crumb from the leg of her trousers. "I asked you earlier why you followed me."

He turned his golden eyes fully upon her, but there was something guarded in his gaze, in his casual shrug. "I saw you traveling alone in the woods, dressed as one of the simple folk. I have been—interested in the simple folk. I knew one of them once." He glanced down, frowning, then shrugged. "I was afraid you would come to harm. So when you ran, I followed."

Dara frowned, feeling from his manner that he had told her less than the full truth. But then, what had she told him? "Well, now I've told you why I was alone." She glanced down at her hands.

"Yes, now you've told me," he said, without emphasis. He gestured to the trees. "Do you intend to feed your friends? Is that why they follow you?"

"My friends?" she said blankly. They were alone except for the grey-duns that had gathered in the branches to watch their meal.

"I saw them yesterday, perched in the trees while you slept. I saw them again this morning, back there, trying to protect you. And now they're here."

"Then surely Chanona sent them," Dara said with deliberate irony. "The birds belong to her, don't they? To the wind?" If he was a priest of Tith, that must be his belief.

His eyes narrowed. "The birds belong to themselves. Tell me, young lady of the simple folk, why aren't you with your people?"

The abrupt question caught her off guard. "I'm—I told you that."

"You gave me an answer, but there wasn't much truth in it." He challenged her with a long, close glance. "Your lips lie better than your eyes and your eyes lie far better than your complexion."

Dara flushed. Was she so transparent? "Perhaps you aren't always entitled to answers."

"Then why not just tell me so? I know from experience that the simple folk can be plainspoken to a fault. So why not speak what you mean to me? Can you tell me where you're bound?"

She hesitated. What right had he to know that?

What right except that he had saved her life. "I'm going to Hendarra—to the mountainside."

The pupils of his golden eyes shimmered with quick, concentrated interest. "You're going among the savages? They don't permit strangers, do they? I heard in Port Calibe that anyone who wants to reach the inland should go to the south, around the mountains—unless he wants to be blinded by the Ilijhari's birds."

Was that where he was bound? To the inland? "The Ilijhari don't permit strangers, but I'm expected."

Kentith leaned back. "Ah, so yesterday you were stolen by escaped prisoners and today you're expected by the Ilijhari. But of course I'm not always entitled to answers," he continued when she flushed violently. "Did you know that in Hemnistora, an unmarried woman always takes an escort when she travels—if she doesn't want to invite the wrong kind of attention?"

"Then it must be as ugly there as it is in Port Calibe," Dara said sharply, flustered. What good was the story she and her father had devised if it didn't convince the first person she met?

He shrugged, withdrawing slightly. "Which do you prefer? To be victimized by priests and aristocrats on the old shore? Or by traders on this side? In the temples, the priests give you music and ritual while they pilfer your earnings. If it's a holiday, the priests of Tith will surely entertain you with a public burning—perhaps an entire series of them, if the tides of fire are running high. And the aristocracy robs the people with such a fine manner, some of them never guess they've been robbed.

"While on this shore, the brawlhouse keepers sell dusts and drinks twice as strong as any man can handle, then set thugs on him when he falls unconscious—and call it good business.

"Which of course it is, for them. But where's the drama? Where's the show?"

Dara studied him, puzzled by the way he spoke—with such light, smiling detachment. "You are a priest of Tith," she said. Did he think she was too ignorant to understand that?

His eyes narrowed fractionally. "No. I'm Tithtouched." He indicated his bright hair, his golden eyes. "I carry his image as well." He touched his chest. "But I'm no longer his priest. Now I'm only an escaped prisoner from the Port Calibe prison."

"Why were you jailed?"

He touched his chest again. "Because I stole an image of Tith from the temple at Chindora. This one."

She stared at him, more confused than before. "But the image is etched on your skin." How could he steal his own skin?

"It's drawn there with dye and needles, permanently. And so I am just as permanently pledged to the temple. If my family had been poor and I had been born this way—touched with the colors—I would have been permitted to remain with them until I was ten. Then they would have taken me to the priests and made a formal offering of me, and they would have received dispensation from the tithe for seven years afterward.

"But my family was not poor, not at all, nor humble either. And so when I was ten, they offered not only me but my weight in valuables—and received enough favor from the priests to make it an excellent exchange for both."

"Favor?" Dara said blankly.

"How does the aristocracy remain strong but through the favor of the priests?"

"You're one of the aristocracy?"

"I was until I was pledged to Tith instead. Now I'm a fugitive."

"That's—" Dara could find no word for it. That any family would give away a child in exchange for favor. "But there are no temples in Port Calibe. There are no priests. Why would you be thrown in jail there for deserting the temple at Chindora?"

"Do you imagine the authorities below distinguish between a priest in good standing and a renegade? I shaved my head before I ever sought passage from Hemnistora. Once I was hired aboard ship, I volunteered for night duty. My eyes are my own then. The color fades when the sun sets. And so I passed myself off as an ordinary sailing man until I made shore here.

"Then I was foolish enough to take a drink in one of the brawlhouses below and to let myself be stripped when I fell unconscious. I woke in the port prison. And the authorities recognized quickly enough, once they understood my story, that they could collect a handsome reward for returning me to my order.

"I expect they are annoyed that I escaped at such a late date. The ship carrying my escort should arrive before the end of festival month."

"Your escort?"

"No captain could keep a crew if he tried to carry a renegade priest without the proper escort, no matter how slight the priest's power. You saw the effect of just one of my chants this morning. There was no fire in my eyes when I sang it, but those three knew the verses of vengeance when they heard them—the verses my former brothers sing when they call down the fire at public burnings."

"Just by—just by singing those verses, you can call the fire from the sun?"

He shook his head. "Not I, nor most of my brothers. But a firemaster can, with the help of the lesser brothers, when the tide runs high enough in him. There are even some of the master class who can draw fire without tapping the power of the lesser brothers—and without using the lenses.''

"The lenses?''

"Every temple has them. Large specially ground glass lenses. An offender is brought to the platform wrapped in heavy shrouds soaked with oil. The brothers fall into trance with the first movement of the song, and the sun begins to grow. With the third movement, the firemaster appears and the lenses are turned. When they are positioned correctly, they catch the light of the sun as the firemaster calls it to full flare. They concentrate the light into a beam so intense it ignites the shrouds. As it might very well do without the brothers, without the chant, without the firemaster. But where is the theater in that? Do we want the people to worship a glass lens?''

Dara shuddered. "You've done this? You've set people afire?''

He gazed into the trees for a very long time before answering. "I'm a dark brother. I can sing whatever verse I choose and the fire never rises in my eyes. I give nothing but my voice to the ceremonies. Only one firemaster has ever called the tides high enough to draw fire from me. And the day after that happened, I left my temple forever.'' He gestured lightly with one hand. "And so you see me here. What have you decided?''

"Decided? About what?''

"Do you want me to travel with you to the mountainside?''

"I—I didn't know you had offered.''

"You shouldn't be alone out here, you know. We've seen that. And I've been told that the shortest route to the inland lies directly through these coastal mountains. Will the Ilijhari consider me an intruder if I come with you? When you are expected?''

"I don't know,'' she admitted.

He shrugged. "Well, you have the offer of my services.''

Dara glanced up and saw distractedly that the storm had passed, leaving behind clear sky. Suddenly she recognized the one thing about Kentith that confused her most: his smile. He had told her things that should have been bitter, that should have been painful. Yet he had spoken as lightly as if they discussed the weather.

"Tell me why none of this upsets you," she demanded. "Tell me how you can talk about being drugged and thrown into the port prison—and about the burnings—without being angry. Or afraid."

His pupils narrowed abruptly. So did the line of his lips. "Tell me who in this world cares if I'm angry or afraid. No one. No one at all cares. So why waste my time on feelings that will get me nothing?"

She glanced down. "I—I see."

"But do you?" he demanded.

"I think I do. I think—" Why shouldn't he protect himself against anger and fear by refusing to admit to them? By simply setting them aside and smiling? She would do as much if she could.

But she could not. She stared down at her hands. Finally she looked up again. "Will you come with me to Hendarra?"

He slid down from the fallen tree and extended one hand. "I was only waiting for to ask," he said, his tone as light, as careless as it had been earlier.

But Dara could not help noticing as she took his hand, as she jumped down beside him, that there was still tension in the small muscles of his face and that the grip of his hand was firmer than it might have been. And as they left the fallen tree behind, there was a residual grimness in his face that made her think of her father as she had seen him last.

CHAPTER FIVE

It was calm that morning in the woodland. The night's rain had washed the air and left it clean. Occasionally the sun reached bright fingers through the trees, throwing yellow streamers across the damp, spongy soil. Flocks of grey-duns and yellow-beaks flew after Dara and Kentith as they walked.

Near midday they found a stream and sat beside it to eat, and the birds gathered noisily in the trees nearby. Dara glanced up, puzzled by their numbers. There were always birds in Wahonin, hopping along stone walls and sills, calling from the trees, pecking industriously at the soil. But she had never seen flocks as large as these or as noisy.

At least the lightness had not overtaken her while they walked. There had been no absent spells, no sudden wakings, no disorientation. "Have you ever dealt with a sprite?" she asked impulsively when they had finished their meal.

Uncannily the flocks fell into a long silence. Kentith peered up at them quizzically, then glanced at Dara. "What do you know of sprites?"

Dara glanced away from his frankly assessing gaze. "I— my friend thought once that she had one. She wondered if there was some way to drive it out."

"So, do the simple folk believe in such things on this shore?"

"No, of course not," Dara said sharply. If he always

smiled, how could she tell when he was laughing at her
and when he was not?

Kentith shrugged. "Well, no need to be embarrassed.
Almost everyone in Hemnistora has paid one order or another to cleanse them at some time. And that, in many
cases, only after first paying a divine to discover whose
sprite was making the trouble. Whose sprite does your
friend think she's host to?"

Dara frowned at the skepticism in his tone. "Do you
believe in sprites?"

"No. I believe in illness, accident and the tides of the
Four. And insanity and plague and the general ill nature
of mankind. And imagination as well. But mischievous
little supernatural spirits who can only be exorcised at great
price? No."

Dara licked her lips, wishing she had never spoken. "I
don't think my friend imagines the things that happen.
Everything she told me seemed real. Other—other people
have seen." He had seen himself, when the grey-duns
flocked to her defense.

He studied her closely. "I don't mean your friend imagines the things that happen to her. I mean she should look
for the real reason those things happen instead of blaming
them on a sprite."

"But what could that be?"

"Why don't you tell me more about the things that happen?"

And have him think she was insane? Or so caught up in
her own imagination that she couldn't distinguish fact from
fantasy? She caught her lip between her teeth. Then,
briskly, she stuffed food packets back into her pack and
stood. "I think this may be the stream that cuts down the
slope north of the watchtower at Wahonin. If we follow
it, it should lead us to the edge of the woodland."

"Wahonin? Is that the name of your valley?" He didn't
seem surprised by the abrupt change of topic.

"I come from there. The stream passes north of there,
but close enough that—" She hesitated, recognizing too

late the snare she had laid for herself. "—that we must be careful not to be seen."

"We must not be seen from your home valley?"

She drew a deep breath. "We must not."

His brows rose, then settled back into place. "If I were entitled to answers, I would ask you why."

"But you aren't, are you?" she demanded, more sharply than she had intended.

For a moment he was very still. His golden eyes shimmered, the pupils narrowing to points. Then he smiled. "So I'll keep my questions to myself."

And so he did for the rest of the afternoon. But Dara was aware, as they followed the stream through the trees, that he studied her. And she was just as aware of the flocks that followed them, darting and calling noisily, as if they escorted her in some triumphal passage.

It was late afternoon when they reached the edge of the woods and looked up the steep slope toward Hendarra. A second system of storms was gathering behind the mountain's tree-clad shoulders. The watchtower stood to their south, at the upper reach of the immediate slope. The stream tumbled down the slope at the bottom of a deep, green-choked ravine.

"If we keep to the ravine, we can probably reach that cluster of trees before it rains," Kentith said, studying the sky.

Dara agreed and they crossed the narrow strip of open ground cautiously. The ravine was deep, and in places the fissure was so narrow they had to pick their way up the streambed itself, fighting to keep their balance as the swift-moving water rushed over slippery rocks.

Dara climbed after Kentith, her boots filling with water, her feet soon so cold they ached. She hardly noticed when the sun set, when dusk began to shade into night. It wasn't until the first fork of lightning flickered overhead that she realized that the air had changed. "Are we near the trees?" The walls of the ravine were steep. She could see little more than rock and soil and, overhead, the swiftly blackening sky.

"Near enough. I see a place above where we can climb out."

She looked up and saw only brush and shadow. The force and volume of the stream were increasing, as if rains far upstream already swelled it. She watched anxiously as Kentith climbed a shadowy tumble of rocks, then turned and held out one hand. He pulled her up the rough stair of fallen rocks, then pushed her over the upper lip of the ravine ahead of himself. With dusk, his eyes had become shadowy and grey.

Dara glanced around shakily, catching her breath. They had emerged less than halfway up the slope, just below the trees. She turned, catching Kentith's hand as he climbed from the ravine, then started as lightning flickered again.

Running, they reached the trees just as the rain began. It was not angry and stinging as it had been the night before. Nor was there wind. The treetops barely rippled. But lightning played and thunder cracked and grumbled. Huddled under the trees, shivering, it was some time before Dara realized she had never surrendered Kentith's hand.

She was about to slip her hand free when his grip tightened. "Look. Down there. Tith is sneezing."

"Tith—" Puzzled, she looked toward Port Calibe and saw a bloom of pink fire rise in the distant sky. As she watched, the pink flower shivered and began to disintegrate, and a bright white bloom rose in its place. A brilliant green blossom followed and for a few moments the colors mingled as all three blossoms slowly disintegrated.

"They're shooting Tith's snuff-powders. Apprentices' fire bolts they're called—because the apprentices shoot them from the temple grounds at festival. If we were nearer we could hear the charge that sends them up."

"Aren't they dangerous?" The fiery colors dazzled her. She had never seen anything so brilliant, so beautiful.

He shrugged. "Brantith—one of my mates—lost an eye tickling Tith's nose. The powders and charges that launch them are explosive."

Dara caught her breath. Lightning played at the edges of the display, as if attracted. Blue-white fingers probed delicately at the phosphorescent blossoms. "The priests made you do it? They made the apprentices shoot them because it's dangerous?"

Kentith laughed. "They could hardly keep us off the firing ground. Even a firemaster can't ignite the snuff-powders after the sun sets—not unless he finds a lightning stroke and calls it down. Or uses a flame-pot, and what firemaster would be seen carrying fire in a pottery shell? He has his dignity, after all, as do his lesser brothers. But you won't find much dignity among the apprentices. Give the darkest apprentice a flame-pot and sticks, and he can paint the sky any color he wants. Look."

Dara turned her attention back to the sky, entirely forgetting the rain that peppered the trees. "Are you sorry you're a dark brother?"

Kentith stiffened, a bright blossom of fire shimmering on the surfaces of his eyes. "Ask me if I was sorry to be helpless in a world full of greed and malice. Then I'll answer you."

Dara bowed her head, then raised it again at the sound of his sharply indrawn breath.

Kentith stared fixedly at the sky over Port Calibe, his lips parted. Dara followed his gaze and saw that the delicate fingers of lightning that had played among the flowers had become talons. They slashed among the bright blossoms and scratched at the dark land below. Wicked, curling, they leaped and coiled across the sky. The display was silent, but Dara could imagine their hiss and crackle.

She did not have to imagine the shudder of thunder as the clutch of talons suddenly spread wide and then exploded into balls of fire that made even Tith's snuff-powders pale. Blue-white, blinding, the fiery globes raced across the sky above Port Calibe, throwing out sparks and streamers. Like spectral observers, tall banks of storm clouds briefly glowed with reflected light.

Dara shrank against Kentith. She had seen lightning taste at the mountains to the west. She had seen it flicker over the port settlement to the east. But never had she seen a storm like this one. It was like an electrical tantrum, a brief, blinding display of pyrotechnic temper.

The last colored blossoms fell in tatters. No new ones rose. And after only a few minutes, the lightning flickered and faded, too. The sky over Port Calibe darkened.

"I—I've never seen a storm like that one," Dara said, turning. Nor, she realized with a shock, had she ever seen Kentith so pale. All the blood had fled his face. His features were strained, his lips tight and white.

He glanced at her, hardly seeing her, and stood. "I have. I have seen a storm just like that one."

"Not here? Not since you came to this shore?" she probed.

"No." Rigid, silent, he turned and walked away into the trees.

And he would say no more. Dara followed him and, when he chose a dry spot beneath the low-spreading limbs, sat beside him. Occasionally she spoke to him. His responses were tense and distant. Beyond the trees, the rain had settled to a steady fall. After a while, Dara fumbled in her pack and laid out packets of food. It was shadowy beneath the trees, almost too dark to distinguish Kentith's features.

They ate little, then made a bed in the tall grass and rolled up together in Dara's cape.

"You said earlier," Dara said after a while, "that a priest can call lightning from the sky."

"A firemaster cannot make lightning, but if there is a storm near, he can bend the lightning into any shape that suits him. But of course there are no firemasters on this shore, are there?"

"They aren't permitted," she agreed. Nor were renegade priests permitted. Yet one lay beside her in the dark.

She lay awake for a long while, wondering what it meant if there were a firemaster in Port Calibe, wondering if it could be true. Kentith lay awake beside her, saying nothing.

Yet she must have slept eventually, because sometime

later she began to dream. She was walking among the trees of the woodland—walking except that her feet did not touch the ground, walking except that instead of moving forward among the trees, she drifted upward, leaving the woodland floor farther behind with every step. The moon was bright and the woods were rain-washed, clean. Strangely, she felt no fear as she slowly slipped into the air. She knew she was not alone. There were others, sleeping high in the treetops. She could not see them, but she felt the reassurance of their numbers, and after a while she settled among them. They rocked together in the breeze, lulled, and she slept again.

Still something roused her after a time, something she could not name. A faint, unfamiliar scent? A sound, perhaps: first voices, then a crackling somewhere in the shadows below. Or was it heat, rising first in feathery streamers, then in long, yellow waves?

Then there was a piercing scream—not from one throat but from a hundred—and almost immediately the air began to beat with wings. Dara was caught at the center of confusion. *Fire! Fire! Fire!*

The cry wasn't hers. It came from all those other throats, a sound so shrill it all but deafened her. She struggled against swift-rising panic, trying to find her way out of the beating confusion. When the thrashing cloud that surrounded her separated and swept away in shrieking streamers, she glanced down. This time the scream was her own. *Fire!* There was fire below. Fire in the woodlands. *Fire!*

And she was falling toward it. Buoyance had deserted her. Searing air clawed her lungs as she tumbled helplessly toward the flames.

Then she was pressed tight in Kentith's arms, crying incoherently. Startled, she pushed herself away and stared up at him. "The trees—the trees are burning." Her voice was raw, unfamiliar.

He studied her with narrowed eyes, then touched her hair reassuringly. "No, you dreamed it. The storm is over. The lightning is gone."

"No. It wasn't lightning. It was— Something else started the fire. Voices. I heard voices." Human voices. And the fire had started at the base of the trees, not in the treetops. "The trees—"

"But the trees aren't burning. You can see that."

She shook her head. What she had seen, what she had felt had been too vivid to be simply a dream. And it wasn't these trees that were burning. It was the trees of the woodland. Pulling free, she stumbled to the edge of the small grove and peered down.

Below and to the southwest, she saw the orange of flame. Above it clouds of birds rose against the moon. Dara could not hear their cry. It was too far. But she knew their fright.

She hugged herself against the sudden, cold clutch of fear. She had dreamed a fire that was actually burning. She had dreamed its crackle, its scent, the scorch of its heat on her face—and the flurry of wings as flocks of birds burst into the sky.

She shivered violently, remembering the morning, when she had flown at the seamen with the grey-duns. Then she stiffened as Kentith's fingers drove into the flesh of her shoulders. She turned. He didn't seem aware that he hurt her. In fact, he didn't seem aware of her at all. He stared down at the orange flicker in the trees. Slowly he licked his lips.

When finally he glanced from the fire to her, she said quickly, "I must have smelled the smoke in my sleep. I smelled it and dreamed there was a fire. It—it's dying now." In fact, the orange flicker had grown duller as they spoke.

Kentith frowned. "I don't smell anything. And the woods are too wet to burn. Is there anything down that way, a structure of any kind?"

"The road runs near there, I think. There's a posthouse, but it was empty when my father and I passed yesterday. Maybe someone broke in to get out of the rain and set it afire accidentally." But what did it matter how the fire was set? That wasn't the question in Kentith's eyes. He wanted to know how she had known about the fire.

She could offer him no explanation. She had none.

Shaken, she turned back toward the trees and curled up under her cape.

After a while Kentith returned and slipped beneath the cape with her. He lay silently for minutes. Then he said quietly, "Dara, tell me about your family."

Dara frowned up into the dark trees, wary of the question. "My mother is dead. My sister—" She tried to say the words but her voice trembled and broke. "My father is headsman of our valley. He's senior headsman of the five valleys as well. The Council of Five confirmed his life appointment last spring." She frowned, wondering briefly how Kels Rinari had received him the night before.

"And your mother?"

"She was head pharmacist before she died."

"And you were born in Wahonin?"

"Yes." Studying his shadowed profile, she could see her answers gave him little satisfaction.

He turned on his side, facing her in the dark. He was frowning now. "Have you ever thought, Dara, that perhaps you aren't as simple as you've been told?"

"What—what do you mean?" The tone of the question was light enough, but his expression, what little she could see of it, made her wary.

"Just what I said."

Inexplicably her nerves tingled with alarm. "What you said makes no sense. And I can't talk. I'm tired." Tired and afraid—of lightning, of fire, of the inexplicable thing that had just happened.

"Tomorrow then."

The very casualness of the words made her stiffen. She hugged herself and pressed her eyes shut.

The night passed slowly. The sky was pale and the birds began to shift restlessly in the branches overhead before she slept again.

They sat under the trees the next morning until the storm-swollen stream subsided. Then they picked their way up the ravine again. The sun was bright, the sky clean. Yet Dara was so preoccupied she hardly noticed those things. The flocks that followed as she and Kentith climbed the steep fissure cried noisily, echoing her agitation.

Finally the ravine widened and they emerged at the crest of the slope. Standing there, Dara looked down over Wahonin. She felt nothing at first. Then the pain came, like a fist to her chest. Fields and halls spread in the sun, animals grazing, children running in the courtyards— She turned her head sharply, not wanting to see the orchard, where there would be freshly dug soil.

How could she leave Wahonin? How could she leave the stones her feet knew? The courtyards where she and Mirina had played?

Yet what else could she do? She brushed at her eyes, avoiding Kentith's narrowed glance. "No one goes to the old orchard. We can spend the day there if we want. It's there, just below the crest of the slope. If we run, we won't be seen."

"Then we'll run." Catching her hand, Kentith pulled her after him. The old trees stood in grass-choked rows, twisted and gnarled and barren with age. "And now—" Reaching their shelter, he pulled her down in the tall grass beside him. "And now if you must cry, do it."

Stricken, she tried to pull away. *"No.* I'm—"

"You've been like a cloud all morning. Rain and be done with it, Dara."

"Kentith—" But he pulled her against his shoulder, holding her there, refusing to let her go. And the tears came, tears of pain, of confusion, of loss.

She cried until there were no more. Then he released her and she wiped her eyes on her sleeve. "Tell me—tell me how you could leave Chindora," she demanded, her voice breaking. "Tell me how you could leave your home."

He stiffened. "I left my home when I was ten."

"I mean your land. The places where you grew up. Everything you knew."

"How could I stay, once Narkith drew fire from me? Until he came to officiate at the spring burnings, I was dark. I could not bring a scrap of oily paper to flame at midday without a lens. I gave my voice to the chants, but my eyes never took fire. Oh, I was granted the privileges of a full brother. My closet was filled with gold slippers and embroidered gowns—never mind that I only wore them when it was required. I had servants—and my choice of the women at the gates. Any girl, any woman in Chindora can win her family seven years relief from the tithe by bearing a child with Tith's eyes and pledging him to the temple. So women come to the temple gates every night for the apprentices and the priests.''

Dara drew back in confusion. ''But surely—''

''No, my mother didn't go to the priests. It was my grandmother—my father's mother—who did that. Her husband—I don't call him my grandfather because he isn't—sent her, but my father was born without the colors. Tith didn't touch our family until he came to me. And then he touched me with a dark hand.''

Dara pressed her fingertips to her temple. How could such things be? How could a man send his wife to another man's bed—in order to sell the resulting child for advantage? And how could Kentith speak so carelessly of it all? ''You wanted more? You wanted to be like the others?''

''What are you asking me? Did I want the power to burn human flesh?''

''I—''

''No, I never wanted that, any more than I wanted the other 'privileges' of the priesthood. But I got it anyway, the day Narkith came to Chindora. He's the most powerful firemaster born to this century. He confines himself to no particular temple. He travels from place to place, sometimes dressed as a beggar, sometimes as a workman, and he shows himself as he wishes. He came to Chindora for festival, and he raised the power in me and then he used it. I could neither raise it myself nor prevent him from raising it and using it.

''Do you understand? I wanted the power *not* to use whatever latent fire I have. But Narkith brought the tides high and he called it up. And now it will be that much easier for the next firemaster to draw fire from me. The pathways have been forged.

"So that night—the night after he used me—" He drew a long breath and closed his eyes. The lids trembled. "That night, I left the temple," he continued, controlled again. "I deserted everyone and everything I knew. I gave no thought to where I would go or what I would do. I was like the fire running before the wind. And this is where she blew me."

He had forgotten to smile, she saw. He had forgotten irony and detachment entirely. "But didn't you go to your family? When you left the temple?"

Kentith's face darkened. For moments he said nothing. Then he stood, staring hard at the gnarled trees. "This must have been lovely when it bloomed."

"These trees don't bloom much anymore." Dara said, disconcerted. "They haven't been cared for since the new orchard was planted."

He nodded absently, then sat again, briefly silent. Finally he sighed and said, "I was going to ask you which of the buildings below was your home. I was going to ask you—oh, any number of things. But you've shown me how the wrong question stings."

Dara paled, staring down at the ground. "I didn't mean to hurt you. I just—"

"No, no, how could you understand? I came *from* my family, but I'm no longer *of* them. They gave me to the temple in exchange for advantage, for favor. Were they to take me back, even just to feed me a single meal, the disadvantage, the disfavor, they would incur would be far greater than anything they ever gained from me.

"No, I didn't go to them. I'll never see them again, and they'll never see me. I have no family.

"And now you know far more about me than I know about you."

It was true. He had trusted her with everything. Tears trembled behind Dara's eyelids again—and her own story, untold, trembled just behind them. "My hall, the hall where I live, is the third one from the southern end of the group. My window is at the center of the second floor. You can count twelve on either side of it." She drew a deep breath—and then she told him everything else. She told him of her family and her friends, of her work, of the spells of absence and disorientation, of Kels Rinari and the demand he had placed upon them.

When everything was said, she watched anxiously as he leaned back against a gnarled trunk, his golden eyes thoughtful.

"And so your father went—not yesterday but the day before—to give Rinari your sister's decision? When did he plan to return?"

"I don't know. I can't see the wagon yard from here. If he returned yesterday, the wagon would be there."

"And the sprite—" He held up one hand, quieting her. "No, I know you no more believe in sprites than I do." He gazed up at the birds that had gathered in the trees, making the branches sway. "And so there is some other explanation. I think—"

"You think . . ." Dara prompted, when he did not go on.

"I think we'll find the answer."

She frowned, biting her lip. Was that all he had to say? And must he say it so distantly, when it had cost her so much just to speak? Distracted, she glanced at the road, then at the distant windows of her father's office. They told her nothing.

They continued talking desultorily though the heart of the day, exchanging details of life among their separate people. They ate sparingly in the early afternoon. Then Dara settled at the edge of the trees, taking up an uneasy vigil. She wanted to see her father's wagon before she went on.

The road remained empty. Later, at dusk, Dara stood at the edge of the orchard and listened for fifth bell. The fields and courtyards were empty now. The people were gathered for dinner, the windows of the halls softly lit. She saw no sign of unusual activity. Nor did she see anything to assure her that her father had returned from Port Calibe.

Finally dark came and they walked on. Leaving the

stream, they picked their way carefully along the high shoulder of the land by moonlight. Making a broad circle around the valley, they reached the sighing darkness of the lower mountainside in the early hours of morning.

Dara glanced up uneasily as they entered the trees. The simple folk never came this far. She didn't know if that was by choice, by agreement with the Ilijhari, or because they had been warned away from the mountain slopes during their first years in the new land. The distant treetops moved in the wind, cutting moonlight to scattered shreds.

They walked until they rejoined the stream that fed Wahonin. Then they curled up under Dara's cape, shivering from the cold.

The sound of the morning wind woke Dara. She sat and looked around, briefly disoriented. The trees of the mountainside were tall and straight, their trunks long, bare shafts. There were no low-hanging branches here, no undergrowth, no smaller trees. There were only giants, the wind bowing their distant tops and making a sound like the rushing of water. The scent that lingered under the trees was sharp, penetrating.

The flocks that had followed them the day before were gone. The woods were still, alien. Dara could not even be sure how late they had slept. Only a diffuse half-light filtered through the distant leafy canopy.

Kentith sat, rubbing his eyes. "How far from here?"

"I don't know," Dara admitted. "Te-kia told me to follow the stream and cry in voice with those who came with me. But we haven't really come so far from the valley."

"Then we'll have to climb."

"Yes," she agreed, with the uneasy sense that they had entered another world, one that was massively, silently indifferent to them. The only sound was the distant rush of the wind in the treetops. The stillness at the floor of the forest was cloying, unnatural.

They ate in silence. Then, for much of the day, they walked just as silently. Dried leaves blanketed the mountainside. Their boots made no sound and left no mark.

Even when the distant rush of the wind became a roar, no breeze touched their hair.

At midday, splinters of sunlight gleamed briefly overhead. Occasionally, from the corner of her eye, Dara thought she saw a winged shadow gliding among the trees. No matter how quickly she turned, she never caught sight of the bird that cast it.

Then, abruptly, at the end of the day, they stood at the edge of a bald patch on the mountainside. "There—up there. A structure."

Dara glanced uncertainly at the tall mound of stone that stood near the upper boundary of the bald area. "Are you sure?" But Kentith was already picking his way up the rugged slope.

"A tower," Dara said as they scrambled over the last stone outcropping. Someone had fitted boulders and stones together to form a moss-cloaked tower perhaps half as tall as the watchtower at Wahonin. Looking up, Dara saw several irregularly placed apertures near the top of the structure. Uneasily she followed Kentith into the structure.

It was dim and cool inside, the air faintly scented. Poorly placed stones jutted from the interior wall. There was no moss on the interior wall of the tower, although there was a lingering dampness. The stone floor was cleanswept. Dara glanced around anxiously for other signs of occupancy. "It isn't a watchtower. There's no way to reach the windows."

Kentith frowned, testing the lowermost jutting stone with his boot. When it did not give, he mounted it and stepped to the next protruding stone. Picking his way carefully, he circled the interior surface of the wall until he stood at the first window.

So it was a watchtower, however strangely designed. But whose? "What do you see?"

"Trees. And the sun setting." Turning, he picked his way down. "Pull off your boots. You'll have a better grip."

Dara frowned distractedly, removing her boots. Trees—

and the sun setting. Were they to spend the night here? Without knowing if they were welcome?

She felt even more uneasy when she stood at the window. It was as Kentith said. The trees stood in every direction, tall, straight, and empty. And the sun was a sullenly glowing disk. It had already begun to slip behind the flank of the mountain.

When she reached the floor, she pulled on her boots without speaking.

"Would you rather sleep somewhere else?"

"Where?" she demanded. "It will be cold when the sun sets." Dark and cold.

"It's cold now. We just didn't notice when we were walking."

It was cold, and Dara's pack was almost empty. They sat together under Dara's cape while they ate their sparse meal, then they sat longer as darkness came to the mountainside. They tried briefly to talk, but their words echoed hollowly against the tower's bare walls. Bleakly, Dara wondered if Kentith was as hungry as she was. Finally they slept, huddled on the bare floor, Dara's cloak tucked around them.

Before so very long, the moon sent its cold light through the windows. Time changed, and Dara shifted in her sleep, trying to curl tighter against Kentith. But he was no longer beside her. Somehow she had slipped free of the tower. Glancing up, she saw the moon through rocking branches. She felt the rush of wind in the trees. The dull ache in her stomach was sharper, keener; it held an edge of anticipation.

It was time to fly.

She was dreaming. Distantly she realized that and tried to wake herself. But the dream refused to yield. Spreading broad wings, she flew.

She did not like the dream. She discovered that immediately. She did not like the gliding silence of flight. She did not like the tall trees or the way she saw among them when she dipped beneath the leafy canopy. The enhanced clarity of her senses frightened her. The creatures of the forest were emerging now, clearing their burrow mouths of the detritus they were stopped with by day, peering out anxiously. And somehow it was her they listened for, her they watched for. She felt their fear as distinctly as she felt her own hunger.

Because the two were related: her hunger, their fear. The throb of frightened hearts, the scamper of feet—she heard those things with her new, enhanced hearing and tried again to waken herself. But it was too late. She was driving sharply downward through the trees. Air rushed swiftly across her spread wings. Distended eyes, a moment's useless struggle— Her prey screamed as she closed beak and claws on it. It was limp before she reached her perch, before she tore its unresisting flesh and tasted the first warm blood.

No! She had done nothing to invite this. She had done nothing to set herself loose on the wings of a bird of prey.

But the dream rolled on, vivid, detailed, real.

Moonlight on her back. Wind rushing across her wings. Then squealing terror and the snap of bones. And when the bones were picked, she preened herself, drawing each stiff black feather through her beak lovingly before she winged away again.

But she was not sated. She soared briefly above the mountainside, relishing the power of her wings. Then she dipped into the trees again, gliding between massive trunks, sharply alert to the nervous activity below.

Dara moaned in her sleep, trying to shake herself from the dream. If she could move, if she could thrash free . . .

She could not. She hunted until she took her fill and then she winged away over the treetops, her last catch hanging limp in her beak.

Dara woke then, at last. She drew a low, sobbing breath and struggled free of the dream. She stared around with blank, cold eyes.

Moonlight streamed through the high windows of the tower. Quirri perched on the jutting stairsteps that circled the stone wall, their yellow eyes half-hooded, watchful.

By moonlight, she could see the blood that stained their claws and their beaks . . . their sharp, tearing beaks.

"Kentith." Her voice was a broken whisper. She licked her lips and tried again. "Kentith." How could he sleep while the quirri stared down at them? How could he sleep—

—as the shadow fell through the doorway. As the silhouetted form followed it, the bird of prey hunched on its shoulder.

How could he sleep as the Ilijhari stepped into the tower?

Dara pushed herself up, pressing at her temples with trembling fingers. Was she dreaming this too? It seemed unreal: herself sitting helplessly; the Ilijhari moving forward in faceless silence, the moon at his back. Was this simply another part of the nightmare?

Perhaps she would waken if she spoke again. "Te-kia?" she said, dry-lipped.

She didn't waken. Instead the Ilijhari stepped into the light and became a woman dressed in a garment of furs, a string of game draped over her shoulder. Captured moonlight silvered her grey eyes.

"Te-kia?" Dara said again, nonsensically, as a single drop of blood oozed from the woman's prey and scalded her forearm.

CHAPTER SIX

The worst of it was that nothing happened. The Ilijhari woman stood over Dara silently, the quirri hunched on her shoulder. She was like Te-kia, slightly built, with tapering fingers, dark hair caught in a feathered braid, and eyes that were grey by moonlight. Her left earlobe was mutilated, as if it had been torn. She studied Dara without expression, then turned and set the quirri on a jutting stone perch. She draped the string of game from another perch and settled in the shadows.

Dara continued to sit, her heart pounding. Were they trespassing? Should she ask the woman's permission to spend the rest of the night in the tower? Would the woman answer if she spoke? Or would she continue to sit silently, her eyes glinting from the shadows? Dara glanced up at the hunter that had perched on her shoulder and the taste of blood rose in her throat.

If only Kentith would wake. But he did not stir, nor did the Ilijhari woman. Finally, not knowing what else to do, Dara curled up beside Kentith and pulled the hem of her cape over her head.

When she glanced out again, the Ilijhari woman sat with head bowed and knees drawn up, sleeping. Dara pressed closer to Kentith and lay cold and wakeful as moonlight migrated across the floor and finally faded from the tower windows.

She woke at the touch of Kentith's hand on her shoulder and sat bolt upright, her heart racing. "What—" She stared past his startled face. Sunlight streamed through the

73

tower door, laying down a golden carpet. Except for that—except for them—the tower was empty.

Kentith took his feet, his golden eyes quizzical. "What is it?"

"There was a woman here. And there were quirri. There were—" How many had there been, perched on the stone shelves she and Kentith had mistaken for steps? Without thinking, Dara brushed at the tiny crust of blood on her forearm, then closed her eyes against a quick surge of nausea. *The swift dive, the terror-scream of prey, the brittle snap of small bones . . .*

Quickly she pushed herself up and stumbled past Kentith.

She had taken barely three steps beyond the tower door before clouds of small birds burst from the brush and darted at her in sudden, noisy excitement. Startled, she tried to retreat. There were hundreds of them: small dull birds much like grey-duns, darker birds with brightly colored heads and wings, others so brilliantly plumed they were like streaks of color in the bright morning sunlight. They flashed and glinted, calling shrilly as they swept around her.

Dara pressed one hand to her mouth, feeling the wind their wings raised. It coaxed her. It tugged at her. One long breath and then another, she realized dizzily, and she would be swept up in the noisy confusion. She would be torn from where she stood. She would go whirling away. Blindly she reached for Kentith's hand. "Where did they come from?"

"I don't know. I didn't see them when I stepped out earlier."

She drew a shallow breath. The flutter, the din—she could barely keep her feet on the ground. "Please—please, Kentith, bring our things." If they fled the tower, perhaps they could leave the screaming birds behind.

But the whirling celebration accompanied them up the mountainside. Kentith brought her cape and pack and they scrambled away over rock and bare ground. The birds swooped and darted after them, crying in cheerful confusion as they ran through the trees. Finally Dara paused and stared around wildly, beginning to tremble as a series of quick images fluttered through her mind.

Te-kia crossing the fields the day Mirina died, the small birds of the valley surging around him.

His slender, tapering hands—and his eyes when she glimpsed them in the tower, grey by moonlight.

Grey like the Ilijhari woman's.

Grey like her own.

She stared down at her own hands, at the finely tapered fingers. The birds no longer called cheerfully. Their cries were piercing now, as if they wanted something from her. They dived at her, tiny claws catching in her hair and clothes. Dara squeezed her eyes shut and pressed her palms to her ears, suddenly too dizzy to stand, to think. *Her eyes, grey. Her hair, dark. Her stature, slight. Her dreams* . . . Kentith caught her as she slowly sagged to the ground.

Looking up, she saw his lips move, but she could not hear what he said. All she heard was the birds. They teemed around her, their colors so vivid her eyes burned. One breath, just one breath—

She pressed one fist to her mouth, crushing her lower lip against her teeth. But the ache of her lungs was too much. One sobbing inhalation and she was in the air, wings of every color beating furiously around her. Dizzily, spinning, she saw the trees retreat. She glimpsed the tower as it spiraled away from her, a fragmented vision. And then her awareness was scattered to the wind.

Chaos.

Confusion.

She moved too swiftly. She darted too wildly. She saw from too many eyes. She tried to call with a hundred voices at once; all she uttered was a frightened wail. If she still clung to Kentith's hand, she was not aware of it.

She caught glimpses—of the mountainside, of Wahonin, of the woodlands. Then she saw other places she could not name. She didn't see them whole. Instead she caught torn and flickering images of them, bright visions that spun into her mind and were superseded so swiftly they left no impression. Color and form leapt to prominence and vanished. Every desperate attempt to seize some single image, to hold it, brought only more confusion.

Clouds, structures, trees, the rock of some unknown mountainside—

And then, when her mind was so badly torn she thought it would never be whole again, she found an image she could hold. She found the sun.

For a moment she wavered. If it was really the sun she saw, why did she see it twice? With effort, she found her hand and raised it. She directed probing fingers at the twin orbs.

They drew back and, startled, she found herself staring up into Kentith's eyes. "What—" Seizing his hand again, she sat and stared around.

The wind had set her down. She was on the mountainside just where she had been before, and the flocks were gone. She heard them calling as they swept away into the trees.

Kentith licked his lips, visibly shaken. "What happened? Can you tell me?"

"I don't know. I—" She had flown over the mountainside. She had seen Wahonin. She had seen the woodlands. And then there had been those other places, those unfamiliar places. Rocks, grass, trees— "Kentith, how far is it to the inland? What is it like? Are there settlements there?"

He shook his head. "I've heard there are towns and farms, but I've never talked to anyone who went to the inland and returned."

"You were told that you should go to the south, around the mountains?"

"If I didn't want to be blinded by the Ilijhari's hunters, yes. But I also heard that there are tribes to the south who are no more hospitable than the Ilijhari. So perhaps there is no safe passage to the inland. But if there is any chance at all of finding a place where a renegade priest can be free—" He shrugged.

Was there a place where she could be free, too? Dara frowned down at her hands. Because how could she live among the Ilijhari if her throat filled with blood each time she slept? If she could be swept away with the flocks whenever she stepped into the sunlight? Those things had never happened before she came to the mountainside.

But now perhaps they would happen wherever she lived. And how could she even think of crossing the mountains with Kentith, when it hurt so much to leave Wahonin?

She gazed up at the wooded mountainside, aware that he watched her closely. Finally she turned back. "Do you want to eat before we go on?"

He settled beside her, shrugging lightly although his eyes were still alert to her mood. "How long will that take? There aren't more than three bites left."

There was more than that, but very little more. They ate slowly, delaying the moment when the food would be entirely gone. Several small black birds with red heads joined them as they ate. When they were done, Kentith shook the last crumbs from the pack. The birds fluttered around anxiously, then settled to the feast. When Kentith and Dara stood and went on, the small flock accompanied them, uttering a trilling cry.

"Are these the birds you're to cry in voice with?"

Dara listened to the distinctive trilling cry. "I don't know." It was not a difficult cry to imitate, although she felt self-conscious at first.

They followed the stream, whistling and calling. Soon the ground grew rockier, more rugged, and the tall, straight trees gave way to others with low-hanging branches and shaggy bark. Vines and undergrowth appeared. Occasionally wildflowers grew from shadowy crevices. The wind, instead of stirring distantly at the tree-tops, reached to ruffle their hair.

They did not pause at midday. The pack was empty. But in the early afternoon, they stopped to drink and to splash their faces. The water rushed down the rocky streambed now, cold and clear.

It was late afternoon when the first quirri winged

through the trees, scattering the smaller birds who followed them. Dara and Kentith paused, glancing up tensely. The quirri reappeared, gliding past, and a few moments later two more followed it, dipping so low Dara could have touched them.

She clutched Kentith's hand as they continued to climb, holding her breath each time the quirri circled them and winged away.

Te-kia found them at dusk. They knelt at the stream to drink, and when Dara raised her head, he stood at the other side of the rushing water. Dara touched Kentith's arm and they rose together, slowly.

Te-kia wore a shirt of skins over trousers tailored in Wahonin. The black plumage of the quirri that sat on his shoulder glistened. Involuntarily Dara glanced down at his hands, then at her own.

He saw the glance but did not acknowledge it. "Welcome to my mountain, small-song." He addressed the words to her, but his gaze, cool and grey, had shifted to Kentith.

Afraid, Dara laid a quick, protective hand on Kentith's arm. "I did what you told me, Te-kia. I came, and I brought Kentith with me to see that I was safe. I—I invited him." The muscles of Kentith's arm were taut under her fingers.

Te-kia inclined his head briefly to Kentith. "I saw you on the mountainside. You've come from the port prison. Where are you bound?"

"To the inland, if I live so long," Kentith said with forced wryness.

Te-kia's eyes flickered to Kentith's bright hair. "You are leaving your kind behind?"

"I've left my order. I am no longer a priest of Tith."

"But you still bear his fire behind your eyes."

Kentith drew a deep breath. "I bear it but I can't use it. And now I'm going where no one else can use it either."

"And what can you tell me of what I've observed below?"

Kentith shook his head. "Nothing. I was aware of nothing until three nights ago, when Dara and I watched the storm over Port Calibe.''

"You weren't aware of the rumors in Port Calibe that there was a firemaster locked in the port prison?''

Kentith stiffened. "I'm no firemaster.''

"You weren't aware that people have reported sun flares? That small pyres have ignited in public places—with no one seen to light them?'' Te-kia shook his head. "No, I see none of that reached you, even though you were the subject of the rumors.'' Taking his quirri on his wrist, he released it with a deft flip of his hand.

Its broad wings beat the air just once before it glided to rest on Kentith's shoulder. Dara drew a shocked breath, her heart stopping.

Kentith stood very still, his golden eyes blazing, his face white. But the quirri only folded its wings and shook its feathers calmly into place. Dara turned back to Te-kia.

"Have I given you some reason to be afraid, small-song?'' he demanded.

"I thought—'' She frowned down at the ground, remembering that he had used the same words once before. He seemed no more annoyed and no more apologetic this time than then. And his voice held the same authority. "No,'' she said. "I only thought—''

"She thought I was about to become a blind man,'' Kentith said. Cautiously he raised one hand and touched the quirri's folded wing. His smile was forced, his face ashen.

"I believe you have come here in good faith and for good reason. So you won't become a blind man without cause, now that we have the smell of your blood. Yours we must take with more ceremony, small-song. I summoned the necessary participants yesterday, when I saw that you would soon arrive.'' He extended his wrist and the quirri returned to him, wings rustling.

Before Dara could ask what he meant, she glanced at Kentith and saw spreading scarlet stains on his shoulder where the quirri's claws had pierced fabric and flesh. "You're hurt.''

Kentith looked down at his shoulder and licked his lips. "I believe my shirt is ruined."

"The wounds are slight," Te-kia said. "And I believe your shirt was ruined a long time ago. But I require this one, so you'll have another. Small-song, did Pi-neka leave game for you when you met?"

Dara frowned. "The woman who let us sleep last night in her tower?"

"The tower where you slept is only a station. Did she feed you?"

"No, we were sleeping when she came. And she was gone when we woke."

"Then you are hungry. My own towers are above." Turning, he stepped away into the dusk.

Dara hesitated, then followed. Te-kia walked as quietly as a shadow. His feet seemed to leave no print on the earth. Occasionally as they climbed, the quirri vanished from his shoulder, gliding away into the dusk. When that happened, Te-kia paused, waiting until it returned. He said nothing, either as they walked or as they waited.

Dusk had become darkness by the time they saw light ahead. Emerging from the trees, they climbed a series of stone steps to a low-walled courtyard. Twin towers rose from two corners of the yard. They were taller than the watchtower at Wahonin, each of them at least twice its girth. Their windows were dark, but the high, narrow windows of the low, oblong hall at the other side of the courtyard flickered with light.

Kentith and Dara followed Te-kia across the courtyard and into the hall. The interior was low-ceilinged and dim, with rough-cut beams and posts. At one end there was a platform spread with quilts. Dara recognized the weave of the fabric; it had come from Wahonin. Nearer there was a small pit in the floor, half-filled with ashes. Cushions lay around it, as if people sometimes sat there. At the other end of the single low room, bundles of herbs and medicinals hung drying. There were racks with furs spread upon them, other racks holding strips of drying meat.

Tools and implements hung from the beams and from the supporting posts.

Small lamps swung from the beams and stood in the broad sills of the windows. Still without speaking, Te-kia gestured them to take cushions on the floor. Dara and Kentith sat and glanced at each other uncertainly as he disappeared into the shadows at the far end of the room. His quirri left his shoulder and flew back to settle on a nearby beam. It watched them with cold yellow eyes.

When Te-kia returned, he carried a fresh linen shirt. "I have a lotion that will sterilize your wounds and help them close. But first give me your torn shirt. The quirri need the smell of your blood while it is fresh."

Kentith's eyebrow rose as he peeled off the bloodied shirt. But Te-kia offered no explanation. He accepted the garment and left the hall.

Nor did he speak when he returned. But within a few minutes he had rubbed a clear lotion on Kentith's shoulder and produced both food and drink. There were cakes of grain, an unidentifiable fruit, dried meat, and a cold brew that fizzed sharply against the roof of Dara's mouth. At the first smell of food, she forgot her uneasiness and ate hungrily.

While they ate, Te-kia arranged sticks and leaves in the ash pit. When they finished and tried to thank him, he silenced them with a raised hand. "It will be time for talk when the smoke is in the room." He turned to Kentith. "Will you remain while I light the leaves?"

When Kentith only studied him with one raised brow, Dara glanced from one to the other uncertainly. Why did Te-kia think Kentith might want to leave? Where was he to go?

Te-kia's eyes narrowed. He continued to wait for some response from Kentith.

Kentith shrugged. "You could tell me what you're burning, but I don't suppose it would mean much."

"It wouldn't."

"The effect?"

"You'll find yourself drowsy. You might hear the sound

of my voice, but so distantly that you'll understand very little of what I say."

Dara glanced from one to the other of them again, realizing with alarm that she had misunderstood. He wasn't building a fire to warm them. "My people—my people don't use powders and dusts," she said quickly.

Te-kia's grey glance flickered to her and narrowed. "It is customary to take smoke with your guide on the night before your blooding, small-song."

Dara shrank back. "My—"

"There will be a ceremony tomorrow, and I am your guide—your sponsor. It is traditional to make a journey with smoke on the night before, to prepare for the ceremony. You won't remember everything you learn on the journey when you wake, but when you need to know, certain things will return to you. I would be remiss if I did not build the fire."

A ceremony? *Yours we must take with more ceremony,* he had said after his quirri drew blood from Kentith. Quickly, alarmed, she said, "Te-kia, I can't stay here. I can't stay with the Ilijhari. I'll only be here until—"

Again he raised one hand. "Small-song, you have come into the mountains without harm, but only because you were expected—and only because you came directly to me. I cannot let you leave my towers without the blooding. There are too many uncertainties. And the time for talk is when the smoke is in the room. Would I have protected you this far if I intended you harm?"

Dara drew a shallow breath and stared down at the floor. "No."

"Do you think I intend you harm now?"

Have I given you some reason to be afraid? How many times would he have to ask her that? She glanced at Kentith. He was watching her intently.

"Please tell me what—what the journey is," she pleaded, glancing up at the quirri that perched on the beam. "Where will you take me?" Would it be like going with the wind? Or would it be a hunt?

"The journey is to be taken, not discussed, small-song."

Was that all he would say? For a moment Dara was angry. Didn't he understand how strange this was to her? Didn't he understand—

But she saw that he understood very well. It simply did not matter how frightened or confused she was. What mattered was the ceremony and his obligation to prepare her for it.

Dara remembered the moment the day before when she had had the sense of an alien world, one massively and silently indifferent to them. She had the same sense now. It was useless to quarrel with the authority of ceremony and ritual. They would prevail.

She wavered for a moment longer. Then, impatiently, she stretched her hands to the pit. "It would be cold without a fire tonight," she said. It was as near as she could come to consenting to whatever must happen next.

CHAPTER SEVEN

The wings that came with the smoke were not black. They were wide and white, and they carried the scent of burning leaves. Te-kia introduced the flame to the pit, smoke curled up, and the wings were upon them, so soft, so cloudy, Dara could not tell whether they were made of feathers or smoke.

The land, small-song . . . The voice was Te-kia's, distant, bodiless. *This is the land we are appointed to guard. See how sweet it is.*

The land— As Te-kia spoke, guiding her, Dara touched the land with every sense. Together they soared above mountains frosted with ice and forests so green they shimmered in the clean, hard sunlight. Beyond were broad, rich valleys much like Wahonin. Still farther beyond were broad lands that lay as flat as a spread cloth. They were carpeted with green grasses and, sometimes, brilliant wildflowers. Rivers, lakes, streams, springs—Dara tasted the sweetness of the waters. She let their coolness dash through her fingers.

Far past the watered lands were barren ones, holding little but scrub and sand and, occasionally, fantastic formations of stone, standing free. Sometimes there seemed to be faces in the stones, and Dara tried to see them better. But the wings carried her on to the far, far mountains that rose steeply from the barrens and then sloped, finally, to the sea. Here was another sea, Dara realized, not the one that touched their own shore. She wondered distantly how

far they had come and what lay at the far side of this sea—
the old land or some place she had never heard of.

*All this came once before. The land was here, sweet
and rich. There were trees and grasses, there were great
animals and small ones, there was all the variety and
plenty of life. And there were men and women appointed
to guard the land. Wisely, they treated it as a thing of
soul, living and aware, to be respected, to be preserved.
They thanked it for its bounty, and when it was briefly
ungiving, they made offerings and waited patiently because they knew that one day it would give again. They
called themselves its children, but they understood that
they were its guardians as well.*

*But after a while, others came from far shores who were
stronger than the guarding peoples. The intruders were
greedy and full of destructive powers. They had stolen
those from the earth itself and from its surrounding sphere,
and they thought that whatever they chose to inflict upon
the living earth and its creatures was only their right.*

*So they called upon their destructive powers and swept
the guardians away. They set fire to the grasses of the
plains and fanned the flames with harsh winds. They raised
floods that drowned the land for years at a time. When the
guardians hid themselves in the mountains, they raised the
rocky understrata from the ground in great cataclysms and
crushed the guarding peoples.*

*The land cried with its wounds and its indignities, but
after a while there was no one left to hear its voice, and
so eventually it died, despairing.*

*Yes, the land died. The soil grew barren, the rains
sparse. Sunlight was lost behind great clouds of dust that
traveled for days and days on the wind. Rivers vanished.
And then the people who had brought the land to such
grief began to die, too. Disease took them. Hunger took
them. Their own kind took them. They died in numbers
and left the land they had come to plunder ruined and
bare.*

See how it was then, small-song.

Unwillingly Dara saw it: mountainsides raw and buckled, without trees; valleys without grass; burns and scars and ugly gouges everywhere. In the barren lands, there were places where the land had turned to a coarse, rubbled glass. In a few places, cones that spit fire and ash had thrust up from the soil.

It was not just the new land that died. The old lands died too. But time was long and eventually resurrection came. Lakes vanished and others appeared. Mountains rose and others fell. Rivers found new beds. In places, the sea swept over the land and carved it away. In other places, the sea drew back and revealed new land.

Eventually those few scattered people who had survived it all began to grow in numbers. In the old lands, upon the far shores the old ideas spawned again, although they wore different faces and called themselves by different names. The greed and the cruelty grew. Now there are men and women who trade again in the favors of the land and the sun. They claim even to sell the goodwill of the wind and the waters. And once again they have turned eyes upon our land.

But we are risen again, its guardians. We are made of new blood and new bone, but the old love is in us and we are strong and we are vigilant and we are clear-eyed. More than that, this time we command the magic of the creatures. My own people, the Ilijhari, cast their vision across the land on wings of birds. In other parts of the land are other peoples who have the strength and cunning of their own creatures.

Let them do what they will across the sea. They will not kill our land again, not so long as one of us lives.

Dara groped for an understanding of what he had shown her—of what it meant to her and to Kentith. "But the inland—you have let people go there?" Did she speak aloud or did she ask in some other way? Confused, lost in the smoke, she couldn't tell.

Yes, we have permitted people to go there. We permitted your father to go there. The land is scantly peopled, and what is a land without people?

"My father?" She did speak aloud this time. And dimly,

through the haze of smoke, she saw the room. Kentith had fallen asleep on the cushions. The quirri winked drowsily from its rafter. Te-kia sat cross-legged at the other side of the fire pit. The smoke muffled some of the surprise of what he said. "My father went to Port Calibe."

Harmin went there. But you know that he is only one of your fathers.

"I don't know that," she said, although she recognized, dimly, that she was not surprised that he said it. Her voice rose, breaking. "I don't know . . . anything." She didn't know who she was or why the flocks flew after her as if she were an Ilijhari. Or why Te-kia had welcomed her here.

Then you must learn. Take another journey with me, small-song. See the man walking into the mountains. See his raggedness. See his hunger. See the anger and the bleakness in his eyes. He has come to this land to find a new life, and instead he has been robbed and beaten and driven out of Port Calibe with nothing but the clothing he wears. Not because he has done anyone any wrong. Just because he is one of the powerless people who can be treated so.

Dara shivered. She saw the man, just as he said, limping, half-starved, desperate.

See him on the mountainside, trying to make his way through storm and cold, falling finally to hunger. He is ready to die. He is resigned to it. But a young woman of my people finds him. She looks past the rags and the dirt and sees a spirit that wants to fly.

She is my sister and she bears one of the finest hunters of the forest on her shoulder. Her flock of quirri grows with every season, and the birds of her small-flocks are a rainbow that follows wherever she walks. She feeds the man. She takes him to her tower to shelter him from the coming winter. She washes him and dresses him in clean garments and cares for him in every tender way. All this she does at first because she is so pleased to have his company. You see, our people live solitary lives, but hers is not a solitary spirit. Although her flocks grow with every season, she has felt an emptiness and an ache since the day she left her mother's side. Now she is no longer alone.

Dara nodded wordlessly. She saw the two people, the man leaning weakly on the woman, both of them climbing the mountainside against the bitter wind. Briefly she glimpsed their faces and knew she was seeing the faces of her parents. But she had no time for questions because the tale moved ahead.

Now see the man when spring comes again. He is healthy, he is strong—and he has decided he must go on. He is a farmer, a man of the land, and he goes now to find a land to call his own.

See the man and woman parting. He thinks of dangers, she thinks of loneliness, and they both are torn. There are tears. There are promises. She will send her small-flocks flying after him, so that she will know every step he takes. Her hunter will carry him game each night until he is beyond the mountains. One day, when she has fulfilled her obligation to bear and train a guardian to stand in her place, she will join him.

Does she really intend it? Or is it only a promise torn from her soul to comfort them both through the first hard days of separation? No one will ever know. What she hasn't told him is that she already carries his child.

The small-flocks follow him for as long as they can and the woman uses their eyes to see that the man is well. The quirri take him game until finally he emerges from the mountains and walks away into the inland. From that time, no one here has glimpsed him.

Dara felt a sharp wrench of concern. "You don't know where he went? You don't know if he survived?"

We don't know. He learned much among us. But there are other peoples guarding the inland, and who can say if he assured them of his respect for the land as he assured us. Perhaps he found a place. Perhaps he joined others who have been permitted past the mountains. Perhaps he did not.

"But she went to find him? After—after her child was born?" After she herself was born.

No. Fly ahead with me to the birth and you will see.

Dara stirred uneasily, trying to see him again through the smoke. His voice had become troubled. "My mother—" she said uncertainly. She had not come seeking an Ilijhari mother. But to learn that she had one, to have glimpsed her face for those few instants, then to hear . . .

To hear what she heard.

The birth took place here, in this room. Her quirri gathered in the beams. If you look, you can see them there now, vigilant, silent. Her small-flocks waited outside, in the courtyard. They heard her cry out with the pains. They heard how the cries began strong and then, over the hours, grew weak. Finally they heard the cries of the child. After that they didn't hear my sister's voice again.

Reluctantly, Dara saw the room, the bed, the woman lying so pale with the child in her arms. She heard the terrible silence of the birds before the quirri unfolded their wings and swept out the high windows. Then the smaller birds began to scream and they screamed until dark came.

Among our people, if the mother dies in childbirth, her family offers the child to the father's family. If they will not have it, then it is taken into the trees and left. If the birds tend it and keep it living for nineteen days, then the mother's family will take the child back.

What was to be done with a child who had no father's people? Must it be left for the birds? Its blood was only half Ilijhari. Would we be leaving it to certain death?

We gathered, those of us of closest blood, and took smoke. While the flame was in the pit, a woman cried over a child born dead in the valley below. Our small-flocks heard and saw and so we heard and saw, and we came to an agreement.

The next morning I went to the valley, carrying the child. The woman there received her gladly. There has long been respect between the simple folk and our people. The woman and her mate promised to raise the child as their own.

So she had come among the simple folk when she was

not their kin at all. "And no one ever told me," Dara said.

Where was the need? If you were suited to live as one of the simple folk, what would it serve you to know you were kin to the Ilijhari? But if it were ever necessary, they promised, they would send you here and I would teach you our ways.

Now you have come.

But she had not come to learn Ilijhari ways. She had not come to learn to hunt with the quirri. The taste of blood rose in her throat when she thought of it.

Te-kia seemed not to hear her protest. He dropped fresh leaves in the pit and smoke billowed between them.

Dimly she heard her own voice, rising half-coherently. She heard Te-kia's calming answer, but she could not distinguish the individual words. Nor could she tell how long the conversation ran. It seemed to her they spoke that way for a very long time.

Later she realized, dimly, that Te-kia was giving her instruction. She pressed her hands to her ears, trying to close out his persistent voice, but it continued as clearly as before. Helplessly she slumped by the fire pit and let him teach her. She didn't even know, after a while, if he spoke aloud or in some other way. If he could fly with the flocks, if she could, why could they not talk without speaking when the smoke was in the room?

Finally he put leaves on the pit again and Dara slept, smoke and wings closing around her.

She woke slowly, stiffly. The sunlight that came through the high, narrow windows told her it was late morning. The fire pit held only ashes, but the woody sweetness of the smoke was still in the air. Reluctantly Dara sat. Her mouth was dry and her eyes stung.

She was alone.

She sat uncertainly for moments, a warning tingle at the back of her neck. Then, as if compelled, she turned and her throat closed.

The gown of feathers hung from a beam at the far end of the room. She knew the gleam of it immediately: rich, vivid. She had only to close her eyes and she saw her mother slipping it over her head and stepping through the door into the courtyard. Behind her, she saw her grandmother going to her own blooding. She saw the other women of the family, through the centuries. She saw—

—herself.

Her stomach knotted. Anxiously she slipped to the door. "Te-kia?" She knew he was near. If only he would come and tell her she need not pull on the gown, that she need not step through the door into the courtyard, where her kin waited. "Te-kia, *please.*"

But why would he tell her that when he had so carefully coached her in the ceremony while they took smoke? She didn't remember the details of it now. But once she drew the gown over her head—

Teeth chattering, she retreated to Te-kia's bed and wrapped herself in quilts. But she could not escape. The women of her family had always dressed themselves in these feathers and gone into the courtyard. Today was her day to go. Her kin waited.

Finally, still shivering, she crawled from Te-kia's bed and removed her travel-stained trousers and shirt.

The gown rustled softly as it slid down her body. It sat heavily upon her. There were scattered dark stains upon the individual feathers. If she was careful, she need not see those.

She walked somehow to the door. She paused there, raising her arms. The gown's wide sleeves unfolded into wings. Light-headed, drifting, she stepped into the courtyard.

They waited for her there, her blood kin. They stood silently, stiffly, like people unused to gathering in groups. Their quirri sat on their shoulders, sinister and black, yellow eyes squinted against the bright morning sunlight. And everywhere were the small birds of the mountainside. They clung to the courtyard wall, to the towers, to the exterior walls of Te-kia's hall. They did not flutter or cry. They were still, a bright tapestry of feathers.

Dara stood uncertainly. Her kin were much alike; it

took her moments to find Te-kia among them. Kentith stood beside him, in a shaft of sunlight, his hair so bright that for a moment she couldn't catch her breath. Tith glowed from his golden eyes.

They watched intently, all of them. Numbly she drew a long breath and found the word she must say, the word from the realm of smoke: "Nekinia." She recognized at once that she had spoken too softly. She spoke again, more strongly. "Nekinia!" Inexplicably a pulse began to pound heavily in her throat.

Te-kia stepped forward and called out several words to her. They ended on a note of inquiry.

Uneasily Dara glanced toward the two towers. Quirri were perched in the windows, watching with yellow-eyed attention. She licked her lips, staring up at them. *Blood—there would be blood shed today, and not all of it hers.*

"I have asked you if you are ready for the duel of hunters," Te-kia prompted. "Your response is to be—"

"Ki," she said, the word little more than a whisper.

Te-kia glanced up at the quirri poised in the tower windows. "They didn't hear, small-song."

Leadenly, Dara looked around at the waiting faces of her kin. Then she glanced into the trees and thought with sick urgency of Wahonin. *"Kiiieeee!"* she cried with all the pain in her heart.

Every quirri echoed her scream. Dara felt the rush of air as the two chosen to duel swept down from the trees and soared around her. Their shadows rippled across the paving stones, broad-winged, black.

The duel was swift and furious. The hunters clutched at her gown, ripping away bright feathers as each tried to establish a foothold on her left shoulder. When neither would yield, they engaged each other, screaming, and fell to the pavement. Black feathers flew. Claws and beaks flashed. Dara backed away, but the hunters rolled after her, shrieking angrily. Blood spattered her bare feet, spattered the feathered gown.

And then, almost before she could draw a second breath, one of the two was dead, his neck broken. The other stood over him, bloodied, his chest heaving, his yellow eyes glaring. Dara pressed one fist to her mouth. Her heart no longer raced. Now it thundered.

"Give him your wrist, small-song."

Dara stared at the quirri. He stared back, arching his neck, spreading his wings. His beak was smeared with blood, his claws dark with it. Numbly Dara shook her head. "No."

"Small-song, he has broken his rival. He has won the right to ride your shoulder and to house his flock in any tower where you are welcome. If you complete the ceremony, he will feed you. He will watch out for you. He will protect you. If you do not, you will be a stranger in these mountains. And strangers do not pass here."

Agonized, she glanced at Kentith. He watched intently, lips parted. She drew a fluttering breath, pressing one hand to her heart. Then stiffly, sickened, she raised her arm and extended her wrist.

The hunter screamed once. Then, before Dara could shrink away, he jumped to her wrist and from there to her shoulder to tear at her earlobe.

Hot blood sprayed her neck. At the same moment, the quirri perched in the tower windows gathered themselves to fly. Involuntarily Dara cried out. She tried to clap a protective hand to her ear. The hunter clawed it away impatiently.

They must smell the blood, and then you can walk anywhere in these mountains and no quirri will draw blood from you again. And if any of your flock ever smells your blood, they will fly to you and they will defend you against all harm. If they must, they will call out other flocks as well.

Yes, Te-kia had told her that. He had told her in the smoke. And how many other things like this had she heard and forgotten? Forgotten because they terrified her, because they revolted her, because she wanted never to have heard them? So weak she could hardly stand, Dara let the blood from her wounded earlobe trickle down her neck as the quirri came in black clouds to catch its scent.

They screamed as they came. Their black wings beat, their black feathers rustled. Desperately Dara squeezed her eyes shut and drew a long, sobbing breath.

A giddiness, a moment's swirling confusion, and she no longer stood at the center of the quarreling birds. Instead she looked over the courtyard from the eyes of the small-flocks who clung to the walls. Dizzily, her heart fluttering like a bird's, she welded a thousand splintered images into one and gazed at the black column of quirri, at the lone figure that stood wilting at it center. Somehow the figure managed to hold itself upright as the quirri surged and screamed around it and finally rose in a long black streamer to the trees.

Distantly she saw the bloodied figure sag to its knees, its face white and fainting. In the last moments before it crumpled entirely, she saw Kentith desert his shaft of sun-light and run to its side.

After that came darkness, although it seemed to her that in the last fraction of a moment before she fainted, a soaring shape far larger than a quirri appeared against the sun and glided near, skimming across the courtyard on leathery wings. She glimpsed its hooked beak, its crested head, its cold white eyes, and fear sang briefly in her blood. Then there was only darkness.

CHAPTER EIGHT

Dara remembered little more of the day beyond the bitter taste of the drink Te-kia gave her each time she stirred and the dull ache of her head. She dreamed fretfully of quirri and of a darkness that came on leathery wings. When she woke, she lay in Te-kia's bed, wrapped in quilts, and once she recognized that the drink brought sleep, she took the cup eagerly.

The ritual had been fulfilled, the necessary ritual that cared nothing for her. The quirri that had won her shoulder perched on the beam above the bed, squinting down at her. He was her guardian now, no matter how little she wanted it. So long as she remained within sight of the mountains, they were blood-bonded.

During the heart of the day, she heard her kin talking in low voices in the courtyard. She understood nothing they said. Their voices were distant; they spoke her mother's tongue, not hers. Later they went away, and soon after that the cup that held the draught was empty. Reluctantly Dara woke and sat. Her head no longer ached. It felt empty now, a hollow shell. If she shook it, there would be echoes.

She stood carefully, not trusting her legs. It was late afternoon and Tith sent dusky swords through the high, narrow windows. Kentith and Te-kia sat beside the fire pit, not speaking. Dara watched them, wondering distantly which of them had dressed her in her own clothes again. Absently she raised one hand to her torn ear. There was no pain. Yet if Te-kia had treated it, she didn't remember.

95

Finally, when she had stood there for a very long time, Kentith glanced up and saw her. He jumped up and helped her the short distance to the fire pit.

She sat beside him, huddled and cold, and stared up at the quirri on the beam. "You've taught me to fly. You taught me in the smoke how to use the birds."

Te-kia shook his head. "No. You came to me prepared. You had already been touched by the daylight wings and you had slept the winged dreams. And so I gave you the preliminary lessons in the smoke. Now you must undertake the later lessons—the lessons that grow from experience."

She had been touched by the daylight wings? Was that what the Ilijhari called the absent spells? And the winged dreams— Dara shuddered. "If I don't want to learn more?"

"Then how will you watch over your home? How will you guard the roads and paths that lead to it? How will you know who approaches and what his intention may be? If you don't learn to use the birds, you may never learn why Harmin hasn't yet returned from Port Calibe."

Dara drew back, her heart contracting. "My father hasn't returned to Wahonin?" It was four days, perhaps five, since he had gone to Port Calibe.

"I've watched the valley and the road. I haven't seen him."

"But how can Kels Rinari hold him? How—" But it was useless to ask Te-kia that. "Can you see as far as Port Calibe?"

"So long as Ri-chi-ki stays within sight of the mountains, I can see what he sees. If he goes farther—or if I go farther—I can neither see with his eyes nor command him. The bond is broken."

"Then my father—do you know where he is? Do you know what has happened to him?"

Te-kia made a steeple of his fingers and rested his chin lightly upon it. "I don't. I have other responsibilities. I cannot neglect them now to search as far as Port Calibe, no matter how grave the situation there. But with a few more lessons, you can learn for yourself why he hasn't returned."

Dara stared at him. "What do you mean—'no matter how grave the situation there'?"

"I mean that first there were rumors that a firemaster had entered the settlement secretly. Now there is clear evidence that he has done so. You saw it yourself, four nights ago."

She had seen talons of lightning turn into rolling fire. Dara glanced quickly at Kentith. "But why would a firemaster come to Port Calibe?" And what did it have to do with her, with her father?

"To frighten the people who live there. To show them how little he cares for the authority of the local council," Te-kia said. "To prepare the way for others of his kind."

To introduce temples and tithes and public burnings to the new shore. And did Te-kia think Harmin's failure to return to Wahonin was somehow related to the presence of a firemaster in Port Calibe? "I—I won't use the quirri."

Te-kia's brows rose slightly at the wavering defiance in her voice. "Then you must learn to use the small-flocks very well because they are much the lesser of your two tools." He glanced up at the beam where his hunter perched. "And I'm sorry that you have let your feelings estrange you from the quirri when you know so very little of them. We've watched over these mountains together for many centuries now, the quirri and the Ilijhari. We've developed a bond that serves us both. Did you know that if you do not release your hunter to fly, he will starve himself waiting for your command? That's how strong his loyalty is to you, now that he's won your shoulder."

Involuntarily Dara looked up at the quirri. Intent yellow eyes returned her gaze. His feathers were intensely black, highlighted with blue. His beak and claws were a clean, bright yellow. "I won't go with him," Dara said, her voice wavering again.

"You need not go in order for him to feed."

"Then how—how do I release him? Can I command

him not to come back? Can I command him not to come to me again?''

"He'll always come back, unless you go beyond sight of the mountains. And you can release him simply by closing your eyes and letting him go.''

Was that all he would tell her? Dara glanced again at the intent bird, then closed her eyes and frowned—frowned so hard the muscles of her face hurt.

"No, you're holding him here. Let him go," Te-kia said softly. "Open your mind and let him fly away. Imagine—imagine that he's perched on your shoulder. And then feel his weight lift away as he spreads his wings and flies. Listen for the rustle of his wings as he follows Ri-chi-ki through the window.''

Dara's eyelids trembled. "If he takes me with him—''

"Have you ever tried to guide someone who refuses to trust you, small-song? He won't take you unless you want it.''

Reddening, Dara bowed her head and tried to do as he instructed. Tried to open her mind. Tried to imagine the bird's weight upon her shoulder. Tried to hear the rustle of his wings. Tried so hard to send the quirri away that her neck ached.

The only sound she heard was Te-kia softly rising from his cushion and crumpling something brittle into the fire pit. A moment later, the faint scent of smoke was in the room. Another moment and tension slowly left her. And then she felt the quirri's weight. She felt it so distinctly she could count the individual claws that dug at her shoulder. She choked back panic and drew deeply at the smoke.

Slowly the weight lifted from her shoulder and she heard the muted rustle of wings. Looking up, she saw the two quirri wing out the high, narrow window. Momentarily, as they vanished into the dusk, she felt the sting of an emotion she had not expected. Confused, she turned to Te-kia.

He sat cross-legged by the pit, his hands resting lightly on his knees, his eyes closed.

"He's gone." Kentith spoke softly, as if afraid of breaking a spell.

But there was no spell. Te-kia had simply gone with his hunter, leaving a few crumbled leaves burning in the pit. Dara studied his unguarded face and wondered where he flew. Was he in the treetops now, gliding among Tith's swords? Or did he soar high above the mountains, looking down over secret places no one else had glimpsed? Why did she feel he had deserted her when he had gone where she did not want to go?

She had not wanted to go until she saw the quirri winging away.

Kentith touched her hand. "You haven't eaten since last night. I'll bring you something."

Dara took only a few bites of the meal he set out. Nor did she stir when he brought wood to build up the fire for the night. She could not keep her eyes from Te-kia. He sat there with them, solid flesh. Yet somewhere he flew.

Why did it disturb her that she did not? Why did it disturb her when a few minutes ago she had felt only panic at the prospect of riding the quirri's wings?

Kentith tried several times to talk with her. Dara answered distractedly. After a while, she noticed with faint surprise that he had made up his bed and gone to sleep.

She kept vigil over Te-kia's inanimate body for a while longer. Then she slept too and dreamed of distances and space and of the wind that rushed restlessly at the mountainside. But there were no winged dreams tonight. She did not fly.

When she woke again, it was morning and Kentith and Te-kia were gone. Dara lay very still, studying the quirri who sat again on the beam above her head. It was clear from his posture that he guarded her.

When she sat, the quirri relaxed from his exaggerated sentinel's posture and leaned down to study her. They gazed at each other, the quirri's eyes bright, watchful, Dara's wary. At the slightest sign of invitation, Dara realized, he would take her shoulder.

Why shouldn't he be eager to claim his place? He had

broken his opponent for the right to sit upon her shoulder, but he could as well have been broken himself. After a hesitant moment, Dara drew a deep breath and extended one hand.

She felt his weight first. Then, strangely, she felt his pride as he stretched himself erect on her shoulder and drew his wings sleekly against his sides. She expected to feel his claws as well. But when she glanced down, she saw that he had carefully drawn them in. He gripped her shoulder with unarmed feet.

Gingerly she touched the feathers of his chest. He cocked his head, ruffing his plumage, and tilted a boasting glance at her. "You're young," she said, surprised. She hadn't seen it before, but it was clear this morning. He was like a young cock strutting his wall, bright-eyed and haughty and, in his way, comical in his exaggerated pride. "Ti-ri-ki. I'll call you Ti-ri-ki." The name was as cocky as he was.

She could not tell from his shimmering yellow gaze whether he understood. Nor did she understand why she felt different about him this morning. Why she had invited him to take her shoulder. Why she found herself thinking now of stepping into the courtyard, of loosing him into the sun. Of gliding with him down the mountainside.

Had her dreams prepared her for this? Or was it some belated effect of the smoke? She glanced around the hall and saw nothing to tell her where Te-kia and Kentith had gone.

She would find them if she flew with Ti-ri-ki.

The small-flocks came in shrieking waves when she stepped into the courtyard. They swooped around her, a rainbow in flight, but she did not whirl away with them this morning. The weight of the quirri on her shoulder held her in place, and the small-flocks darted noisily away without her.

And then she flew. She drew a long breath, closed her eyes, and loosed Ti-ri-ki to the wind. Te-kia's hall, the courtyard, her own still figure standing there—she glimpsed them all briefly before she went winging away.

Ti-ri-ki flew swiftly, exuberantly, eager to show her the power of his wings. Trees, sky, rugged mountain peak—for the first few minutes, image tumbled upon image, dizzily. Before Dara could bring one to focus, another displaced it. Even the air was different from what she had guessed from her winged dreams. It was not trackless, featureless. Instead it had weight and substance and contour. Currents ran through it, as through a body of water. And there were invisible peaks and troughs, like shifting landmarks in the sky. Ti-ri-ki rode them expertly, dipping and rising.

By the time Dara's stomach steadied, they had left the hall and towers behind. They flew high over the mountainside.

Morning sunlight was an intoxication. Dara lost herself in it, quickly forgetting why she had loosed the quirri. Ti-ri-ki's wings became hers, and she spread them to the air. They were as broad as the mountainside, as wide as the earth. They could carry her anywhere—to the peak of the mountains, to the inland, to the other side of the earth.

To Wahonin.

She steadied with that thought. If she could direct the quirri, if she could send him where she wished . . .

But she didn't know how. She only knew that suddenly she wanted keenly to see familiar places: halls, courtyards, fields and orchards. And faces. She thought of people she knew: of Piroka, who had taught her to mix ink, of Wina, who had tried so hard to teach her to cook, of Firin and Glea, who had let her sweep the halls with them when she was so small she could hardly push the broom. If she could see only one of them this morning . . .

Ti-ri-ki faltered and for a moment bobbed unsteadily in the air, buffeted by the wind. Then he wheeled and glided purposefully down the mountainside.

Trees and vegetation fled swiftly below. Stream waters glinted in the sun. Once Dara thought she saw a tower standing at the center of a bare patch. Then they soared over the tall, straight trees of the lower mountainside and Wahonin lay below.

The fields were no more than patches of plowed earth, the people who crawled among the furrows infinitely small. The halls and courtyards were compact, square, fastidiously laid out. The watchtower was a small shaft at the edge of an orchard of foreshortened trees.

Nearer. Please take me nearer.

It was that simple. She had only to think clearly of what she wanted and Ti-ri-ki faltered momentarily, then described a graceful spiral toward the tower. A moment later he perched on an upper sill, preening himself in the sun.

Dara laughed softly at his pleasure. He took a cock's pride in his feathers. He drew them through his beak lovingly and then fluffed them back into place with minute care. Only when he had completely groomed himself did he raise his head and glance around.

Dara had not realized until that moment, when Ti-ri-ki's yellow gaze spanned the orchard, how much keener his eyes were than hers. She could never have distinguished such detail from the uppermost tower window with her own eyes. But with Ti-ri-ki's she saw the curl of individual leaves, the green of tiny, hard fruits, the crispness of the spring grasses that grew under the trees. And there, near the center of the orchard, she saw freshly turned earth—a raw mound of it.

Her response was so sharp, so bitter that Ti-ri-ki burst into the air, shrieking. Dara had only a dizzying impression of the next moments. The world fell steeply away as Ti-ri-ki spiraled and climbed, spurred by her sudden distress. Trees, field and stock pens grew small again. Briefly the woodland road was below. Dara glimpsed a place where there were charred timbers and scorched trees, glimpsed red-clad figures in a mounted group, glimpsed the ravine she and Kentith had climbed. She hardly saw any of it.

How could she have forgotten? How could she have glided over the mountainside with Ti-ri-ki as if she had nothing to do but learn new pleasures? How could she have savored the spread of his wings, the buoying force of the air? How could she have laughed as he groomed his ruffled feathers in the sun? Had she forgotten there would be a fresh grave in the orchard?

A briefly glimpsed image flashed back into her mind. *Red-clad figures on the woodland road . . .* But she was too caught up in fresh grief to fully understand. It wasn't until Ti-ri-ki flew over the tall trees of the lower mountainside that fear struck like a fist to the stomach. *Kels Rinari's men were riding toward Wahonin.*

Ti-ri-ki stiffened and uttered a piercing cry, as if torn by her alarm. Then, before she could urge him back to the woodland, his wings dissolved. She stood again in Te-kia's courtyard. She blinked, stunned, as quirri burst from the twin towers, from the surrounding trees, and formed a screaming column around her. She saw Kentith run toward her, saw Te-kia pull him back. Far overhead she saw soaring shapes far larger than quirri, their eyes blazing with cold white light. Then the curtain of birds closed around her.

She was at the center of a funnel cloud. She pressed her hands to her ears, trying to shut out the scream of the quirri. She hardly noticed that after the first stunned moment she screamed too, too frightened, too confused to do anything else.

The quirri swirled around her until finally Ti-ri-ki breached the curtain they formed and settled upon her shoulder. Then the other quirri rustled away into the trees of the mountainside and Dara gazed blankly around, her knees so weak they sagged. Te-kia and Kentith stood together at the far end of the courtyard. Te-kia still grasped Kentith's arm, holding him back. A rapid pulse beat in Dara's head. She could not tell if it was hers or Ti-ri-ki's.

Te-kia approached cautiously. "What happened, smallsong?"

"I—I don't know." She pressed her temples with trembling fingers. "I flew with Ti-ri-ki to Wahonin. I saw Kels Rinari's men on the woodland road. I wanted Ti-ri-ki to go back. I wanted to know why they were coming to Wahonin. But he screamed—and then I was here. I was—"

Lost in a cloud of shrieking quirri, while far overhead, casting broad-winged shadows . . .

"What did you feel when you saw Rinari's men?"

"I was frightened."

Te-kia nodded. "You were frightened, so Ti-ri-ki called for his flock to guard you until he could get back to your shoulder. And then he flew as hard as his wings would carry him. He is your protector. He felt your fear and he protected you."

Dara glanced at the quirri. His feathers were ruffled. His dark chest heaved. "But I wasn't in danger. Kels Rinari's men are on the woodland road, not here."

"You were afraid, weren't you?"

"Yes. But not that they would hurt me. They're riding to Wahonin. They—"

"Yes, I understand that. And after Ti-ri-ki has carried you longer on his wings, he will understand too. Until then, until the bond between you has matured and refined, you must govern your responses carefully. Ti-ri-ki's first concern is not to evaluate your situation, not to understand the reason for your panic—but to protect you. Simply to protect you."

And by his lights, he had done so, surrounding her with a screaming curtain of quirri, then flying back to her shoulder. Dara nodded shakily. "Will he take me back to Wahonin?"

"Now? Tell me how many men you saw. A large group? Was Rinari with them?"

"I—" Pausing, frowning, Dara was surprised to find how much detail she could call back. "There were just a few of them. Three or four. They were riding hard. Not because they were in a hurry—just for the sport of it. I could tell. Rinari wasn't with them."

Te-kia nodded thoughtfully. "If there are so few, they have come with a message. So you will be as much interested in what they say as in what they do when they reach Wahonin. And in that case, the quirri isn't your best vehicle. His vision is acute, but his hearing is not so very much keener than yours or mine. He won't be able to hear what's said without drawing attention to himself.''

Dara nodded. Certainly a large black hunter, hovering at the edge of whatever group gathered, would command attention. But no one would notice if a grey-dun or a yellow-beak perched on a wall or a sill, listening to everything with bright-eyed inconsequence. Dara caught her lower lip in her teeth. ''The small-flocks?'' She glanced distractedly at Kentith, hardly seeing him.

Te-kia paced toward the courtyard wall. ''You've barely mastered the first steps of flying with the quirri. You must be far more artful to use the small-flocks.''

''But I have to go, Te-kia.''

He thought for a moment, head bowed. ''No,'' he said. ''Your father—Harmin—is a friend. I will go.''

Dara hesitated, relieved and disappointed at once, uncertain she could simply wait while Kels Rinari's men rode into Wahonin. ''Can you really listen to what people say through the small-flocks? Can you understand?''

''How do you think I learned your language? Wait here.'' He sat on the courtyard wall, legs crossed, and held his arms wide. The small-flocks swept to him noisily from the trees. They eddied around him for a moment, bright feathers glinting in the morning sun. Then they gathered themselves into long streamers and darted away down the mountainside.

When they had gone, Te-kia remained, head bowed, eyes closed. Ri-chi-ki crouched protectively on his shoulder.

Dara drew a long, sighing breath and met Kentith's eyes. Neither of them spoke. The mountainside was suddenly very still.

As if it had been deserted. As if *she* had been deserted.

And she had. Te-kia had simply flown away and left her helpless and wondering. Dara glanced at his inanimate body, frowning. Then, shaking her head, she spread her own arms and drew one long breath and then another.

The wind came first, sweeping lightly at her feet. Then the small-flocks burst from the surrounding trees and swept around her and she was torn in a hundred directions. The courtyard, Te-kia's hall, the mountainside were fragmented. They became nothing more than flickering images. *Ti-ri-ki, stay here,* she called back and hoped he understood.

She had only one clear vision before the small-flocks swept her away. Kentith stood beside the body she had abandoned, his face taut and still. Looking down at him, she felt a sharp sting of misgiving. She was deserting him just as surely as Te-kia had deserted her.

But it was too late to turn back. The small-flocks were already darting away down the mountainside, carrying her with them.

CHAPTER NINE

Sunlight splintered as Dara flew. Trees were torn into green slivers and Dara caught flickers of rocks and sky from hundreds of swiftly changing perspectives. Dizzily, she tried to shut out the racing fragments of vision, but she could not. The flocks flew in shimmering waves. Individual birds were bright particles dancing in the sky. She saw only chaos.

Did the flocks understand where they must take her? Dara struggled to call up images of the downward sweep of the mountainside, of the valley cradled below. *My home—take me to my home.* Halls, courtyards, fields—

She could not fix the familiar scenes in mind. Detail was swept away, displaced by fluttering shreds of color and light: clouds, the sun, an occasional glint of water. Desperately Dara tried to weld the rapid-flowing flickers into coherent images.

She had done it in the courtyard after Ti ri ki tore her earlobe, when the quirri swarmed to smell her blood. But the small-flocks had been still then. Now they swept through the morning by the hundreds, tearing her among them.

In fact, she realized dizzily, the wave of birds was broader and deeper than it had been just a few minutes before. *Te-kia?* she called. Had her flocks overtaken his? *Te-kia, please, if you hear me . . .*

There was no response. But a few confused minutes later, the flow of shattered images slowed. Dara saw the mountainside below, the tall trees bowing in the wind.

There were thin clouds to the north, clear sky to the east and south. The flocks bobbed and darted around her.

Had Te-kia heard and helped her slip into the perspective of a single pair of eyes? She had only the faintest sense of the bird that carried her. She could not measure its wingspan or guess its color or breed, even though she commanded its vision—and its other senses as well. Strangely, its eyes found colors in sunlight she had not seen there when she flew with Ti-ri-ki. And the earth itself seemed to generate subtle messages. She could not interpret their significance, but she felt their shifting tug and pull as she flew.

Wahonin. Take me to my home.

The bird that carried her gave no sign it understood, but a few swooping minutes later the flock flew over the outermost fields.

The woodland road.

Much of the flock fell away as they crossed the valley, settling to the fields, to the courtyards, to the orchard. Only a handful of small brown birds with white-ringed necks and speckled chests remained. They swept down the road in loose formation, scooping tiny insects from the air as they went. Briefly Dara lost herself in their darting pleasure. Then she saw red uniforms below and heard the strike of hooves. Quickly, effortlessly, she winged across the road.

The messenger who had come the first day was accompanied by two younger men. They wore their uniforms carelessly, the coats unbuttoned. Their horses danced down the road with exaggerated vivacity, their flanks dark with sweat as they mounted the rise and approached Wahonin.

Dara followed. People came warily from the halls as the three men pulled their horses to a skittish halt in the central courtyard. The guardsmen laughed as they dismounted, but their blades flashed in the sun. "Who governs here?" the messenger demanded loudly.

Ebin, Harmin's assistant, crossed the flagged pavement. His broad face was grey, guarded. "Harmin is headsman, but he cannot speak to you today."

The messenger laughed again, sharply. His face was brightly flushed and his voice held an edge of intoxication. "Of course he can't. He's in the deep hold of the port prison. Thrown there for setting fire to the seventh posthouse. I'm here to speak with the man who succeeds him."

They accused her father of setting fire to the posthouse? When it had burned more than a day after he passed? Stunned, Dara settled to a nearby sill.

Ebin crossed his arms over his chest, but the very stiffness of his posture betrayed his ill-ease. "No one succeeds Harmin. He holds a life appointment."

"Then you'll want him back, won't you? And here's the master's word for you. The master is a man of some influence, you know. The prison governor takes dinner with him regular, and the master keeps two constables on his payroll. He will do what he can to buy off the charges against your headsman, but he needs someone to testify for him. He needs the girl who was seen riding down to the port with him."

Ebin frowned sharply. "Dara? His daughter? They left here together seven days ago. Isn't she with him now?"

"Would the master need her if she was? No, your headsman sent her back here for safekeeping. The master knows it and you know it. Give her over and you'll soon have your man back. Don't and he's locked in the bottom hold for as long as anyone cares to keep him there."

So Kels Rinari had no more believed Harmin's story than Kentith had believed hers. He had thrown Harmin into the deep hold and sent his men to be sure she learned it.

The deep hold, where black water washed in with every tide, where the rodents were more vicious than anywhere else in Port Calibe. No man lived long in the deep hold. Kentith had told her that much.

The bird's tiny body shivered with Dara's urgency. What could she do? Go to Rinari? Plead with him to release Harmin? What did he care for her feelings?

Offer him what he wanted then?

She couldn't. But if she didn't, her father . . .

Her father?

Her father wasn't shut in the prison at Port Calibe. Her father had walked away over the mountains more than seventeen years ago. And her mother— How badly would Kels Rinari want her if he knew she was half an Ilijhari?

Half a savage. She had called the Ilijhari savages herself.

Caught up in her thoughts, Dara scarcely heard the remainder of the talk on the plaza. It was not so hard to see what she must do. Draw her hair back in a braid. Dress herself in skins. Go to Kels Rinari and confront him, Ti-ri-ki on her shoulder. He would have no reason to hold Harmin then. No reason to demand that she honor the *damen-kest*. Because how would it enhance his status to take an Ilijhari as his wife?

The three uniformed men gave their horses to the care of stock workers and followed Ebin into the hall. Dara hesitated on the sill. But there was no reason to stay when her path was clear.

To Te-kia's hall.

Her thoughts flew as rapidly as the bird that carried her. They would need three days, perhaps four, to reach Port Calibe by foot if the weather held. Te-kia would give them food. When they arrived, they would ask directions. And when they reached Rinari's door—

Preoccupied, she had no warning. One moment she was caught up in her plans. The next she was torn again in a hundred directions. Sky and mountainside shattered and the fragments whirled around her. Trees, sun, clouds— She saw them from a hundred sets of eyes in swift succession.

The small-flocks surged around her again. Their colors danced in the sun. Half-blinded, she tried to find her escort, but she could not pick it from the others, could not slip safely back into its senses. Sick, terrified, she tumbled forward through the air. Briefly she saw the blaze of white eyes, heard the rush of leathery wings.

Stop! Te-kia, make it stop! Did he hear?

It did not stop. Instead earth and trees surged steeply

toward her as the flock dived toward the mountainside. Dara screamed, silently, and heard the shrill of a hundred voices.

And then she stood in Te-kia's courtyard, Te-kia's fingers digging into her forearms. His grey eyes were cold with anger. "Didn't I tell you to wait here?"

Dara stared up at him, too shaken to respond.

"Would I have given you instructions if I didn't intend you to listen? No, don't argue with me. Give me an answer. I'm your guide. I'm your sponsor. And I told you to wait."

Dara drew a shivering breath. "Yes. Yes, you told me. But I had to learn why Kels Rinari's men came. And I did. I—"

"You learned for one reason. Because I drew the flocks away from you and left you a single set of wings. If I hadn't done that, what would you have learned?"

So he had heard her plea. And whatever she had learned, she owed to his intervention. Reluctantly Dara met his eyes. "Nothing," she admitted. "But, Te-kia, you did help me, and now I have to go. To Port Calibe. I have to go now. If you will give us food—"

He released her abruptly. "You intend to give Rinari what he wants?"

"*No.* I'll go to him and tell him I'm not Harmin's daughter. I'll tell him I'm adopted. That my mother was—" She caught herself and glanced away, embarrassed.

Te-kia's lips quirked. "You'll tell him your mother was a feathered savage?"

"I'll tell him she was an Ilijhari."

"Yes? And then?"

"Then he won't want me. He'll free my father and we'll go back to Wahonin. We'll—"

"You don't think this is exactly what Rinari wants? To bring you to his door?"

"Of course it's what he wants! But once I tell him—"

Te-kia shook his head. "Small-song, you have fledgling fever. You've flown once with your quirri and you think you're master of earth and sky. The truth is, you've learned

the very first lessons. You don't even know how many
more there are to be learned. The revenants—you've seen
the revenants. Don't you even intend to ask me about them
before you go bolting away? Or do you remember so well
what I told you of them in the smoke?''

''I don't know what you mean.'' But she glanced up,
remembering hooked beaks, crested heads, the blaze of
cold eyes.

''They come from another plane, from another time. If
you must, you can summon them fully into the material
plane. You can use them, just as you use the quirri. But
you must employ them far more carefully. Their abilities
are different and much greater than those of any living
species. You must not fly too long upon their wings, and
you must never permit them to taste blood.

''You must not use them unless you have no other alternative. The risk is too great—to you, to all of us.

''That is one lesson, the bare beginning of it. There are
many others—and Port Calibe is a poor place to master
them, particularly now. The situation there is far more
volatile than you recognize.

''And Ti-ri-ki is as newly fledged to the shoulder as you
are to the sky. It's customary for quirri and master to spend
twelve days training under the sponsor and his hunter before they make their way together. And that is the custom
for those who have grown up among us, who already have
an understanding of the disciplines involved.''

Dara shook her head. ''Te-kia, I don't have twelve days.
And I don't intend to make my way—not the way you
mean. I'm not an Ilijhari, and I'll never live as one.''

''Oh? Then how will you live?''

''As one of the simple folk. As I always have.'' Because
nothing had changed. She saw that with quick, saving clarity. She was not an Ilijhari simply because she had come
to Te-kia. Nor had the blooding made her one. She had
glimpsed her natural parents only once, in the smoke. Her
other kin she knew not at all, except for Te-kia. Harmin,
Mirina and her mother had shaped her—shaped her as one
of the simple folk.

"Dara, you have a power that is not simple at all," Te-kia said softly. "You can't set it aside because it comforts you to go on thinking of yourself as one of the simple folk. The Ilijhari gifts are awake in you now, and you'll learn just how great they are if you leave me without training them correctly, without learning to discipline yourself to them." When she did not respond, he shrugged. "But you don't want to hear those things. Tell me, small-song, can you use the small-flocks well enough to find Kentith?"

She looked at him blankly, then glanced around the courtyard. She hadn't even noticed that Kentith was gone.

"No, he's not here. And you won't find him in the hall. Call down the small-flocks, why don't you, and discover where he's gone."

"Ti-ri-ki—"

"Call down the flocks. Ti-ri-ki will go with you to Port Calibe, but the small-flocks will be your best eyes and ears there, simply because you can station them wherever you wish. If you go to Port Calibe without learning to use them, you are foolish."

"Will they come so far with me?"

"The forest flocks won't follow you, but the local small-flocks will be at your command wherever you go, even if you wander beyond sight of the mountains. If you can discover how to command them."

She flushed at the dry note in his voice.

"One hint, small-song," he said, before he turned away. "Don't give yourself to the entire flock. Find the leader and fly with him."

Dara stared at him, tight-lipped, as he disappeared into the hall. When he had gone, she coaxed Ti-ri-ki from her shoulder and loosed him to join the other quirri in the tower. Then she retreated into the trees. Kentith had probably gone no farther than the stream.

Rebellious, preoccupied, she did not begin to worry until the first hour had passed. Then she remembered the tautness, the stillness of his face earlier, when she flew after Te-kia. She remembered that moment in the smoke when her father had turned away from her mother and gone alone toward the inland. Was that what Kentith had done? Had he gone on alone?

Uneasiness settled in the pit of her stomach, a cold weight. She glanced up at the small-flocks gathered in the trees. They watched over her nervously, fluttering and chattering.

How was she to pick the leader from the flock? She counted at least a dozen different breeds. Did the flock as a whole have a single leader? Or was there a separate leader for each breed?

Anxiously she watched the birds. Some were cocky, some reserved. Some sprang from perch to perch; others gathered in stable clutches.

"To find the leader, you must summon him."

Dara jumped. She had not heard Te-kia approach.

"You must ask silently for him. Imagine your hand extended. Imagine the touch of his claws as he settles on your finger. Then open your eyes and you will know which is the leader."

Dara looked up at him in confusion. Could it be so simple? "Is there just one leader?"

"No, there is one from each breed. But you want to fly with the pale-nape, the one you flew with this morning. He's the most responsive. Can you find him?"

Dara gazed up into the branches. Half a hundred small birds with fastidious white collars and speckled chests mingled with the larger flock. She could not pick any one from the others. Nervously she licked her lips and closed her eyes.

"No, don't move your hand. *Imagine* it extended, the thumb against your palm, the fingers parallel to the ground. No, you're trying too hard. I can see the muscles of your face tighten. Inhale deeply, then release a long breath. As you do so, feel your hand float away from your side. Slowly, slowly . . . Do you feel it?"

"Yes," Dara said faintly. Her hands were cupped in her lap. She felt them there. At the same time, one had risen to float weightlessly before her.

"Now very quietly—silently—ask the leader of the palenapes to come to you. When he hears, you will feel his claws."

Come. Come please.

"Another deep breath," Te-kia coached.

She nodded and inhaled. Monitoring the tension of her facial muscles, of the muscles of her shoulders and arms, she slowly exhaled. *Please come to me.*

Before the breath was gone, invisible claws closed around her extended forefinger. Startled, Dara opened her eyes and found one of the white-necked birds watching intently from a low branch, poised to fly. Her mouth was suddenly dry. "I've found him."

"Good. Now go with him. Extend your arms to the flock and let him carry you."

Could it really be so easy? Dara licked her lips again and held her arms wide.

The wind touched her and lifted her. And then she was darting away through the trees on a single pair of wings. Elated, she slipped into the pale-nape's senses. Light changed and sensory organs she could not name began to record unfamiliar messages. The earth spoke to her, tugging and pulling. Even the sky had distant, keening things to say. She spiraled upward, then sternly drove the pale-nape back down into the trees. They soared around Te-kia's towers and then described a series of widening circles through the forest. Rocky outcroppings, shallow streams, scrub and trees

She did not know how long she flew before she found Kentith trudging up the mountainside, his hands thrust deep into his pockets, his bright hair tied at the nape of his neck. He placed one foot before the other mechanically, taking little notice of his surroundings. His face held no expression, but Dara could guess what he felt.

Kentith had saved her from the seamen. He had walked with her through the woodland and up the mountainside. He had shared hunger and danger with her—and so much more. But she had scarcely spoken to him since reaching Te-kia's hall. And this morning she had abandoned him without a word, going where he could not go. She had deserted him, leaving only her still body behind.

And so he had gone on his way, and she could not even call him back. He only glanced up absently when the pale-nape darted around him, crying.

She fluttered anxiously, helplessly, for minutes longer before she urged the pale-nape back to Te-kia's hall.

The flocks that had flown with her streamed back to the trees in noisy agitation. Dara opened her eyes. Te-kia sat nearby, cross-legged, silently watching her. "Te-kia, I've seen him. I found him. But I don't know how to reach him." He must have left Te-kia's hall two hours ago or more, and the mountainside was broad and featureless. "I—if I had spoken to him this morning, if I had said something—" But she hadn't. And so he had gone on alone without even saying good-bye.

"Another deep breath—and then tell me why it is so important to reach him."

"I—" Dara paused, staring at him blankly.

"Because you want him to go to Port Calibe with you?" he prompted.

"Yes." But she frowned as she said it. Kentith had just come from Port Calibe. He had just escaped from the very prison where Kels Rinari had thrown Harmin. How could she ask him to go back there?

"No," she said. "I'll go alone. But if I don't find him first . . . If I don't find him, how will he reach the inland with no one to show him the way? Without warm clothes? Without food?"

"It will be difficult," Te-kia said. "But if you remain here while he makes the journey, I'll teach you to guide him yourself. When you learn to use the birds, you can send the quirri to him with food. You can direct him to shelter and to places where our kin will give him what he needs."

If she remained here. "You sent him away."

"I told him I thought it was time to begin his journey. He cannot remain on this side of the mountains, small-song. He is a priest, and there is a firemaster in Port Cal-ibe.''

"You sent him away so I'd have to stay here with you while he travels through the mountains. So I'd have to train with you." Because Te-kia had guessed, even before she returned to the plaza, that she would insist upon going to Kels Rinari to free her father. "What will happen if I refuse? Will you let him starve?"

Te-kia sighed. "No, I will not let him starve. I will not let any danger overtake him that I can prevent."

"Then tell me how to reach him. If he must go, I can't let him go this way. Without even saying good-bye." And perhaps if she found him, it would not be necessary for him to go today. If she found him and brought him back to Te-kia's hall, if she promised him that once her father was free she would go to the inland with him—

Did she want to do that? Could she leave her home and her people for Kentith?

How could she even think of it when she had met him only six days before?

Yet she was thinking of it.

Dara bowed her head in confusion, and the small-flocks began to flutter noisily from branch to branch. An hour before, she had told Te-kia that once Harmin was free, she would return to Wahonin and live as one of the simple folk. She had told herself that she *was* one of the simple folk. How could she think of going with Kentith if that was true?

"I have to see him," she said in a low voice. "I have to see him again before he goes." Something had begun between them: a friendship, or something more. Perhaps the bond must be broken now, but not this way, without a parting word.

Te-kia studied her silently, then stood. "Then come with me to my hall. I'll give you supplies for the night. And I'll give you something else as well. Something that will help you sort out the confusion of your heart."

"Something?" she said blankly.

"Something to burn in the fire. It will help both of you

come to a clearer understanding of who you are and what you must do.''

"Will it work? He didn't hear when you spoke to me in the smoke, did he?''

"That was a different smoke. This one has worked for others who weren't Ilijhari.'' He turned back to the courtyard. "Come.''

Still she hesitated. Te-kia's mood, his ungrudging capitulation, puzzled her. "Aren't you angry?''

He turned back. "Because you insist upon going to find him? No, I guessed you might. Are you angry with me for hiding him?''

Dara met his cool grey gaze. "No,'' she said finally. "You are my guide.'' And in this, whether it had been his intent or not, he had guided her to the knowledge that she was not so simple as she had thought, nor so decided. Nor were her objectives as clear as she had thought.

"Yes, I am your guide, and I am guiding you as well as I know how. I hope when you look back later, you will see that I did what I could.''

Dara nodded and bowed her head. Except for the slight flavor of misgiving, his words seemed much like her father's last words when he left her on the woodland road seven days before.

Seven days—or a lifetime?

CHAPTER TEN

It was cold on the mountainside. The moon floated among the stars, a remote silver disk, and the treetops rustled and stirred. Small animals scampered for hiding as Dara passed. She didn't see them, but she felt some echo of their alarm. She was dressed as an Ilijhari, in furs and skins, but tonight when she loosed Ti-ri-ki into the trees, it was not to find game. It was to plot her course, as Te-kia had shown her, to the place where Kentith slept— to the place where they would take their parting if he chose to go on to the inland tomorrow.

Dara's throat closed when she thought of it. Her mother had gone to her father just this way, Te-kia said, and burned heart-leaves while he slept. They had dreamed together and talked in their dreams and briefly her mother had thought that he might relinquish his dream of a plot of land beyond the mountains. But her father had been a plain man, and the very strangeness of the experience had hastened his parting.

Dara touched the small leather pouch Te-kia had given her and loosed Ti-ri-ki into the dark trees again.

It was late when she found Kentith. He slept in a small clearing, curled in a bed of leaves against a mossy log. Dara looked down at him and shivered under the cold touch of the wind. His face was pale by moonlight. He seemed thinner than when they had met. She wished she could curl up beside him and share the furs Te-kia had given her. But the heart-leaves told the heart best, Te-kia said, if one of them slept when the fire was kindled.

So instead she placed the furs carefully over him, then set Ti-ri-ki loose in the trees while she dug a small pit and gathered stones to line it. Kentith stirred only once, the bed of leaves rattling as he huddled deeper into it. When the pit was lined, Dara filled it with twigs and sifted dried leaves around them. Then she crumbled the heart-leaves over those and opened the tinder pot Te-kia had given her.

The fire caught, flaring brightly. Almost immediately Dara saw the waver of heat in the air. She hesitated for a moment, kneeling beside the fire pit, then retreated. Bracing her back against the log where Kentith slept, pulling her knees against her chest, she waited tensely for drowsiness.

It did not come. The leaves blazed and crackled. Smoke curled around her, its scent sweet, faintly spicy. Ti-ri-ki perched nearby, the light of the fire briefly flaring in his eyes, then fading. A few crackling minutes, and leaves and twigs were gone, consumed. There were only threads of fire crawling among the ashes.

Dara watched them, disappointed. Had Te-kia been wrong? Were heart-leaves only for full-blooded Ilijhari?

But her father had dreamed with them. Perhaps if she stirred the ashes . . .

But to do that she must get up from where she sat. And, she discovered, she could not. She instructed her muscles carefully, but they refused to respond. She could only stare helplessly into the fire, listening to a faint, distant sigh she recognized finally as her own breath.

Was this the beginning of the dream? If it was, she did not like it. She did not like the sensation of limbs suddenly so slowed in their response that they might have been frozen. She did not like the occasional remote concussion that was her heartbeat or the dry grittiness of her eyes. She tried to blink them against the smoke that still hung in the small clearing and could not.

When she felt the tear, she did not know if she cried at her own helplessness or if her eyes had simply begun to water. The single drop of moisture trickled slowly from her left eye and stood cold and still on her cheek.

No, don't cry, Sister.

Mirina? But how could Mirina speak to her here? And when had the moon glided into the clearing? The concussion of Dara's heart speeded, jarring at her breastbone.

Have no regrets, Sister. You thought I left you and you shed tears for me. I felt them upon my hand. But it is as I told you. I still live for you. I am in the smoke and in the stones and in the wind that blows through the trees. I have light to give whenever you need it. Ask and I will shine for you tonight.

Paralyzed, disbelieving, Dara watched as Mirina stepped from the moon's bright disk. She was dressed as Dara had seen her last, in the shirt their grandmother had stitched, their mother's hair clips in her hair. Her face was misty, her arms pale, but her presence was calm and strong.

Dara found her silent voice, the same voice she had used when she took smoke with Te-kia. *Mirina, I didn't cry only for you. I cried for myself too, because you left me.*

That isn't such a terrible thing. Surely I would have cried if you had left me. But now you know that I did not truly leave you, Sister. So why do you cry still? Tell me what disturbs you.

Distantly Dara felt a second tear course down her cheek after the first. She tried to find some excuse for it, but she knew Mirina wanted the truth. *Mirina, I've lost myself. I don't know anymore if I'm truly one of the simple folk. I don't know if I belong to Wahonin. I'm not even your sister, not really. I don't understand who I am.*

Mirina glided nearer, her features shrouded in radiance, her voice as firm, as certain as it had always been. *The answer to that is simple. You are the person you always were—the sister I love, different from me because our blood is different, but dear to me for your differences.*

Yes, I am different from you! Dara cried in pain. *You always knew what to do, and then you did it, and it was so simple. But I don't see as clearly as you do. And now I don't even know what I want to do. Or what I should do.* If she was one of the simple folk, then surely she must go to Port Calibe and free Harmin. If she was an Ilijhari, she must remain with Te-kia and train herself to use the birds. And if she was neither—

But how could she examine her obligation to Kentith in those terms? He had walked with her, he had listened to her troubles and reassured her, he had held himself ready to protect her. Surely her first obligation was to him.

But if she left her father in the port prison while she helped Te-kia guide Kentith safely across the mountains—

Here is what you must do, Sister. You must give close attention to the path that lies at your feet. When it forks, you must quiet yourself until you discover the way that beckons you most clearly. For this is what your life will be: a series of paths, some of them straight and clear, some obscure, some splitting and leading in different directions at once.

You must search your way from hour to hour and day to day, discovering each successive step in its turn and then taking it—until finally there are no more steps. Until finally you have taken them all.

Dara's heart jarred distantly. Was Mirina telling her she must die too? *When will that be?*

You'll know, just as I knew. You'll pick your way down the pathways of your life, and they will seem precarious and long. Sometimes it will seem you've lost your way, as now. Other times you will stumble. But if you pick yourself up and look around carefully, you will find your way again.

So that is what you must do. And I will be with you as you do it, just as I'm with you now.

But you aren't really here! Dara protested. *You've come from the smoke. You're a dream.* How could she take counsel from a mirage? From a phantom?

I've left my body. My hands are cold and my heart is still. But does that mean that I am dead to you—my dearest sister?

The paralysis had eased. Dara drew a long, shivering breath and lowered her gaze from the radiant face. Did she want it that way? Did she want to believe nothing of

Mirina was left? *You'll never be dead to me,* she said. *I thought you were. I thought you were gone. But it isn't so.* Because how could she dream so vividly of Mirina if there weren't something of her left? And the light—

Mirina had swept up the moon's light and mantled herself in it. Her features were lost. Only her arms remained, reaching from the boiling silver mist for Dara. Dara sighed deeply, drawn. From the corners of her eyes, she saw that Kentith lay watching, saw that Mirina's brilliant silver arms reached to enclose him too.

Their touch was cool, bodiless. They drew her into a place where time and dimension became meaningless, where there was only light diffusing in every direction. Mirina was there. Her mother was there. So was her grandmother and the Ilijhari mother she had never met. Dara could not see them. They were no more than indistinct shadows lost in the moving light. But she felt their touch at her heart and tears slid down her cheeks.

After a long while, the light began to change. It became not moonlight but sunlight, and Dara no longer knew the person who cast her shadow against it.

Son, I saw your face when you went with the priests. You were angry and you were afraid, but you showed me only a smiling mask—a mask that haunts me every day I live.

Dara felt Kentith stir. He was near. Briefly she thought she felt the touch of his hand. *No, Mother.*

You showed me a mask and I know it, because when did I ever show you my true face? When did I ever show you what I felt at seeing Tith's eyes look out at me from your face on the day you were born? When did I ever show you how it frightened me to love you as you grew, knowing that one day Tith would demand you? I never offered myself at the temple gates. I never wanted a priest's child. But I bore one anyway and there was nothing I could do to make you different. So I hid my face and showed you only empty smiles, and you learned from me to wear masks.

No.

Yes. All through your childhood, you woke with night-

mares. You never told me what you dreamed. You only sat rigidly in my arms as I tried to comfort you. But I knew what you dreamed because I had the same nightmares—that the sun had come in a priest's robes to take you away.

Mother—

And then the sun did come in a priest's robes and when you left, you showed me nothing but a mask. Now I want to think that you've forgiven me. But can a mask forgive? Son, son, take away your mask and show me what you feel. If you hate me still, I want to see it.

How can you see anything? Dara made a fire and you've come out of the smoke. You're not real. You're—

I've come out of your heart. You carry me there wherever you go. And I want to see your face.

Dara's heart contracted with distant shock. She could not see Kentith in the moving light, but for a moment she glimpsed his mother and saw what she was: one of the simple folk—a bride of the *damen-kest*. And Dara understood then why Kentith had followed her that first night in the woodland. She understood the bond that had formed so easily between them. She groped through the luminous mist for his hand.

Their fingers touched. He clutched her hand. And then they were together, running toward a place where not light but moisture boiled in the air. Running so fast their feet never touched ground, they plunged through a rainbow gate into a swirling rain.

Why wouldn't you show her your face?

She's seen it. There is no mask.

There is, Dara insisted. *I've seen it myself. You laugh at things that make you angry. You hate the priests, but when you speak of them, your voice says you don't care at all. You told me yourself—*

I told you that there is no one in the world who cares if I'm angry or afraid. So why should I bother feeling those things?

But you do feel them, and I care, just as she cared. Don't you know that?

For a moment he did not answer. Then he said softly,

*Yes, you do care. You care about me just as I care about
you. But didn't you heed what your sister told you? Didn't
you look yet at your path—and mine? They are clear now.
All you have to do is look and you will see them. Yours
leads back to Port Calibe—and mine across the mountains.*

Dara hesitated, gazing blindly around, suddenly uncertain whether the moisture on her face was rain or tears. *I
don't want to look now.*

Look.

Dara drew a long breath and gazed into the swirling fog
that enclosed them.

The path was there, a broad mossy track. They stood
side by side upon it. Yet a short distance away, it forked,
and it was as Kentith said. One branch led to Port Calibe.
She could see the port settlement in the distance. The
other led into the mountains.

She shook her head, trying to deny what she saw. As
she did so, the moisture that had boiled around them
slowly became moonlight again. They sat together, leaning against the log, the moon standing before them. *Must
you go to the inland?*

There is no other place for me.

*Then will you wait and take me with you? When I've
freed my father from Kels Rinari?*

No, Dara. Your path does not lead there.

One day it might.

*It will not lead you to me. Because I am meant to go
alone, and I am meant to be alone, except for what travels
with me.*

And what is that?

It is this.

Dara drew back from the sudden scorch of heat. Kentith
stood before her now, and at first she thought that it was
he who blazed so fiercely. Instead it was a man in golden
robes. He stood behind Kentith, his wide sleeves blazing.
His arms spread wide to embrace Kentith. His eyes were
twin suns. They glowed so violently that their light obscured his face. Dimly Dara saw that he was tall and an-

gular. His fingers were bony and his bare scalp wept with angry red sores.

Who—who is he?

This is Narkith, who raised my fire. Until he came, I was dark. I wore the gowns of a priest and I sang the verses, but I had no compunction when occasionally I went to the gates to meet the women who gathered there. Because I had been told that Tith had touched me so slightly that he could never afflict a son of mine through me.

Near the end, there was a woman who came often—for me. Only for me. I loved her, and she wanted my son even though she knew he would be dark.

But Narkith came and my eyes burned and I knew then that I had been told wrong. There is more of this terrible gift in me than anyone saw, and clearly it can breed through me. And so what did I give my love—I left her carrying my child—but the same pain my mother knew? And what did I give our son, if the child was male? And the other sons I may have given those few other women?

I cannot take back past acts, but I will not give this gift new flesh. When I leave you, I will walk alone. You cannot join me on my path because it is a solitary path. I will not have you there.

Then tonight . . . she said, her voice fading. Was tonight all they had?

Tonight is the closest we will be. Let it be good.

Yes, let it be good, she echoed faintly.

As if at her will, the fire blazed in its pit, communicating warmth to every part of her body. Kentith sat with her again and they talked, their voices ringing silently against the surrounding trees.

They spoke as friends, as kin, as lovers whose union could be consummated only in the smoke. Later, when they had said everything that needed to be said, when they had spoken an entire lifetime to each other, the moon took wing and carried them among the stars. The sun raced after them, its light so tightly contained it fell in a brilliant cone. Each time they dipped near the earth, they saw brilliances gleaming from broad, dark surfaces and shadows lying heavily upon light ones. After a while the stars changed in their configuration and bombarded them with darting needles of light. Soon after that they slept.

Dara woke at midmorning, cold, stiff and hungry. At first, when she opened her eyes, she only stared blankly at the empty pile of leaves beside her. Then her heart clutched. Had he gone on with no further word?

"What did you put in the fire?"

Kentith stood nearby, pale and unsmiling. Dara met his eyes and her shoulders tightened. "Te-kia calls it heart-leaf. Do you—do you remember what happened? What we said?"

There was no tenderness in his face. There was only hard tension. "I remember very well. Kels Rinari is holding your father in the port prison. You told me that, but not why."

Dara paled. She had not intended to tell him that, but the smoke had loosened her tongue. "He accuses my father of burning the posthouse."

"That burned long after your father reached Port Calibe. We saw it together."

"Yes. I think Rinari sent someone to burn it himself. And now he won't free my father from the port prison unless I go to testify for him. And so I'm going. I'm going dressed as an Ilijhari, and he'll see then how little he wants me as his wife." There was grim satisfaction in that at least.

Kentith frowned. "Have you discussed this with Te-kia?"

"We talked about it."

"And he said?"

She glanced away. "He wants me to stay and train with the birds." She frowned down at the ground. "But he sent me here with the heart-leaf himself. He sent me here to find my path. I can't leave my father in prison, not even for the twelve days Te-kia wants. Kentith, they've put him in the deep hold. The men who came from Kels Rinari told Ebin that. And you told me—you told me about the deep hold."

"I told you," he agreed. He studied her for a long moment, then slowly relaxed, as if he had reached some decision. He glanced toward the heavy pack. "Supplies? For us?"

"For you. For your trip through the mountains."

He shook his head. "Do you think I'll go there now? And leave you to go to Port Calibe alone?"

Dara glanced up in sharp alarm. "You can't come with me. There is a reward for you. You told me that yourself." When he only shook his head again, she hurried on. "And your path—you saw. You saw just as clearly as I did where your path leads."

"My path will wait while I follow yours for a few days farther."

"If I won't let you?" she demanded, remembering how firmly he had refused her his path.

"But you will, Dara," he said softly.

"You said last night was all," she said in confusion.

"I said last night was the closest we would be. And it was. When I leave you, I walk alone. But you won't force me to walk alone before I'm ready, not if you care about me." He moved nearer, placing one hand on her arm. The touch was light, cool, compelling. "I've been close to very few people, Dara. If I go ahead into the mountains alone, you can send the quirri to see that I'm well. You can watch over me until I reach the inland. You can help me make my way.

"But if you go to Port Calibe without me, I will never know if you freed your father, if you returned safely to Wahonin, if Kels Rinari felt as you think he will feel about taking an Ilijhari wife. I'll go through the rest of my life not knowing if you yielded to the *damen-kest*, as my mother did.

"I can't let you go to Port Calibe alone."

"My flock will protect me," she said faintly. "I won't be harmed."

Kentith glanced toward the tree where Ti-ri-ki perched. The quirri's yellow gaze was bright and watchful. "Then they will protect me too."

"And the firemaster? Can you go to Port Calibe when there is a firemaster there?"

Kentith released her arm. His face became grim. "Only one firemaster has ever raised my fire."

Narkith, whom she had seen in the smoke. "But now that he's done it, it will be easier for the next one." Hadn't he said that himself?

"Yes. It will be. But not so easy, perhaps, that a lesser master than Narkith can do it. Because now I will guard myself."

Could he do that? Dara hesitated. "Will you promise me that if you feel any danger from this firemaster, you will leave me?"

Kentith's golden eyes flickered and narrowed. "I promise you." He stepped across the small clearing and took up the pack. He weighed it speculatively in one hand. "We must stop at Te-kia's hall on the way. We must tell him we are going together."

"Yes," she said, accepting Kentith's decision reluctantly. Te-kia would be displeased that she chose to make the journey now. But he had given her the heart-leaves that had told her what she must do. How could she turn from the path the smoke had shown her?

She glanced up. Ti-ri-ki was poised on his branch, ready for the leap to her shoulder. But for a moment she only stared at him, recognizing the very alienness of her last thought. Five days ago would she have considered herself bound by a decision reached by throwing a handful of leaves on the fire?

She would not have. But she was no longer the person she had been then. She extended her arm, summoning the quirri to her shoulder.

CHAPTER ELEVEN

Dara and Kentith remained one more night in Te-kia's hall. In the morning, he accompanied them to the edge of the stream. Dara and Kentith filled water jugs and placed them in their packs. "One thing, small-song," he said, when they stood. "If Ri-chi-ki comes to you while you are in Port Calibe, give yourself to him and we will share his wings."

Dara glanced at the hunter poised on his shoulder. "What do you mean?"

"I mean that if I want to speak to you, I will send Ri-chi-ki to Port Calibe. He can carry us both on his wings for a short time, for a minute or two. We can talk that way, briefly." He shrugged. "It's the best I can do."

"I'll remember," Dara said, feeling some of the weight lift from her own shoulders.

They turned then and made their way down the flank of the mountain. Wind and rain played with them as they went. Vagrant showers tickled the fur cloaks Te-kia had given them and the wind laughed in the trees. Small-flocks appeared, made bright celebrations around their heads, and then darted noisily away, Ti-ri-ki crying after them in mock pursuit.

It was a calm as false as on the morning when Kels Rinari had come with the *damen-kest*. But it followed them down the mountainside, around the rim of land that bounded Wahonin, and through the woodland. It followed them for the four days of their journey, and occasionally Dara thought perhaps it was real.

As they walked, Dara seldom glimpsed more than one or two quirri gliding high above the trees, but at night she heard the rustle of many wings as the flock went to the hunt. Ti-ri-ki waited nearby each evening as she and Kentith made camp, watching closely to see if she would accompany him. Each time, she released him to hunt alone and sat in the dark of the trees with Kentith, aware of the vigilant eyes of those quirri left to guard them.

She was aware of Kentith's vigilance, too. He watched the trees as keenly as Ti-ri-ki did as they walked. When they paused to eat or drink, he peered up at the sun, tense and watchful, alert for some brightening, some intensification of its light. Somewhere along the way, he had shed his light, smiling bitterness. Now, when he spoke of the old land, he did not smile at all. Strangely, the change created a distance between them.

Or perhaps he created the distance himself, deliberately. Dara wondered.

Then the days of the journey were done. Late on the afternoon of the fourth day, they stood at the edge of the woodland looking down over Port Calibe.

The harbor settlement sprawled beside a grey sea, a disordered collection of timber structures, weathered piers and wind-crippled trees. Tall-masted merchant ships stood at port. Dockworkers, seamen, and women in bright clothing moved through the rutted waterfront streets or picked their way along wooden walkways. There was a festival gait to their activity: quick, exaggerated, convivial. Occasionally a rider drove his nervous mount through the streets and celebrating pedestrians jumped from the animal's path.

A walled compound stood on a narrow street near the waterfront district. There, Te-kia had told them before they left his hall, Kels Rinari made his home.

So at least they need not ask on the street for his house. It was there behind the walls of quarried stone. "The port prison," Dara said reluctantly. Even looking down over Port Calibe from the edge of the woodland, she was glad for Ti-ri-ki's weight on her shoulder, for Kentith's presence at her side. There was something tawdry and something sullen about the harbor settlement. She would not want to walk there alone, especially at festival time.

"You can't see it from here. It's just above the tidemark, north and east of the last row of warehouses."

And built on a shelf of land that sloped sharply to the narrow, rocky beach, so that the lower hold, standing at sea level, flooded with seawater at every rising tide. Dara pulled her fur cloak close, counting the days since her father had set her down on the woodland road. Kels Rinari had surely locked him in the lower hold soon after that— perhaps even before the posthouse burned.

Ti-ri-ki shifted restlessly on her shoulder and a passing flurry of duns screamed. "We'll go when it gets dark."

They sat in the shadow of the trees and, as the last hours of afternoon passed, Dara's mood grew increasingly brittle. Kentith laid out food, but she could not eat. Nor did they talk. Small-flocks began to gather as if called, until the trees grew noisy with them. Sunset came and Dara waited for them to fall still. But the woods darkened, and hundreds of small birds continued to cry restively.

It was time to go. Below, night and damp had driven the festivities inside. Windows lit and chimneys belched sparks and woodsmoke. Closing her eyes, Dara loosed Ti-ri-ki.

She flew with him down dark streets, picking a course to the compound where Kels Rinari made his home. There was activity everywhere in the compound, men coming and going among half a dozen small structures, horses shuffling their feet in the dark, voices. Dara searched out the largest building, a house with exterior walls of quarried stone, and paused on the sill of a lighted window. She saw only an empty room, plainly furnished with bed and bureau. She visited other sills and saw little more. There was no sign of Rinari.

Her chest was tight anyway when she opened her eyes, and she felt a heavy reluctance to leave the shelter of the trees. "We'll go when the moon rises," she decided. Surely there was no harm in delaying that much longer.

Kentith crouched beside her, his bright hair tucked under the cap Te-kia had given him, his eyes grey, watchful. When the moon rose and Dara continued to crouch in the dark, he touched her arm, prompting her. She stood, reluctantly, and did as Mirina had told her she must. She pulled her cloak close and took the next step.

Her throat was dry. There was a tremor deep in her chest. She had not guessed, until they stepped from the trees, how many birds had gathered. The quirri burst from the dark branches first in a long, rustling streamer. The small-flocks followed, darting noisily toward the lights of Port Calibe.

She had never known grey-duns and yellow-beaks and catch flies to fly after sunset. It was not natural that they did so now. Dara looked after them, disturbed.

She had promised Te-kia that they would slip into the port settlement by dark, that they would pass inconspicuously down back streets, that they would speak to no one until they reached the walled compound where Kels Rinari lived. But by the time they reached the outskirts of the settlement, there were people at doors and windows, drawn by the shrieks of the birds.

Uneasily they made their way into the warren of streets, the flocks sweeping back to escort them. Dara tried to walk easily, as if she belonged on the streets of Port Calibe, but her back was rigid, her shoulders taut. If only one of the dozens of people who had come to doors and windows looked out and recognized Kentith—

The street twisted. Somewhere ahead a man called out and a woman answered. From another direction came the ragged, runaway rhythm of a horse's hooves. Glancing around, Dara saw that while they walked in moonlight, the opposite side of the street was deep in shadow. Dara caught Kentith's hand and drew him across the rutted street, pulling him into the shadows.

People saw them anyway, framing themselves in windows to stare. Behind them a burly seaman burst from a lighted doorway and looked after them, licking his lips speculatively. A woman called to him from a door across the street. What she said brought laughter from all along the street.

Dara clutched Kentith's hand, knowing she must quiet the flocks. But how? It almost seemed they screamed with her own unease. And that was growing sharper with every moment.

"Wait—wait," she urged Kentith. If the birds screamed with her unease, then she must quiet herself. She glanced around. Ahead the street narrowed. On one side stood a dark, sagging building with boarded doors. The other side of the street was lined with straggling trees. Catching Kentith's arm, pulling him after her, Dara slipped into the shadow of the trees and closed her eyes.

She paused several minutes there, standing as quietly, as calmly as she could, but the birds continued to cry. Finally, instinctively, she bowed her head and drew a long breath, then a second.

The lightness, the calm, were slow in coming—and tentative in their approach. Gradually the moon turned the color of ashes. The cries of the small-flocks first grew distant, then faded as the birds settled into the trees.

Hooves—she had heard the undisciplined rhythm before, pounding down some back street. Now she heard it again. But was the sound nearer? How could she tell when the world itself had receded into the distance?

Whatever the barrier that separated Dara from the world, the horse ruptured it. It burst from the dark, the uneven clash of its hooves jarring Dara alert. Startled, disoriented, Dara stared up at the runaway animal. Moonlight reflected from its rolling eyes. Its teeth were bared in a silent scream. It was upon her, so hard upon her that she smelled its breath. All she saw of its rider was boots and spurs.

Dara could not move, could not cry out. Her heart had knotted tight in her chest. Kentith caught her arm to pull her from the horse's path, but her feet slipped. The horse shied and reared, startled by the shadowy movement beneath the trees. Dara stared up helplessly at its dancing hooves, too frightened to move.

The quirri descended upon the rearing horse then, descended in a cloud, screaming with her own unarticulated fear—and with an anger purely their own. Dara watched, still helpless with shock. The dancing hooves were momentarily suspended in the air. Then the panicked horse twisted and crashed to its side. It wallowed, shrilling, and struggled to regain its feet. The quirri did not permit that.

By the time Dara struggled to her feet, still too numbed to understand, the horse was no longer a horse. It was something else, blood-pocked and blind, with stripped flesh and torn muscles. And after that—it seemed to happen just that quickly—it was a quivering carcass sprawled in the muddy street, the quirri and the small-flocks beating furiously around it. Far above, leathery wings were dark against the sky. White eyes burned.

Her mouth dry, her heart pounding furiously at her breastbone, Dara pressed her eyes shut and opened them again.

Nothing had changed. The quirri and the small-flocks swarmed and screamed, and the horse lay dead from hundreds of wounds, its neck arched, the bloody shreds of its lips retracted from its teeth. Its rider sprawled in the narrow street, his eyes as glassy, as uncomprehending as Dara's.

People came from everywhere. They appeared from lighted doorways, from darkened buildings. Seamen, dockworkers, laborers, women with scarlet-stained cheeks and trailing scarves— A small child with avid eyes pushed among the people and stared in fascination at the savaged horse. A blind man groped along the edge of the crowd, his eyes bandaged, his bony hands extended. Briefly Dara stared at his bare, inflamed scalp. Then two men in sea wear elbowed him aside. The people gathered in a wide, wary circle, too shocked to speak, too wise, for the moment at least, to dare the vortex of screaming birds.

That was as well. Let them step closer and the flocks would be on them. Dara knew it with knife-thrust certainty.

She knew with the same chilling certainty that she must

still the birds again. But could she quiet herself now, her body trembling, her heart hammering against her breastbone? She drew one long breath, then another, but the screams of the birds only grew louder.

Instinctively she did the only other thing she could think to do. She drew a third long breath and held it until her vision faded and her knees sagged. Weakly she crumpled toward the ground.

She knew dimly what happened around her after that. She knew that Kentith caught her and lowered her carefully to the ground. Knew that Ti-ri-ki took up vigil on her chest. Knew that the small-flocks, released from her fear, calmed themselves and settled in the trees again. Knew that the people who came near then, slowly, breathlessly, as if drawn, were safe, at least so long as none of them tried to touch her.

Men with rough authority in their voices arrived almost immediately after that and the people melted back. For a while the men spoke over her, saying things Dara could not understand, and she imagined Kentith being snatched from her side. *Leave me! Run!* she cried, but the only sound that emerged was a raw scream—and that from Ti-ri-ki's throat, not her own. And Kentith did not abandon her. Instead he spoke levelly to the men and then lifted her and carried her.

To the port prison? Were they both being taken to the port prison? Confused, afraid to care, Dara released herself into total unconsciousness.

She returned to awareness slowly, one sense at a time. She lay upon a firmly padded surface in a lamplit room. Male voices argued in low tones nearby.

"Why do you think those keys were dropped at your feet? So you could turn yourself free—and then show yourself on my doorstep not twenty days later?"

"You paid Watts to drop the keys when he took my bowl? It was no accident?"

"I paid him to see that you got free of your cage and went on your way. Did you think I would sit tamely in my office and let myself be undercut by the rumors? Sun flares, pyres burning in odd corners of town—a fallen priest ready to burn the town from his prison cell? Superstitious nonsense.''

''Not so much nonsense if there is a firemaster in Port Calibe.'' It was Kentith's voice, light, faintly ironic.

Kels Rinari answered him with hard exasperation. ''Did I know when I let you free that I was dealing with anything more than festival-season rumors? It wasn't until two days later that I saw the sun flare myself, with my own eyes. By then you were gone. And where did you go? To the simple folk, and they gave you shelter. They sheltered a fugitive.''

''No one gave me shelter. I went—''

''Well then, you have shelter now. A locked room where no one will see you but my own men until I've decided what I must do with you next. You'll take it and be grateful, unless you want me to sell you aboard the *Temple Star.*''

''The priests are in port to escort me back?''

''They've been there since yesterday, standing at the rail of their vessel, turning the light against us with their lens, making every man and woman in town start every time the sun comes from behind the clouds. They're offering a good price to the man who delivers you to their ship bound and gagged, ready to sail. Shall I claim it?''

Dara drew a frightened breath and struggled to sit. Kentith and Kels Rinari stood at the far side of the dim, plainly furnished room where she lay, Rinari's face white and angry.

''Claim it if you please,'' Kentith said with a shrug, his very indifference a challenge.

Rinari stared at him. He wore dark trousers and a gleaming white shirt, his blade holstered at his belt. For a moment his hand hovered over its carved grip. Then he shook his head. ''I'll give them nothing. What any priest wants from me, he can come and take.'' His eyes darting, he saw that Dara had wakened. He snatched up the bell that stood on a nearby table and shook it.

A tall woman with greying hair and deep-set eyes hurried into the room.

"Didn't I tell you to take her up and wash her clean?"

The woman's thin lips contracted in annoyance, but she closed lean fingers upon Dara's arm. "You come with me."

"No. No, I'll—" Dara's protest was useless. Unwillingly, she was tugged to her feet. She swayed, looking desperately to Kentith, to Kels Rinari. Why was she so weak? "Please—he only came because I asked him to come. He didn't want me to travel to Port Calibe alone."

Rinari's dark brows rose. "And was he so much help to you when you arrived here?"

Dara struggled to pull free of the woman's grip. "Yes," she said angrily. "*Yes*, he was a help to me. If you harm him—"

Kentith stepped forward. "Dara, he won't harm me. He'll give me a private room, and in a day or two he'll send me away again."

Dara raised one hand in a disbelieving gesture and was struck mute. Her fingers, the backs of her hands, were spattered with dried blood. She stared down at them and licked her lips, too shocked even for nausea. *The horse, the quirri . . .*

"Let me take her up," Kentith said quickly, moving to support her.

Rinari's response was sharp. "My woman has her instructions."

"Does your woman know how to deal with the quirri?" Kentith demanded. He nodded to Ti-ri-ki, poised on the back of the padded bench where Dara had rested, his feathers ruffed in warning.

Rinari's eyes darted to the hunter. He frowned and glanced at the woman, who had stepped back, her eyes narrowing. "Do you?" he demanded of Kentith.

"He won't hurt me."

Rinari shook his head in irritation. "Then wash her yourself and get her to bed. There will be two men just outside the door."

Dara knew little of what happened after that. Kentith carried her up the stairs and into a dark room. Kels Rinari's woman hovered a safe distance behind them, bringing a lamp, towels and cloths. Dara heard Ti-ri-ki utter a low warning as he settled into place on the bedpost. Distantly she heard voices: Kentith's, the woman's, Rinari's. She did not stay to listen. Kentith helped her to the bed and she let the world go.

It was morning when she woke. The room was clean and bare, with rough-textured walls and windows open to the sunlight. There was a pitcher and mug on the bedside table, extra quilts folded over the back of a nearby chair, unfamiliar clothes hung on a hook driven into the wall. Dara lay very still, testing the ache of her body. It was dull, diffuse, without focus.

Men's voices, the nicker of a horse, the ring of a hammer against metal— Dara closed her eyes to listen more closely and quickly opened them again. Because now that she was fully awake, there were images of blood etched on the backs of her eyelids. One glimpse brought sharp nausea and a hoarse, low cry from Ti-ri-ki. Dara sat up unsteadily, and he jumped from the bedstead to her shoulder, his claws carefully drawn.

Dara hunched on the side of the bed, swallowing down the sourness in her throat, then went to the window and looked down.

She was in the walled compound where Kels Rinari made his home. There were uniformed men gathered below, their horses standing in unaccustomed calm under a cluster of trees. The grounds, what she could see of them, were like the room where she had slept, clean and bare and sunlit.

She did not see the quirri of Ti-ri-ki's flock, but she knew they were near: in the trees, on the roof, on the compound wall. And when she closed her eyes, the runaway horse was there, too, teeth bared, eye sockets empty.

"Master is waiting for you. The morning meal is set below."

Dara started and turned stiffly. She had not heard the

woman enter the room. She met the woman's dark-eyed stare and licked her lips. "My friend?"

"He's just where he belongs, where no one will see him. And he should give thanks he's not aboard the *Temple Star* instead."

Dara relaxed slightly despite the grim satisfaction in the woman's tone and glanced at the unfamiliar clothes hanging on the hook. "Where are my own clothes?"

"Hanging in the washroom if you want them." The woman gestured distastefully toward a door on the opposite wall, then leveled a long, calculating gaze at Dara before she withdrew.

Puzzled, uneasy, Dara glanced out the window again, then stepped into the small room that opened off the bedchamber. She retreated immediately, fighting fresh nausea. Her fur cloak hung stiffly against the wall, like the badge of some recent savagery. Her clothing was crumpled on the floor. Everything was spattered with blood, even her boots. Dara closed the door and leaned against it, fighting for breath.

She gave herself minutes to recover. Then, still shaking, she pulled on the clothes that hung from the hook and braided her hair.

Six doors lined the corridor outside her room. Dara paused, listening for some sign that other rooms were occupied. She heard nothing. Pausing, she bowed her head and disciplined herself to a precarious state of calm. Then she made her way down the stairs to meet Kels Rinari, Ti-ri-ki hunched on her shoulder.

CHAPTER TWELVE

Kels Rinari turned from the dining room window at the sound of her footsteps. As when he had come to Wahonin, he was taller than Dara remembered, the lines of his face starker, his eyes more deeply set. Again he wore dark trousers, a white shirt, and a holstered blade. A heavy shaft of sunlight fell through the tall window and parted around him, as if the sun blessed him.

Ti-ri-ki shifted on Dara's shoulder and uttered a low warning. "No," Dara said, placing her fingertips on his bristling breast feathers. She met Kels Rinari's eyes. "You sent for me."

His brows were like wings, broad, arching, black. They rose slightly at her words. Otherwise his face remained controlled, unbetraying. He made no more reference than she to the night before. "Harmin refuses to speak for you, so it was necessary that you come and speak to me yourself. And before we begin, let me say that I am sorry for your sister's death."

He was sorry? Did he think she had come so far to hear empty words? "What can I say to that?" Dara demanded, trying to keep her own voice level.

Rinari's shoulders stiffened. "You can say whatever you please. The *damen-kest* is traditionally presented in a certain manner. I presented it in that manner and your sister gave me one of the three traditional answers. I am sorry for the answer she gave me, but she chose her own reply."

"She chose her reply, but you posed the question. I want to see Kentith."

Rinari's face darkened. "I gave him a room in the men's quarters. He has been instructed not to try to leave it."

"He's your prisoner then." Hadn't he said the night before that the room would be locked?

"He is under my guardianship, and he should give thanks for it. By now some who were there last night have realized just who it was they saw with you and what he's worth—and where to find him as well. But they won't get past my men. He was foolish to come here."

Dara stiffened. "Then he was foolish on my behalf. What do you intend to do with him?"

He gestured impatiently. "Just what he told you. At my best opportunity, I will supply him and send him on his way. Perhaps this time he will have sense enough to keep going."

"And my father?"

Rinari's brows rose. "Yes, your father. Well, which first? A visit to the port prison or your morning meal?"

Dara glanced at the table. There were two places laid. "Have you eaten?"

"I was waiting for you."

Then it would do him good to miss his meal. Certainly she did not intend to eat with him. "Take me to the port prison."

"Of course," he said readily. "I have a cloak that will fit you. The wagon is waiting."

As if summoned, his woman came with cloaks for them both. Rinari shrugged into his and seemed to grow even taller and starker. He spoke privately to the woman, turning his back on Dara as if deliberately. Then his boots struck the flagged floor sharply as he led Dara through the house.

The morning was cool and faintly misty, the tang of salt sharp in the air. Dara hesitated at the door, willing the small-flocks to be quiet. But they came flying anyway as soon as she stepped out, bright squadrons of them sweeping across the gravel drive. They whirled and called as she approached the wagon, catch-flies and yellow-beaks and grey-duns and others she could not identify. Their voices were querulous and confused.

Kels Rinari watched the birds briefly, darkly, then offered Dara his hand. He said nothing as she settled herself on the wagon seat. He spoke only to the team, urging them down the drive.

Men in and out of uniform worked on the spacious grounds, raking and sweeping soil that already seemed clean. Several bent over the long, straight furrows of a newly planted garden. Others weeded in the small orchard. They averted their faces, but Dara knew from the prick of her neck that they looked up again when the wagon passed and stared after it. She pressed steadying fingertips to Ti-ri-ki's breast. From the corner of her eye, she saw other quirri gliding just above the compound wall. "How many people live here?"

"Within my gates? *I* live here, along with the woman who keeps my house. No one else holds tenure beyond the hour."

She glanced at him in surprise. In addition to the house, there were a dozen smaller buildings within the compound. Te-kia had not warned her that the entire compound was Rinari's.

Frowning, Rinari offered a quick inventory of structures. "Stables for the horses, quarters for those men who present themselves sober at the gates, a cookhouse for their meals, tool buildings, storage buildings, a carriage hall— and here, outside the gates, a second barracks for men who are sobering up to come back inside."

A uniformed guard raised a stiff hand as they passed through the gate. Turning, Dara saw a long, low shed built against the rear wall of the compound. "You make them sleep out here if they've been using dusts?"

"Or brews. Or if they're simply feeling quarrelsome. The horses are admitted at any hour, no matter how drunk," he said dryly.

"Was it—was it one of yours the birds killed in the street last night?" Why had he said nothing of the incident? Surely he understood well enough now what she was. Why not speak of it?

"None of mine. Any man of mine who rides his horse that hard in the streets has lost tenure with me."

Order and discipline vanished at the gate of the compound. Port Calibe was even more tawdry, even more sullen by day than by night, its timber buildings crooked and sagging, its streets rutted, its plank walkways treacherous with rot. And the festival celebrations lent it no charm. Even at midmorning there were groups of men on the streets, drunk and quarrelsome. Loud music thumped from open doorways and women with glittering eyes trailed bright scarves and provocative glances.

"Do you like what you see?" Kels Rinari demanded, taking the wagon slowly through the winding streets. "Today we are celebrating Tith again."

"No, I don't like it," Dara said, aware of Rinari's frowning tension beside her, aware of the glances and the long silences that followed them.

Those were not so surprising, considering the cloud of birds that trailed the wagon. And they weren't just quirri and birds of the small-flocks now. Seabirds had joined them, screaming hoarsely, sometimes flying irritably at the quirri. Dara closed her eyes and bowed her head, trying to calm them all.

"Have there been other signs of the firemaster since the storm?" she asked, when the screams of the birds grew less shrill.

"Yes," Rinari said, and did not elaborate, even when she glanced questioningly at him.

He guided the wagon through the main streets of the settlement, as if determined that everyone see her. Then he left the boardinghouses and brawlhouses behind and urged the team down the deeply rutted thoroughfare that served the piers. Ships stood in the water, tie-ropes creaking, wind-wings folded. Men pushed crates and cartons on wheeled carts or loaded the wagons that lined the streets, waiting to be dispatched north or south with imported goods.

"Which is the *Temple Star*?"

"There," Rinari said, pointing out a vessel anchored near the center of the harbor. "You can see the lens. It sits on its own raised platform. It's covered this morning. They'll remove the cover later and turn it on us."

Dara frowned at the slowly rocking vessel. "Can they set fires with it?"

"Here, on the piers? From there? No, not if they are the lesser brothers I take them for. But even so, they manage to make everyone who must work down here anxious—even men born to this shore, who have never seen a burning."

Dara drew herself straighter on the wagon bench. "Have you?"

"Was I born on this shore?"

"No. You came here from the old land."

"Then I've seen the burnings, and all the rest of it as well."

He did not say more. He steered the wagon past a series of warehouses to a place where the sea had eaten sharply at the shore, baring a steep rocky declivity. Below, the water washed quietly at a narrow, stony beach.

The prison stood there, its entryway fortified, its stone walls pitted and stained and grown with dark mosses. Its uppermost story stood at street level. Its second and third stories stood below the grade of the street and even now, with the tide receding, seawater washed the lower foundation of the structure. Bleak stone walls were set at intervals with narrow, barred windows. Dara looked down and felt anger and revulsion.

She made no effort to conceal what she felt as Rinari helped her down from the wagon. He either did not notice or did not care.

Nor did he speak as he led her past the guards and into the cavernous interior of the port prison. There he nodded cursorily to a uniformed jailer who stood behind a low counter.

"Master Rinari." Nervous, anxious to please, the jailer

slipped a key from a hook and placed it in Rinari's hand. "You know the cell, Master."

Rinari had no more to say to him than to Dara. Silently he led her down a corridor that smelled of salt and damp and things Dara didn't want to name.

They descended two sets of slippery stone stairs to the lower corridor. The salt smell of the sea was stronger there. So were the smells of damp and waste. The corridor floor was littered with debris, as if no one had ever bothered to remove garbage and offal. Rodent eyes winked boldly from the shadows.

Without speaking, Kels Rinari directed her to a door at the far end of the corridor. Unlocking it, he took her elbow and guided her into the cell.

She glanced around the tiny cubicle. Sunlight shone weakly through the single barred window. Dark water sheeted the floor. The walls were slippery with mossy growth. The smells of damp and waste were stifling.

The cell was empty.

At first Dara thought she was mistaken. But the shadows were not deep enough to conceal a man. She turned to Rinari in sharp alarm. "My father—"

Rinari crossed his arms over his chest. His winged brows converged. "Did you expect to find your father here?"

"You said—"

"I asked if you wanted to take your meal first or visit the port prison. You chose to visit the prison."

"Because—" She stared into the dim, empty corners of the cell, fighting panic. Where was her father? Why had Kels Rinari brought her here if not to see him? Dizzily she closed her eyes—and saw Rinari's face etched on her eyelids.

She forced her eyes open at Ti-ri-ki's warning cry. Desperately she choked back the salt taste that had risen in her throat. Her voice shook, angry and frightened at once. "Where is my father?"

Kels Rinari strode past her to the window. He stared out at the tide for long moments. Then he turned back, standing as he had in the dining room that morning, with the sunlight behind him, parting around his shoulders. He spoke with heavy precision. "As I understand it, no one can say where your father is. He went into the mountains before you were born. No one has seen him since. But that's no matter because it's Harmin you're asking after. He is a guest in my home—and has been since the night he arrived."

Dara stared at him, trying to understand. He knew the details of her birth? Had known, presumably, before he sent his messenger to summon her here? And her father had never been confined here? He was safe in Rinari's home? She pressed her fingertips to Ti-ri-ki's breast. "If that's true, if my father was never locked up here—why did you bring me here?"

No expression touched Rinari's face. He seemed impervious to her bewilderment, to her indignation. "What better place to talk? Harmin brought me a missive from Mirina. She suggested something valuable to me, your sister. She suggested that some things can be given but never taken.

"A meaningless principle in my world. But you come from another world, a world where apparently that notion carries some weight. And so I've decided to show you some of the things I've already given you, things you could never have taken from me. Harmin's freedom. His health. The life of the young man who brought you to my compound. And Wahonin— Have the halls been stormed? Are the people dead? Have the crops been destroyed and the livestock driven away? No. None of those things have happened. Everything that you want, you have—from my hand.

"Now it is time for you to consider what you would like to give me."

Dara drew a slow breath, not able to take her eyes from his face, his stark, dark face. There was a twisted logic to what he said. Harmin, Kentith, Wahonin: they were his to destroy, or at least so he saw it. But he had not destroyed them. Instead he had bestowed them upon her.

Now he expected her to bestow something upon him—something she had been convinced he would not want once he understood what she was. "You know I'm half an Ilijhari," she said. "My father told you that too."

"If you mean Harmin, yes. He thought it would make a difference if I knew. And it has. It has made this alliance far more necessary than it was before."

"Necessary—because I'm half a savage?" Dara said disbelievingly.

"Half a savage? What does that mean? I've arrived at my present position by snatching every advantage that came my way, no matter whose hands I had to wrench it from. I've made enemies like lesser men make casual acquaintances.

"I don't need more enemies now, with the firemaster here, ready to show himself and demand we raise a temple for his order. I need allies, and with you in my house, I will have those. Because with the simple folk allied to my household, I can promise any man who sides with me that he will have food to eat and a safe valley retreat, no matter what passes in Port Calibe. Everyone knows that once the *damen-kest* is accepted, the simple folk will honor their pledge, no matter what the circumstance.

"And your birds? They will earn me just that much more respect when we ride through the streets together." He glanced at her, meeting Ti-ri-ki's irritable yellow eyes keenly. "In Hemnistora, Chanona's priestesses release the temple flocks to fly over the city when they perform their wind ceremonies. The birds fly in white clouds, and later, when the people are gone, they return to their lofts in the temple yard. They're tame from the egg, bred to fly and return, and everyone knows it.

"But your quirri don't come from cages. And now, after all the stories my people have heard of the Ilijhari and their birds, they have seen with their own eyes what the quirri can do. Perhaps that will give me the kind of authority I need, if I'm to keep Tith's men off this shore."

Dara stared at him. "How can you expect me to be your wife when you killed my sister?"

Rinari's eyes blazed. "Your sister killed herself."

"Yes, because you came to Wahonin with armed men and threats. Because you—"

"Yes? And how did you want me to come, once I had seen the sun flare with my own eyes? I had been thinking of the *damen-kest* since I first saw your sister. I had been considering the advantages of a marriage, and I had been considering how little I would enjoy a refusal and all its consequences—which I would surely get if I approached too softly.

"So I did not approach softly. I did what I had to do and I said what I had to say—or so I thought—in order to win what I required. Do you have some difficulty with that? You're the same, aren't you? Tell me who isn't."

He had lost himself in the darkest corner of the cell. She could see only the angry glint of his eyes. "I am not the same. None of my people are."

"Are they not? Your sister wanted so badly not to come to me that she killed herself. Your people want so badly to be separate from mine that they let her die. Her own father let her die. And you—what would you do to have *your* way if I were to change my mind? If I were to tear up your sister's missive and forget her message?"

If he decided not to "give" her Harmin and Kentith and Wahonin. "Are you going to do that?" Dara demanded, her mouth dry.

He advanced from the shadows, the line of his mouth hard. He did not speak for moments. Then he paid out the words deliberately, as if he were controlling a fierce anger. "I could easily deliver your friend to the *Temple Star,* if I were inclined to touch a priest's gold." He shook his head impatiently. "That I am not, but I have decided what I require, and I am going to have it. You are going to give it to me. Oh, you think you are not. But you haven't troubled to think of the full consequences of a refusal."

"You will come to Wahonin with armed men," Dara said—weak, ashamed of her weakness.

"If I must, yes. But do you think my men are the worst threat your people face? Haven't you heard any word I've said? There is a firemaster in Port Calibe. He hasn't shown himself, so we don't know his name or the dimensions of his power. Perhaps he is weak, perhaps he is strong. Perhaps he can raise his tides high enough to burn the town down around us. Perhaps those few moments in the storm were the most he's capable of.

"But he doesn't need to burn the town to win his way. All he needs is to frighten the Council—and to persuade enough of its members that they might gain favor and titles by acceding without resistance. And then they will vote to let the temples rise in Port Calibe, the first on the new shore.

"Think beyond that. There is no better natural harbor than this one along the entire northern half of the coastline. Just a few years, and Port Calibe will be the major seaport settlement on this shore. Who commands Port Calibe will command the new lands.

"If your folk don't want the priests of Tith to command Port Calibe, to command the entire new land, it is better to make me an ally now than to remain uncommitted. Certainly you won't find another ally as much kin to your folk in standards and principles as I am."

Dara stared up at him, not believing what she heard. "You are not like us at all."

"Am I not? You want to believe I'm something black and evil, a looter from across the water. But tell me how I'm different from your father—from Harmin. List me the ways."

She shook her head weakly. Did he really think that he was like Harmin in any way at all? She seized upon the most obvious difference. "The blade you wear—"

Rinari drew it from its holder and tossed it aside. It clattered against the stone floor. "An ornament, useless against a firemaster. I don't need it."

"You don't need it because you keep armed men," she said immediately. "Will you discard those too?"

He shook his head irritably. "When they come into my

compound, they leave their blades with my gatekeeper or they do not enter. Because with weapons at hand, they fight, and within my grounds I will have order and I will have discipline.''

"But when they go out—''

"Then the choice is theirs, whether they ride with me or go alone. It's a different world outside my gates. You've seen that. Do you expect me to tell another man how he is to survive there? I will no more speak for my men when they step into that other world than your father will speak for you.

"And if you think I am completely unlike Harmin, consider this: I am strong, as he is. I am disciplined, as he is. And I am fair. Not to your sister, do you say? I think I was. I approached your sister in a manner that would have served me well in the old land, but it would have served her well too—in this land or that. No one could have faulted her for accepting me if her other choice was to see her folk destroyed. Why make a show of force but to permit the enemy a bloodless surrender?

"But your sister demonstrated to me that the simple folk do not respond in a normal manner. And so I have altered my approach.''

This time he had chosen to soften his demand with reason and generosity—at least, generosity as he saw it. But his reason was so rigid, his fairness so stringent, so alien, so anger-driven, that they were more threatening than reassuring. That he could consider himself Harmin's like in any way—

"If you had spoken to my sister of the firemaster—''

"I tried. Your father preferred not to listen.''

Dara sighed, remembering. "The things you threatened my sister with—would you have done them?''

"Of course. I always do what I say I will do.''

Dara pressed one hand to her temple, suddenly oppressed by damp stone walls. "Then these things you have given me—what if I choose to give you nothing at all in return? Will you take everything back?''

Rinari strained a long breath between his teeth. His

hands tightened on his cloak, the nails clean and scrupulously groomed. He was like that in every particular, she noticed. His clothing, his hair, his teeth, all were immaculate. Distractedly Dara remembered the childhood he had mentioned, his face scrubbed in the mud.

"I don't intend it now," he said in a controlled voice, "because I think you will soon enough see the necessity of what I want."

"But later? Some other time?"

"I can't answer you today for tomorrow. Why should I?"

"If you are as fair as you say you are—"

"I'm fair with those who are fair with me."

A blunt pronouncement, almost an accusation. If she was so unfair as to refuse him, what did she deserve? Dara closed her eyes. The images she had seen there earlier—the horse, Rinari's face—had faded. She was too confused now to be angry. How was she to deal with a man whose life had been so different from her own, whose sense of reason and fairness was so alien? Sighing, she opened her eyes—and surprised an unexpected bleakness on Rinari's face.

"Is it really necessary that there be a marriage?" she asked. "Surely there are other ways to structure an alliance."

"Surely there are, but none of them carry the weight of the *damen-kest.*" He turned away. "I have one requirement: that you remain in my home overnight. You need not give me your answer until the morning meal tomorrow."

So she had that long to consider the consequences of refusal. And those had grown far more complex, now that she understood what the firemaster's presence could mean to her people. Dara stepped to the window and gazed out. Black shadows glided across the narrow, rocky beach. Her quirri. She watched them for a long moment, then turned back.

Kels Rinari studied her without expression. She stared at him just as dispassionately, and something struck her about his face, about the lines it displayed and the ones it did not. ''Do you never smile?''

No muscle moved. The pupils of his eyes did not contract. The corners of his mouth did not draw down. Finally he demanded, with a hard undertone of bitterness, ''What will smiles ever win me from this world?''

CHAPTER THIRTEEN

So they wore their two masks, Kentith smiling because it would win him nothing to be angry, Rinari frowning because he saw no profit in smiling. Kentith at least had learned to set his mask aside these last few days. But was it even a mask Rinari wore? Or was his habitual starkness simply his soul showing bare?

Dara wondered as they rode through the busy streets toward the compound. She wondered and by the time the wagon reached the compound, the small-flocks were screaming so loudly the gateman could summon no more than a stiff, nervous salute.

And when they entered the house, there were still just two places set at the table. Kels Rinari pulled out a chair and sat. "My woman will serve us."

Dara hesitated, staring at the long, bare length of the table, licking her lips. "My father?"

Rinari's dark brows contracted in irritation. "He has eaten and gone. My woman sent him on his way while you and I were out." Seeing her stricken expression, he stood again, angrily wadding the napkin he had placed in his lap. "And tell me what's wrong with that. Can't you sit down without him?"

Dara recoiled from his sarcasm. Harmin was gone? Rinari had sent him away before she could even speak with him? Before she could even discuss with him the import of the firemaster's presence in Port Calibe?

Why had she ever expected Rinari to do otherwise? "How do I know he was ever here?" she demanded angrily. "How do I know he's not at the prison after all? In some cell you didn't show me?"

Rinari's lips tightened. "You'll know from the note my woman had him write before he left." Deliberately he sat and shook his napkin into his lap again. "You'll see it when we've eaten, so you may as well sit."

When she did so, stiff, angry and helpless, the woman brought platters of food. Rinari served Dara himself, then addressed himself to his own meal. He did not look up again until he had cleaned his plate. "Is there something you would prefer?"

"Nothing." Dara stared at her untouched plate, then glanced up. The woman stood behind Rinari, her gaze as stark, as critical as his. Startled, Dara glanced from one to the other and had the brief, uncanny feeling that the same eyes watched her from two faces.

Dara's hands tightened on her napkin. The woman's height, the proportions of her face, her dark, deep-set eyes— Did Kels Rinari trust the world so little he concealed his closest kinship?

What else could she think, seeing the resemblance? Certainly he knew how easily pressure applied to one member of the family could move another. "Have your mother bring my father's note now, will you?"

Rinari's face darkened but he made no denial. He nodded and the woman left the room.

Harmin's note was brief, just a few lines expressing regret that he must go without seeing her. Dara read with little satisfaction, wondering what he would have written if he had been assured that only she would see the note. Frowning, distracted, she pushed back her chair.

Rinari's brows rose. "Are you ready to tour the compound?"

Dara glanced up, meeting his gaze levelly. "I am ready to go back to my room."

Rinari stood, wiping his mouth—carefully, she saw, as carefully as he did everything. Just as carefully, he folded his napkin and tucked it under the edge of his plate. "Later, when I've gone to the warehouses, you can rest.

This morning I will show you how my men live when they win their way past my gateman. Your people are concerned with things like that, aren't they? Cleanliness. Order. Dignified living conditions.''

Dara frowned. He was concerned with those same things, apparently. So why the tone of mockery—and of barely subdued anger?

She couldn't guess. Yet his voice held the same tone through much of her reluctant tour of the compound. He showed her the barracks where the men slept when they came home sober. The floors were swept and scrubbed and every bunk was made up with clean bedding. He showed her the cookhouse where meals were prepared and it was as clean as the kitchens at Wahonin. He showed her orderly storerooms and carefully organized workrooms and toolsheds. He led her through stables where elegant, fine-boned horses stood calmly in freshly swept stalls. She had the sense, as he led her into each successive facility, that their condition today was in no way out of the ordinary. This was how they were always kept.

Yet every step of the way he challenged her to find fault.

Finally they stood at the far corner of a newly planted orchard, Dara's flocks ranged in chattering agitation on the compound wall. ''This is where it ends now,'' Rinari said, indicating the tall stone wall. ''Later I will extend my walls. Then, when my position is secure, I will take the walls down and the entire settlement will be mine.'' He glanced up at the midmorning sky, the small muscles of his face tightening. ''It will be mine,'' he repeated, frowning.

The entire of Port Calibe would be his if he could keep it from the priests. Dara bowed her head, trying to see the vision he saw, wondering if it was in any way workable. ''How? How will you make Port Calibe yours?''

''The same way I've made this piece of the world mine—whatever way I can. I'll buy what property is for sale at a reasonable rate, beginning with my associates' interest in Fidler, Wasson and Rinari. When the Port Council is securely in my pocket—three years, perhaps four—I'll annex whatever other commercial facilities I require. If there's anything left after that, I'll take it.

Dara frowned. "Is there some difference between annexing and taking?"

"A little."

Not enough, she guessed, to make his intermediate step popular with the proprietors of the facilities he intended to annex. "And when you have it all?"

He frowned intently, not at her but at his own vision. "Then there will be one place in this world where I set the terms people live by."

"But what if they don't want you to set terms for them?" Dara protested. The people she had seen in Port Calibe today, drunk in the streets at midmorning—how happily would they trade their rowdy freedom for the kind of order Rinari surely intended to impose?

He shook his head impatiently. "Then they can live elsewhere. Here things will be done my way. Because once I control Port Calibe, I control the development of this entire sector of the coast. And that I intend to do, if I don't die instead. But for you it isn't good enough, is it?"

Dara stiffened at the abrupt, bitter demand.

"Your father wasn't even one of the simple folk. He was a farm helper from the old land and your mother was a feathered savage. Still you're too good for me and my world."

Dara drew an unsteady breath, puzzled by this new grievance. "I never said that."

"Your eyes say it. The way you stand there says it. You look at me and you see the dirt on my face, just as your sister did. Well, look closer—*look closer*. Look for what I've made of myself, not what I came from. And then ask yourself—isn't it just possible your sister made a mistake in refusing me?"

Dara stiffened. "Mirina did not make mistakes."

"Did she not? Then why is she dead while we stand here alive?"

Dara stared up at him, at his rigid features, at his glinting eyes, and bit back an angry response. Because—

reluctantly—she recognized something deeper, something far more painful than venom in Kels Rinari's words. She recognized remorse—an angry remorse, all the more powerful because it ate at him silently, like an unacknowledged cancer.

Why else speak so angrily against Mirina's decision? He was not trying to convince Dara of his innocence. He was trying to convince himself. And he never would.

Never would, never could. Because it was just as he had said earlier: Along with a rigid sense of discipline and order, he was cursed with a sense of fairness, however tortuous it might be. And he recognized the wrong he had done.

"If my sister could speak to you now, she would forgive you," Dara said softly. Surely she would, given the circumstances.

Rinari turned back, his face turning ashen. But he did not protest. Instead he stared at her as if struck. Then he drew himself up stiffly, his lips a tight, pale line, his eyes bleak and bitter at once. "I have a meeting with my associates. Look around here or go back to your room. I don't care. But don't try to leave the compound. We will take the evening meal together." Turning, his shoulders rigid, he strode away.

Dara stood among the young trees until his horse cantered out the gate. Then, weakly, she slumped to the carefully raked grass.

She must deal with him. She had no choice. But he was not just a man at odds with the world. She saw that now. He was at odds with himself as well, and the more she understood him, the more he confused her.

Dara pressed her hand to her ears. With Rinari's departure, the small-flocks had swept down from the wall and ranged themselves noisily in the trees. Quirri ranked themselves along the compound wall, watching her with intent yellow eyes, as if they could read her very thoughts. Tiri-ki bobbed restlessly on her shoulder. If only she could send them all away.

But she could not. They were her self-sworn guard, down to the tinest and the least effectual.

Bowing her head, closing her eyes, Dara released a long breath. She sat with her arms wrapped around her knees, as empty, as still as she could make herself. After a while the flocks quieted, too. The quirri's eyelids drooped and Ti-ri-ki huddled close, his feathers warm against Dara's cheek.

Slowly the sun burned through the morning mist and brightened the trees. Opening her eyes, Dara gazed up until she thought she saw a momentary brightening. Or did she only imagine it? Frowning, she looked around the small orchard. Tender leaves hung upon the young trees like translucent green panes. Looking down, she saw tiny white flowers in the grass. Dara touched them with a careful fingertip and wondered absently how a man so bitter, so turbulent as Kels Rinari could create a place like this. Did he ever come here alone? What did he think of when he did?

Perhaps the orchard was in some was as much a manifestation of his soul as his stark, unsmiling face. But what did it mean to her if that were so?

After a while, she stirred impatiently and glanced up at the flocks. Would anyone notice if a single dun fluttered toward the house and landed on a sunny sill? And flew from there to the men's quarters that stood at the other side of the house?

Closing her eyes again, Dara summoned the leader of the grey-duns. When she found him, she spread her arms and felt the familiar lightness as they took wing.

They made their way around the house, darting from sill to sill. In the kitchen, Kels Rinari's mother wielded her broom, pursuing some invisible enemy across the tiled floor and out the door. Apparently the rout gave her no satisfaction. A moment later she was scouring at the chopping counter, her lips pulled back in a fierce grimace.

From the house, they flew to the main barracks, a long, low structure with high slotted windows. Dara directed the dun from window to window. She found Kentith quartered alone in a small room furnished only with a straw mattress. He sat cross-legged on the mattress, gazing toward the high window. His expression was tense, troubled.

At first he seemed not to notice the grey-dun on the sill. Then his eyes narrowed. He pushed himself up and approached the window, almost warily.

Did he know her? Briefly he extended one hand, then pulled it back. She turned, realizing that his gaze had shifted, that suddenly he was staring not at her but beyond her.

The sun was brightening again. Its circular disk did not expand, but the quality of light was changing, intensifying so rapidly that Dara squeezed the dun's eyes shut and turned briefly away, hunching the tiny bird's shoulder protectively.

When she dared look back, the sun burned even more fiercely in the sky. Dara shrank on the sill, confused. She had seen the sun brighten before, once just a few minutes ago, once on the day Kels Rinari had come to Wahonin. This was not the same. She could not ascribe this to imagination. She could not call this a trick of the eyes.

Because now long, fiery arms were peeling free of the sun's disk and reaching lazily across the sky toward Port Calibe. Dara turned back to Kentith. *What is it? What's happening?* The dun's voice was shrill, useless.

Kentith shook his head. The motion seemed a mute plea. Abruptly his back arched, snapping back so sharply Dara heard the crack of joints. Staring at the twisting arms of fire that arced down the morning sky, he backed from the window and pressed himself against the far wall of the narrow room. His hands were extended, palm outward, as if to fend off a blow.

Dara stared—at his tightly drawn lips, at the stiffly trembling hands, at the golden eyes that had begun to blaze so fiercely in his face. The shirt he wore was open at the throat. She saw the upper portion of Tith's face on the exposed flesh of his chest. Eerily, grotesquely, the etched image began to writhe, although Kentith himself did not move.

Kentith said one word: "No!"

Or perhaps he said, "Go!"

Whatever the strangled word, its tone was agony. And beyond the window, long arms of fire rippled as if infused with fresh energy. They licked downward toward the ground.

Stunned, Dara heard a sharp explosion somewhere beyond the compound wall. She could not judge the distance. It was followed immediately by another, by an entire host of others, until the entire structure of the men's quarters shook. The concussions were isolated at first. Then they came in strings, some sharp, others dull, muffled, massive.

Dara glanced wildly at Kentith, at his arched back and burning eyes. Then she was in the air.

The eastern sky was already dotted with clouds of smoke that swelled like so many dark flowers opening in the sunlight. Dara took no notice of her body sitting cross-legged in the grass, guarded by quirri. As she darted toward the compound wall, she swiftly exchanged the dun's wings for Ti-ri-ki's and flew from the compound.

In the streets, people stood shocked and still. Near the spot where the quirri had savaged the runaway horse the night before, a heavy wagon lay overturned, its team shrilling as they struggled to regain their feet.

Ti-ri-ki's wings quickly carried Dara to the rutted thoroughfare that served the dock and warehouse area. Men scattered in every direction from the docks, shouting hoarsely.

Dara saw it all in one swift pass: the long wooden warehouse, its roof blackened and torn, its walls shattered; shreds of wood splayed in every direction, as if blown by a swift, violent wind; a man in bloodstained coveralls sprawled near the street, a long splinter of wood buried in his abdomen; horses that screamed and bolted, dragging wagons and carts after them like wheeled toys.

There were screams from within the shattered warehouse. Two men scrambled through a torn wall, flames streaming after them, and ran toward the water. Their voices were thin, agonized. Gliding near, Dara smelled burned flesh and clothing.

The explosions had grown less frequent, but now flames licked through the warehouse, tasting the splintered wood hungrily. The heat drove back the half dozen men who had come running with water buckets.

". . . snuff powders." Dara did not see Kels Rinari at first, but she picked his voice from the others. A group of men had gathered at a distance from the burning warehouse. Rinari paced before them. "If there are powders in any other warehouse, they are to be thrown into the harbor. Now, before the flames spread. And no one is to waste water on Brimmer's holdings. They're lost, and he deserves it. No man stores powders in that quantity in a wooden structure without deserving this." He paused, glaring at the shocked, unresponsive men. "Every bucket goes to wet down the roof of the nearest facilities to his. Or do you intend to stand and watch the entire dock area turn to smoke?"

The men only stared at the blazing warehouse. Rinari turned away in exasperation, directing a dark-eyed scowl at the *Temple Star*. It stood where Dara had seen it the day before, near the center of the harbor. The big lens was uncovered now. A figure in golden robes tugged at the ropes that turned it in its frame, and it caught sunlight and played it across the water in a wide, diffuse beam.

Rinari's jaw tightened. He strode away.

Flaming debris had already ignited two smaller structures near the burning warehouse. Dara hovered near, watching as Rinari summoned other men to form bucket gangs. By then, people from the nearby streets of the settlement had come.

They pushed near, impeding the bucket gangs, and were angrily shoved back. Two small boys ran shrieking toward the warehouse and were snatched back just as a final deafening volley blew out the front wall. A woman in gaudy satins screamed as a splinter of wood pierced her fleshy forearm. The blind man Dara had seen the night before groped toward the sound of her cries, the bandages that swathed his eyes pristine despite the soot that already streaked his bare, ulcerated scalp.

Dara glanced up. The sun had not faded, leaving the day half-lit. It only seemed so, obscured as it was by dark smoke.

Alarmed, Dara remembered Kentith. Quickly she coursed back to the compound.

He lay crumpled against the wall of the small room, his eyes dark again, vacant and staring. She paused for a moment on the sill, then abandoned Ti-ri-ki's wings for her own legs. Jumping up from the grass, ignoring the momentary protest of stiff muscles, she ran to the men's quarters.

She found Kentith's door easily, but she found no one to open it for her. Rinari's men were gone, all of them. Nor had they left keys where she could find them. She pounded on the locked door, calling Kentith's name, until finally she heard him stir. "Are you all right?"

"Yes." His voice was faint, dazed.

"I can't find a key. I'll go to the docks. I'll find Rinari. I'll—"

Kentith's voice grew nearer, stronger, as he approached the heavy door. "What happened?"

"There were snuff powers—Tith's powders—stored in one of the warehouses. For festival season, I suppose. They ignited. One large warehouse is burning and several smaller sheds. There may be more by now." Most of the waterfront structures were of wood.

"There are people hurt." It wasn't a question.

"Yes."

A moment's silence. "Tell Rinari that it's Narkith. He will know the name."

Narkith—the firemaster who had raised Kentith's fire in Chindora. And now he was here, on this side of the sea? "Are you sure?"

"There is a—there is an identity to a firemaster's touch. This touch was Narkith's. Tell Rinari I must leave. Narkith can use me again, whenever he wants. And if his tides are rising, it will be worse next time.''

"Does that happen at festival season? Do the tides rise?'' She understood the priests and their powers so poorly.

"It happens. Just go—and tell Rinari I must leave.''

Dara lingered for a moment longer, torn. There was carefully controlled panic in his muffled words, and that made it hard to go. Yet she could do nothing for him here. Quickly she turned away.

CHAPTER FOURTEEN

She did not call the flocks to her. They came as soon as she stepped from the men's quarters. Her quirri, hundreds of small birds, scores of larger ones—they swept to her from every quarter, crying and screaming. She left the compound at the center of a winged cloud, and the few people who still lingered in the streets cowered against weathered storefronts or hid themselves indoors as she passed. Soot and ash hung in the air. Smoke drifted through every street.

The waterfront was chaos. Men and women groped through dense smoke, stumbling over each other, cursing. Dara's escort screamed and whirled as she pushed her way through long, snaking bucket lines. Startled men froze, staring at the birds, buckets forgotten in their hands. Others dropped their buckets and retreated.

Dara did not have to seek Kels Rinari. He found her. His white shirt streaked and smeared, his face strangely pale beneath the soot, he loomed through the smoke. "Get your birds away from here! Get them back to the compound! You're tearing my gangs apart!"

Dara caught his arm, coughing so violently she could hardly speak. "Rinari—you have to get him away from Port Calibe."

Rinari's winged brows rose steeply, angrily. "Yes? And how do I do that when he hasn't shown himself?"

Dara stared at him blankly. Smoke stung her nose and throat. Thick, choking, it had many flavors; she could identify wood, linen, flesh. "No, not Narkith. Kentith."

Rinari sucked a long breath. "So it's Narkith we have here—the man we least want to deal with. Kentith told you he's the one?"

"Yes. Please, if you will just give me the key to the room where you've locked him, I'll let him go. If you keep him here, Narkith can use him again. I'll—"

"You'll turn a renegade priest loose in a burning town? In my name? And then how many other ways do you propose to damage me? I should have disposed of him last night." Seeing her shaken expression, he gathered one hand into an angry fist. "Yes, I should have strangled him in his sleep and sent the body to the *Temple Star* before the morning fog burned off. No one could blame me for this had I done that."

"Surely no one blames you," she said, incredulous and afraid at once.

"They will when they've had time to think. Who else harbored a renegade from the priests? And with a firemaster known to be at large in the settlement? Who else gave those vultures such good reason to strike the town with flames?"

"But it wasn't even your warehouse they struck, was it?"

"My buildings are safe at the far end of the street. But we're going to lose half the facilities at this end. How do you think it will go with me when my buildings emerge intact from all this? With my enemies on the Council— these are their holdings you see floating around you in ashes—claiming that it was my stubbornness that brought the fire down on them? If Watts tells any person why he dropped those keys—" He looked around, squinting through the smoke. "Figgins!"

A soot-smeared apparition stumbled through the smoke, peering up fearfully at the cloud of birds that beat the heavy air. The whites of his eyes glared in his blackened face.

"The two smaller buildings where I've stored the last of the fall grain consignment— Go, set them."

The man blinked at him, mute, uncomprehending.

"Torch them, man. But let no one see what you're doing. I'm truly damned if I come out of this holocaust without damage. Get them burning and then grab a gang and wet down everything near them. Don't lose more than you have to." He glowered at the dumbstruck man. "I can trust you to keep a sealed mouth, can't I?"

Figgins glanced up at the screaming birds again and bobbed his head. Licking his lips, he backed away into the smoke.

"Good man," Rinari said absently as he turned back to Dara. "And you—take your birds and get back to the house. No one will bother you, not with this guard around you. We'll settle this when I can get away from here."

A quick, hard chill ran down Dara's spine. They would settle this—how? "What do you mean?"

Something in her tone brought Rinari's attention to narrowed focus. He frowned, his eyes dark, bitter. "What do you think I mean? That I'll give your friend over to the priests?"

Dara licked her lips, and the birds fell into sudden silence. "Will you?"

"I'll give the priests nothing!" Rinari said fiercely. "Neither will I send your friend walking out my front gate in broad daylight. Are there men at the compound? Did any of them remain behind?"

"No."

"Then if you value your friend, why have you left him unguarded?"

Dara stared up at him, stricken. "Do you think—" Would anyone dare trespass on Rinari's property to take Kentith?

"I think you have a renegade priest with precious little fire to call his own and a reward on his head, and you've left him locked up alone—in exactly the place where he's known to be. And that is extremely foolish."

"Yes," Dara said, with a cold sinking in the very pit of her stomach. She glanced around. Her eyes stung and watered. Her throat felt as if she had inhaled raw flame.

Ghostly figures stumbled through the dense smoke, choking and coughing. ''You'll come when you can?''

He peered into the dark smoke, then glanced absently
down at his own hands. He extended the fingers and stared
at the blackened nails with fleeting distaste. ''I'll come.''

Dara ran through the streets, not daring to pause long
enough to send Ti-ri-ki ahead. Reaching shelter of the
compound, she slumped in the grass and took wing.

Kentith slept in his room, slept so heavily he seemed
drugged. There was no one else within compound walls.
Even Kels Rinari's mother had gone.

Dara searched the compound twice, using first Ti-ri-ki
and then one of the smaller breeds. Then she hovered
briefly over her deserted body. Her face was streaked, her
hands smudged. She carried the smell of smoke in her
hair, in her clothing. Abandoning her wings, she roused
herself and went to the men's quarters to wash.

When she had done that, she found trousers and a shirt
small enough to fit her in a supply room, where piles of
clothing lay. Changing, she took up watch outside Kentith's window.

No one approached the compound through the afternoon. Only clouds of smoke breached its protective walls,
drifting through the orchard, down the driveway, between
the buildings. Horses stirred restlessly in their stalls. Occasionally one shrilled and the other animals answered,
stamping their feet.

Smoke and mist hastened the dusk. Dara retreated to
the house. Leaving her body curled up on the padded
bench where she had regained consciousness the night before, she returned with Ti-ri-ki to Kentith's windowsill and
stood sentry as dark came. Her small-flocks retreated to
the trees of the surrounding settlement and subsided into
sleep. The quirri divided themselves, some rustling away
to hunt, others remaining near, black specters hunched in
the trees and on the compound wall. When the moon rose,
Dara saw the watchful glint of their eyes.

Men began to drift into the compound soon after that.
Black-faced, coughing, they stumbled into the quarters and

collapsed into their beds without washing, without even pulling off their stained and sodden clothing.

Rinari returned an hour after the moon rose. Dara heard his horse at the gate, heard his voice from the dark. ''Parilli, you're to stand gate duty until I find someone to relieve you. No one is to enter who wasn't here at wake-up today. No one, for any reason.'' He coughed heavily, then dismounted and led his horse toward the stables.

Dara glided through the darkness and watched him brush down the animal and measure out its hay and grain. He stood watching the animal eat, his arms crossed over his chest, his expression abstracted, thoughtful. Finally he turned and trudged toward the house.

He stood over her when she returned to her body. He had stopped somewhere to wash his face. It was smeared and grey, stiff with fatigue. Looking up, Dara realized she had never seen him like this before, with neither anger nor irritation coiled somewhere just beneath the surface.

''The fires are out?''

''Yes. We lost no less than half the harbor facilities. Warehouses, work sheds, offices, ships standing at dock . . . Sparks and debris ignited two of them before anyone thought to remove them to a distance—and caught four others with their wings spread. They went like torches. And we lost most of the men we loosed from the prison to help fight the fires.'' He shrugged. ''They'll brawl their way back into lockup without ever sobering up long enough to hear that we commuted their original sentences. Still, altogether a heavy price.''

Yet his mood was not angry or even particularly somber. He seemed only tired and thoughtful. ''And your colleagues blame you?'' she asked.

''Of course they blame me.'' He paced across the room. ''Do you cook well enough to prepare our meal? My woman has remained in town. There are men who need care for their burns.''

''Your mother has remained in town,'' Dara corrected him.

His eyes glinted. ''Does it matter? Can you cook?''

"I can prepare a meal," she said. "And if it doesn't matter, why not call her what she is? What do you intend to do with Kentith?"

"Prepare dinner for three. We'll discuss it when we've eaten." He glanced down at his hands, studying the darkened nails with the same distaste Dara had seen that afternoon. Frowning, he left the room. His boots struck heavily at the stairs.

By the time she had assembled a rudimentary meal, Rinari had returned, his face and hands scrubbed clean, his nails freshly groomed and trimmed. His inflamed eyes and a raw, oozing burn on his neck were the only stigmata of the afternoon. He moved crisply, decisively, as if he had shed fatigue along with soot and grime. "I will go see who's fit for night watch and then bring your friend to dinner."

He returned a short time later and they sat to dinner, Ti-ri-ki watching from his perch on the back of Dara's chair. Tense, silent, Kentith ate sparsely. Dara ate hardly at all. Rinari's mood confounded her. He seemed neither angry nor discouraged. Instead it was as if he had found fresh energy somewhere.

At last he folded his napkin and placed it precisely beneath the edge of his plate. Pushing back his chair, he turned to Kentith. "Well, we have a formidable enemy here, and we haven't yet so much as glimpsed his face. Tell me how a man who's Tith-touched, just as you are, can lose himself in a settlement as busy and full of rumor as this one. How long were you ashore before we had you in lockup?"

Kentith studied him levelly, then shrugged. "I made the mistake of stepping into a brawlhouse for a drink on my first night in port. But remember that before that I made an entire crossing without arousing suspicion."

"And how did you do that?" Rinari leaned forward, keenly interested. "Tell me what we should be looking for, man."

Kentith frowned. "In general, you should be looking for a man who is only seen at night, when his eyes have dulled, who covers his chest, who tucks his hair up under his cap, dyes it, or shaves himself bald.''

"And in particular?''

"Narkith is tall and lean, and he suffers from a condition that produces raw skin lesions. But that is transitory. The condition may not be active now. As for the rest, he knows well enough how to disguise himself. So his clothing will tell you nothing. He seldom takes robes.''

"In the old land, I've heard, he goes from place to place garbed as a beggar.''

"Or as an aristocrat. Or as an itinerant scholar. And no one ever knows he has come until he steps among the brothers as they chant on the temple steps. But of course there are constant rumors—in every township, in every province—that he has been seen, that he is about to burn the granary of some farmer who has not given generously enough or the property of some aristocrat who has displeased the local priests. Let a house burn, let a haystack catch fire, even let a summer day be brighter and hotter than usual—''

"So he manages by rumor to be everywhere at once, to keep an entire populace terrorized without showing himself more than a dozen times a year. And to keep the offerings flowing to every temple in the land.'' Rinari glanced from Kentith to Dara. "He is a large enemy, a large enemy indeed. Did you know—have you thought of this?—that from a small enemy, a man can snatch only a small victory? But from an enemy like this one—'' He extended one hand and snapped it shut. The knuckles blanched and his fingertips turned scarlet, as if he had captured something he did not intend to loose again.

His dark eyes glowing, he turned back to Kentith. "I've told people that Dara is to return to Wahonin tomorrow to prepare for our wedding. When she has had time to reach there—''

"I never consented to that!''

Rinari shook his head impatiently. "Are you going to hear me out? Don't you understand that I'm the only thing standing between your friend and an angry mob? The townspeople would like very much to appease Narkith by handing the renegade over to the brothers aboard the *Temple Star*. And they know very well where to find him. Here. You brought him here. In fact, the only reason they are not here for him now is that I have promised to turn him over voluntarily tomorrow afternoon, when you, Dara, are safely out of the settlement.''

Dara stared at him, the blood running from her face. So that was why he seemed so little upset by the situation now. He had worked out a resolution. ''So your word means nothing.''

''My word means everything,'' he said, rising from the table, pacing to the darkened window. ''At least sometimes it does. And you still have not heard me out. You will have an escort back to Wahonin: one man to drive the wagon, six armed men on horseback.'' He glanced questioningly at Kentith. ''You do ride?''

''Yes.''

''And will you agree to carry a blade? You aren't afflicted with Dara's principles about weapons?''

''I wore a blade when I was five years old. I can wear one again.''

Briefly Rinari's brows rose. ''When you were five? Then you come from a better class than any other man who will ever wear my uniform. You will ride with Dara half the distance to Wahonin. Then you will discard your uniform and enter the woodland. And if any man or woman sees you after that, the fault is yours, not mine. As is the loss.''

So he intended to keep his word to her. Dara relaxed momentarily. ''But tomorrow afternoon, when the people expect you to turn him over to them?''

Rinari paced across the room and paused before her, but it was the quirri he studied. He extended a curled hand, coaxing. Ti-ri-ki shifted on his perch and uttered a low warning cry. Rinari's eyes narrowed keenly.

''In the afternoon?'' Dara prompted. ''What will you do then?''

''I don't know. But that is many hours from now. If my men could find Narkith—'' His eyes narrowed even more keenly as he turned again to Kentith. "He has no power by night."

"None at all unless there is an active storm near. Then he can draw some fire from the lightning."

Rinari nodded thoughtfully, then raised his shoulders in a shrug of dismissal. "Our chances of finding him tonight are slight. What clues do we have? So far as I know, he has revealed himself to no one. Would either of the priests aboard the *Temple Star* know him?"

"Who are they? Do you know their names?"

"I sent men out to warn them that they were not to step ashore. There are three of them: Hanarith, Feltisith, and an apprentice who calls himself Renkith."

"I know them, and I doubt any of them would recognize him any better than I would. If they were more senior, if they had spoken to him privately when he came to Chindora—but they weren't among the few called into the senior brother's chamber to meet with him afterward."

"You wouldn't know him?" Dara said, surprised. Hadn't she seen Narkith herself when she and Kentith used the heart-leaf? But, she remembered, she had scarcely glimpsed the firemaster's face. The fierce glow of his eyes had obscured his features.

"I wouldn't know him," Kentith said. "He changed the entire course of my life, and all I can tell you is that he is tall and lean and sometimes has weeping sores on his face."

Weeping sores. Dara frowned, briefly touched by some elusive memory.

"And these others, the ones aboard the *Temple Star*— what is the level of their power? They are lesser brothers to Narkith, of course."

"Every brother born to this century is lesser than Narkith. Renkith, the apprentice, is gifted but not yet particularly disciplined. Hanarith and Feltisith have minor gifts."

Rinari nodded. "So we haven't much to fear from these men individually. If there were no firemaster here—"

"If there were no firemaster here, you would have very

little to fear. But there *is* a firemaster, and he can use them again—and me—just as readily as this afternoon."

"And even without them, and you—" Rinari glanced at Kentith questioningly.

"He *needs* no one. And if he is on a rising tide, as he may well be at this season—"

Rinari caught his tongue between his teeth, peering intently at Kentith. "So I won't cripple him in any way by disposing of the other three immediately. And my chances of finding him tonight are slight. I would as well let my men sleep." Quickly, fiercely, he smiled. "This is a very large enemy indeed. And that means there is a large prize here. If I can bring this man down, I can win a lifetime's advantage in one afternoon." His glance flickered to the quirri again. "A large, juicy prize—but who is the hunter? Narkith—or me?"

The bird gave him no answer. Rinari paced back to the window and gazed out into the dark. When he turned back, he was thoughtful again. "Let us get to bed. Tomorrow we will be up well before light. You will sleep in your own bed tomorrow night, Dara, and I will come for you when I can—when I dare leave here that long again."

Dara stood. "You will come to hear my answer."

He did not respond. "Let us get to bed," he repeated. But he did not wait to see that they obeyed. Nor did he mount the stairs to his own room. Instead he went to the front door and stepped out into the dark.

Kentith met Dara's eyes. He raised his shoulders in a light, questioning shrug. "Which is he? Hunter or hunted?"

Dara frowned, summoning Ti-ri-ki to her shoulder. "I don't know." Rinari's presence was still in the room, strong and perplexing. Was it the prize he saw at hand, the advantage, that had buoyed his mood at dinner? Or was he simply excited by the prospect of the hunt? She glanced up into Ti-ri-ki's shimmering eyes, as if she might find some answer there.

"And what will your answer be—afterward?"

"I can never accept him."

Kentith glanced thoughtfully at the quirri on her shoulder. "You may not have to," he said. "If he routs Narkith, he won't need you. He'll be strong enough in this community without you and the simple folk. And if he doesn't rout Narkith . . ."

Then he would be dead. Dara had no doubt that Rinari would pursue it to that extreme. He had wanted assurance that his supporters would find refuge in the valleys if necessary. But take refuge there himself? Dara stared down at the floor, troubled. "Where will you go tomorrow?"

"To Te-kia. I'll stay with him until this is resolved."

Dara looked up with quick hope. "And then—"

"And then I will go on. Alone," he said firmly.

Yes, alone. Hadn't she already accepted that? Their paths parted tomorrow, and they would not join again.

She had accepted it. Yet, going to her room, releasing Ti-ri-ki to hunt, she lay awake for a long time.

When she slept her dreams were troubled. She woke deep in the night at the rustle of wings. She glanced up as Ti-ri-ki settled on her bedpost. Meeting the yellow glint of his eyes, she realized with faint surprise that it wasn't only Kentith she was concerned for. Improbably, she was concerned for Rinari too.

Sleep came doubly hard after that.

CHAPTER FIFTEEN

Morning came too soon. The moon set, and soon afterward Kels Rinari's mother appeared in the doorway, lamplight from the hall casting her shadow across the floor. Starting awake, Dara sat and glanced out the window. She saw no sign of dawn. "Is it time?"

"The men are waiting. The master wants you to come to the table before you go."

"I—I'm not hungry," Dara said. Instead she felt a cold, faint nausea, as if she had not slept at all.

"He wants you to come," the woman repeated coldly. Her shadow spiraled and was gone. Her heels snapped at the hall floor.

Dara hugged herself against the morning chill, then approached the washroom. Her stomach tensed as she opened the door. The furs that had hung so stiffly against the wall yesterday were gone. Only the slight, sharp odor of blood lingered.

Dara splashed her face with water from the basin and frowned at herself in the small glass as she combed her hair and pulled it back. She wondered at her mood. Yesterday she had wanted only to return to Wahonin. Now she felt uneasy at the prospect of leaving Port Calibe. Had Rinari formulated some plan for dealing with the firemaster? Had he any hope of success?

Rinari waited at the table. He stood when Dara appeared, the burn on his neck covered with a fresh bandage, his white shirt spotless. But those things only made his pallor and his distraction more apparent to Dara's quick, searching glance.

Dara knew him well enough not to speak before they had eaten. She knew him well enough, too, to anticipate his disapproving frown when he pushed back his plate at the end of the meal and saw how little she had eaten. But he did not comment. He only folded his napkin, the corners carefully squared, and slid it under the rim of his plate.

Dara stood when he did. "Rinari, if you want me to stay—"

He glanced at her sharply. "Stay?"

"Do you have a plan for finding Narkith? For dealing with him?"

"Nothing firm," he admitted. "I will send men through town to look for him. Later, when it becomes clear that I don't intend to turn your friend over to the townspeople, perhaps he will show himself."

Show himself with what fiery violence? "Then what will you do?"

Rinari shook his head. "How can I say now? All I know is that without a battle, there is no prize—a looter's maxim."

She stared down at the table. Even his uncharacteristic lack of irritability made her uneasy. "I will stay if you want. I don't know what I can do, but—" She shrugged helplessly.

Rinari became very still. His face was immobile, unbetraying, but there was the distinct flicker of surprise in his eyes. He drew a long, thoughtful breath, then released it, shaking his head. "No, you must not, not if your friend is to have some excuse for riding out of town garbed as one of my men." His brows drew together, dark and frowning. "And until this is settled, nothing of mine is safe, even you." He paced across the room to the window, not noticing Dara's quick flush of annoyance. "I have instructed my men. They are not to give their horses anything more than food and water this morning. They are not to stop along the road except at your request. Nor are they to invite anyone else to travel with the party. And surely your friend understands well enough that if he returns here again, I am not responsible for his safety—or his survival."

"He understands."

Rinari nodded, studying her with a long, thoughtful frown. For a moment it seemed he had more to say. Then he shook his head. "Take the cloak you wore yesterday. I'll bring the wagon to the door." He left the room, closing the front door with uncharacteristic restraint.

The morning had grown shadowy with approaching dawn. The grounds stood in grey light, although the air still smelled heavily of night. Dara waited at the door, wrapped in the heavy cloak, until she heard wheels on the drive. Rinari was alone in the wagon, the leads in his hands.

The small-flocks emerged from their perches, crying querulously when Dara stepped from the house. They darted around the wagon. Rinari pulled the wagon to a halt, looking up at the complaining birds thoughtfully. Helping Dara into the wagon, he drove to the gate.

It took only a glance to pick Kentith from the seven men who waited there. He sat on a tall chestnut gelding, his hair tucked into a red hat trimmed with gold. His eyes were still shadowy grey with night. He met Dara's glance and gave her a distant nod, as if they had already parted.

Suddenly the morning ached, just as on the day when she had left Wahonin. Ti-ri-ki uttered a low cry and Dara bowed her head. Kels Rinari jumped down from the wagon and the driver mounted and sat beside her. The gatekeeper swung the gate. The wagon rolled into the street.

Port Calibe was as tawdry, as sullen at dawn as it had been at dusk two days before. Even at this hour there were people on the streets, moving uncertainly from place to place or curled asleep on porches or walkways. Tired, thin music wailed from a nearby brawlhouse, a single musician punishing his instrument. People turned and watched with veiled curiosity as the wagon passed. The smell of damp ashes was in the air.

The guards divided themselves, four riding ahead, two behind. Kentith was one of the two who rode behind. By the time the wagon reached the far edge of the port settlement, the men began to talk and joke. Only the driver maintained discipline, sitting stiffly upright on the seat, watching the shadows that lined the twisting streets. Occasionally he glanced at the clouds of birds that followed the wagon and touched his lips with a nervous tongue. He was a thin man, older than the others, with pocked skin and evasive eyes.

They passed through the outskirts of the settlement and wound up the narrow road into the trees. The sun crested the horizon and became a pale half-disk behind them, but the air seemed heavy, as if night had left some damp residue. No breeze stirred the trees. There were only the flocks, darting in agitation among the still, shadowy limbs. Dara turned and caught the rising of color in Kentith's eyes. He gazed steadily at her as grey became gold. When finally he glanced away, she stared down at her hands, a hard pain in her chest.

Once they entered the edge of the woodland, the men quieted. They reined their horses to order and watched the trees uneasily.

The mounted guard watched the trees, but Dara realized after a while that there was something different in the wagon driver's manner. His eyes darted constantly—from the trees to the road to the birds that escorted the wagon. His tongue darted just as quickly, wetting his thin lips. But he was not alert. He was expectant.

Ti-ri-ki pressed against Dara's cheek, uttering a low, querulous cry. Dara glanced around.

She saw nothing but the road and the trees and the men in their uniforms—and their driver, glancing back at Kentith now, then at her, but evading her questioning gaze. Evading her eyes entirely.

Sensing her unease, Ti-ri-ki cried again and stretched to his full height. Dara hesitated, then bowed her head and loosed him. She felt strangely vulnerable, abandoning her body on the jolting wagon seat.

She did not even feel the quirri leap from her shoulder. Instead she herself leapt into the air and glided away on his wings. Behind her, she heard the driver's quickly indrawn breath. The team broke stride momentarily as the leads slackened in his grip.

Then she was winging through the trees, searching.

What she found, she found quickly. Barely a moment's flight showed her a splash of gold in the shadows below, half-concealed beneath a cluster of bushes near the road. And gathered near, some crouching, some stretched on their stomachs, all waiting silently, waiting—

Men. There were eight men hidden within striking distance of the road, and with them two other men in golden gowns. Two men, Dara saw, swooping nearer, who wore their sun-bright hair in long braids. Two men who glanced up at the screaming quirri with eyes the color of Tith's face at setting.

Ti-ri-ki screamed, but Dara was too shocked for more than a moment's numbed indignation. Kels Rinari had promised her Kentith's freedom, but there were priests hiding in the bushes, armed men beside them. And the driver knew.

Ti-ri-ki's feathers quivered. Dara felt salt and gall rise in her throat. Then, abruptly, she lost the power of Ti-ri-ki's wings. She was sitting on the wagon seat, columns of birds closing around her. Far above she thought she glimpsed the crested head, the hooked beak of a revenant.

She saw nothing of what happened next. The curtain of quirri was too dense for that. Beyond it she heard muffled shouts. She heard voices raised in a long, high chant. She heard the scream of men and horses. The wagon lurched, struck something and tipped. Dara clutched at the edge of the seat. Her head struck wood as the wagon rolled to its side. For a confused moment, she thought the onrushing darkness was only quirri closing near. Then she lost consciousness.

She lay at the side of the road when she woke, the overturned wagon nearby. The quirri kept vigil from the roadside trees, a series of dark, hunched presences. Ti-ri-ki perched on the overturned wagon, his yellow eyes fierce and bright.

Dara stood, stiff and confused. Her head hurt. Her left shoulder ached. It appeared near midmorning. The road was scuffed, the grass along its verges trampled. The wagon had shattered a wheel on a boulder at the side of the road. The team had been cut loose. Men and horses were gone.

There was no blood. No one had raised a hand to her, so the quirri had only swarmed in protective formation. But the priests had taken Kentith, and Rinari's men were gone.

Dara stood at the center of the woodland road, and the small-flocks came to her, crying uncertainly. She could tell from their voices that they were concerned by her long unconsciousness, confused by her waking mood.

Why had she ever trusted him? Why had she expected Kels Rinari to deal honestly with her today when he had not done so before? This morning she had even hesitated to leave him alone against the firemaster. She remembered the flicker of surprise in his eyes when she had offered to stay and bitterness rose in her throat.

It was swiftly followed by sickness. Kentith was in the priests' hands. Perhaps they had already reached the port. Perhaps the *Temple Star* had already spread its wings to the wind.

There was no time for anger, for fear. Yet the woodland seemed changed by them as she ran back toward the set tlement. The sky had the flat blue luster of enamel. The sun was raw and yellow. The trees rasped in the morning breeze. She had gathered great clouds of birds. They flew ahead of her, screaming so loudly the leaves shivered on the trees. The woodland trembled.

It was nearly midday when she saw horse and rider in the distance. They rode down the tunnel of trees, the horse's feet thrashing in nervous rhythm, the rider's dark cape snapping and billowing around him. Then they drew nearer and Dara saw that Kels Rinari rode toward her, his face white and set, his feet spurring at the horse's flanks.

Dara stepped to the middle of the road and the flocks came circling back to her from the trees, the smaller birds screaming shrilly, the quirri shrieking. Ti-ri-ki flexed his wings and ruffed his feathers. His warning cry made Dara's ears ring.

Rinari saw her then, and his face grew starker, whiter. He hauled at the reins. His horse skittered and reared, then danced to a reluctant halt. Rinari dismounted and assessed her with a quick, dark glance. "They told me you were not hurt." Incredibly the words were angry, accusing. He yanked at his horse's reins as it shied and tried to back away. "Send your birds away. Can't you see they frighten my horse?"

Dara stared at him incredulously. "And what will you do when my birds are gone? Sell me the same way you sold Kentith? Is there someone willing to pay a price for me too?" *A lifetime's advantage*, he had said the night before. But he had not said aloud what he must have been thinking: that the advantage could be as easily gained by giving the firemaster what he wanted as by defying him.

Or was it called favor in that case? Was Kentith the price of Rinari's title once the priests established their first temple on the new shore?

Beneath the dark cloak, Rinari's shoulders tightened. His pupils contracted to hard points. "I sold no one."

"Then how did your driver know the priests were waiting for us? I saw him. He was watching for them."

"My driver knew nothing. There was nothing to know. My driver—"

"He knew because this morning before we left, you told him you were going to sell Kentith. And when we had gone, you told the priests where to find him: riding along the woodland road, dressed as one of your own men. You—"

"I told my driver nothing except that he was to leave your friend somewhere in the woodland, then take you safely to Wahonin. What reason did I have to tell him anything else?"

"What reason? When you had everything to gain?"

Dara's voice rose, and the flocks screamed. They screamed for her, they screamed for Kentith.

Rinari's brows arched into a scornful line. "So you think that little of me? You think I am afraid to stand against Narkith? You think—"

"Are you afraid of this?" Dara demanded in a low voice and, goaded, let her birds fly.

Small-flocks and quirri closed around Rinari, forming a broad, whirling vortex of color. Dark and bright they flew. Their voices rose in a piercing shrill, a single cry that ground at the pain centers of the brain. Rinari's horse jerked free. It reared, its eyes rolling, then bolted down the road toward Port Calibe, its jaws wide in a silent scream.

The birds did not draw Rinari's blood. Those that touched him only brushed him with the tips of their wings. But hundreds of them touched him so before Dara's anger receded and the screaming column drew back. The birds spun away in bright streamers, leaving Rinari standing so stiffly that Dara knew only his locked joints kept him erect. He was as pale as if he had been bled. Even his lips were white.

But the glitter in his eyes was fury, not terror. He stood at the center of the road, his shoulders knotted, his breath heavy, and he spoke in a voice she had not heard before. "If you want him back, you'll pay the price."

Dara stepped back, licking her lips. *Look for what I've made of myself, not what I came from*, he had said the day before. And now, she realized, she was seeing what he had come from. Because this was not the Kels Rinari who had ridden to Wahonin at the head of a crisply uniformed guard. This was not the Kels Rinari who had shown her the careful discipline and order of his compound. This was not the Kels Rinari whose meticulously groomed hands folded a snowy napkin and slid it under the edge of his plate at the end of each meal.

This was the boy who had had his face ground into the mud. This was the youth who had robbed and killed on the sea. This was the man who had sworn to take what he wanted, whatever the cost in blood or tears—to himself, to others.

And she had not recognized before just how deep, how cold his anger ran or how closely he held it. She had sensed only the least part of it—and thought she saw it all. "What do you mean?" she said finally, her mouth dry.

He advanced upon her, one hand extended, clutched into a fist. "I mean that if you don't want your friend to burn, you'll yield to the *damen-kest*. You'll pledge yourself to my house and to my bed. You'll ride the streets in my wagon and stand at my back in everything I do. Your father will pledge himself as my ally. We will crush Narkith together. And then you will bear me sons who will be lords of this coast. And if their blood calls to the birds as yours does, the better for them. The better for me. The more quickly the entire coastline will be ours."

Dara stared into his eyes, compelled. There was something dark in his gaze, something living. It moved like a shadow, but it was far more dense. Perhaps it was only anger and intractable will. Or perhaps it was the vision he saw taking brief life of its own. "If I don't want Kentith to burn?" she said numbly.

"What else do you think they intend to do with a renegade priest? They've equipped themselves. They can do the job even without Narkith's help."

The lens. She had seen it herself.

"And they will do the job today. You can count on it. So you can walk on your way free. You can return to Wahonin and let your friend burn. Or you can pledge me what I want."

"And then they will give him back to you?"

"Give?" he said incredulously. "They'll give him to no one. I will gather men and we will board the *Temple Star* and take him."

Dara frowned uncertainly. "Will they let you do that?"

"No, they will not let me do it," he said with heavy sarcasm. "Don't you understand yet what a looter is? He is a man who takes what he wants. I am a looter, and your friend needs taking."

"The danger—"

"I may well lose everything I own for this, including my life. But no battle, no prize. And no pledge from you, no battle. This is the price you pay for not believing what I tell you."

Dara raised a trembling hand to her temple. Was any of this real? She knew it must be from the clutch of terror at her stomach. "Yes," she said. "You—you have my pledge." What other answer could she give him? "But you'll take me with you."

His eyes narrowed. "You will wait at my compound."

"You will take me with you," she repeated. Perhaps she had accused him wrongly. Perhaps it was his driver who had sold Kentith. But unless she accompanied him, she would never be sure. Nor would she be sure he had done his best to free Kentith.

Rinari read her thoughts and his face darkened. "Match my pace then. And if we are too late, remember who lost my horse for us." Turning, he strode back toward Port Calibe.

CHAPTER SIXTEEN

The pace he set was vindictive. Matching it, Dara had no time for terror. She had time only for aching legs and the tight band that had closed on her chest. The small-flocks and the quirri screamed, sweeping back and forth across the road. The sky had lost its flat blue luster. When the breeze touched the trees, the leaves no longer rasped. They rustled.

There was no sign of Rinari's horse along the road. Instead they came upon a dispirited spotted mare trailing its reins. Rinari caught it easily and mounted. Pulling Dara up behind him, he urged the reluctant animal toward the settlement.

They found Port Calibe deserted. Bars and brawlhouses stood silent, their doors gaping. Nor was there anyone upon the rickety wooden walkways. Dara's birds swept through the empty streets.

The horse's wandering, uncertain gait brought them to the waterfront, and there they found all the people they had not seen in town. The *Temple Star* remained at anchor near the center of the harbor. Dozens of small boats stood at a safe distance from it, rocking precariously under the weight of the curious. Ashore, men and women balanced on pier posts to stare at the indistinct figures on the deck of the *Temple Star*. Others milled along the waterfront, restless and excited, while small groups searched the jagged black skeletons of warehouses and other dockside structures for booty. Burned hulks listed in the water. The smell of damp and ashes was oppressive.

Rinari reined the horse to a halt. "So it hasn't begun yet." He glanced up at the sun.

It stood almost directly overhead. Dara stared at the *Temple Star,* recognizing fully for the first time just what he proposed: that they take Kentith from the *Temple Star* by force of arms, in full daylight, with all of Port Calibe watching. "How can you do this?"

"Can you tell me another way to take him back? They'll begin the ceremonies soon. They have the audience they wanted." He glanced up distractedly at the flocks that swirled around them. Seabirds had joined the small-flocks and the quirri, crying in hoarse voices. "Our best plan is to board them after the chants are well begun. The priests will be in trance, more deeply in trance with each successive stanza of the chant. If we wait as long as we dare, if no one raises the alarm until the last moment—"

Dara frowned. Could they possibly board the *Temple Star* without the priests' knowledge? She knew from Kentith that the song of vengeance fell into four movements: the accusation, the judgment, the burning, the song of ashes. During the first two movements, the lens pulled the beam ever tighter, ever narrower. With the last stanza of the third movement, the rope-puller, as deep in trance as the others, made the final adjustments and light became fire.

But even if they boarded while the priests were in full trance, Rinari's men would have to deal with the ship's crew. And where was Narkith? If he were aboard the *Temple Star*— "The firemaster—"

Rinari's shoulders tensed. "My men have been searching since sunup. He's hidden himself—or lost himself among all these people. If we had some clearer idea of his appearance—"

"Could he have gone aboard the *Temple Star?*"

He released a long breath. "If we board the *Temple Star* and he is there, it doesn't matter how quickly we sever the ropes that control the lens. We are dead."

Dead because unlike the lesser brothers, Narkith required no lens to touch them with fire. Dara stared down at her trousered leg. The firemaster would never permit them to remove Kentith from the *Temple Star,* not if he were there to see. Only if he were ashore, only if he did not recognize until too late what was happening aboard the *Temple Star,* could they hope to succeed.

Rinari turned to look back at her. "Do you still intend to come?"

"I'll come."

He tugged the horse's reins and turned the animal toward the far end of the waterfront. Milling crowds parted for them, shrinking from the swarming flocks with sharp fear. Near the end of the street, Rinari coaxed the horse past two harassed guards and halted before a long, wide structure of weathered planking. He pulled Dara down and slapped the animal's spotted rump.

"There should be men here and boats to carry them. This poor beast—" He slapped the horse again. It jerked apathetically but did not move away. "Whoever dosed it this hard doesn't deserve it back. I'll have one of my men stable it later." He vanished into the structure.

Dara hesitated for a moment, then followed. She found herself within a large, shadowy building sparsely stacked with crates and bales. Rinari approached a partitioned area where several men bent over a half-opened crate. The open seaward end of the structure faced directly onto the harbor.

Dara walked quickly through the warehouse to the open water. Two large vessels stood at dock there, the ropes that secured them creaking as harbor water rose and fell. Seabirds streamed from their masts and rails and screamed angrily at Dara's encroaching flocks. Ti-ri-ki shifted restlessly on her shoulder.

She touched his bristling feathers absently, hurrying along the pier until she could see the *Temple Star.* Did she only imagine it, or had the ring of smaller boats drawn tighter around the priests' vessel? As she watched, the lens flashed in the sun, and Dara felt the cold grip of fear. If they were beginning—

"Take me," she said to Ti-ri-ki. Then she closed her eyes, and she flew.

The rocking water seemed solid and fluid at once, a cold green wall that moved and changed beneath her wing tips. Occasionally small walls of foam rose and then spilled from a cresting wave. A clutch of seabirds flew past her, bound for the open sea. Their hoarse cries lingered on the breeze.

The scene that had seemed so static from shore—the ring of small boats, the tiny forms they contained, the larger vessel standing bare-masted, wind-wings furled—began to assume movement and detail. Many of the smaller vessels stood with oars in the water, ready to propel themselves into a more advantageous position. Others had secured their oars. One tiny scull rode bare inches above the water, seven men in sea-gear sitting or crouched inside it. A larger vessel rose and fell buoyantly on the gentle waves, its single occupant a boy no more than twelve. He stood, balancing himself with outspread arms, and stared eagerly—

—stared eagerly toward the *Temple Star,* toward the figure that stepped to the rail, vivid hair streaming, chest bared to reveal the scowling face of Tith. As Dara hung there, the priest raised his arms, fists clenched. The muscles of his chest rippled, and Tith's fierce mouth opened and began to sing in a high, angry voice.

No, no, it was not Tith who sang. Dara reminded herself of that sharply. It was the priest who uttered the song of vengeance, his head thrown back, his eyes glowing as brightly as the sun. And, winging higher above the water, she saw that a second priest stood at the opposite rail. She darted around the ship. The second priest was older. The hair that floated in the wind was thin and streaked with silver. The countenance he bore on his fleshy chest was at once less mobile, yet more malevolent than that the first priest bore.

The third priest stood near the tall framework that housed the lens. He was young, fully robed, and he clutched the ropes that moved the lens, although he seemed scarcely aware of that. He gazed up at the sun as he sang, a strange, vacant-eyed rapture already consuming him. He pulled steadily at the ropes, as if from a dream, moving the lens to catch the sun, to translate its diffuse light into a single wide beam.

And at the focal point of that beam, lashed to a second frame—

Dara screamed as she swooped near, but Kentith seemed not to hear. He did not open his eyes. No muscle of his face shivered as the priests intoned the harsh syllables. Bound, gagged, he lay so still against his bindings that he might already have been dead, pierced by the slowly narrowing beam of light that centered upon his heavily swathed chest.

For a moment, Dara's heart fluttered, a trapped bird. Then she became aware of the scream of many voices, and abruptly she stood on the pier again. The small-flocks, her quirri, and clouds of angry seabirds surged noisily over the water. Kels Rinari clutched her arm, shaking her.

"What is it? What do you see?"

She stared blankly for a moment, the writhing face of Tith still vividly before her. "It's begun. They've begun the chant." Her tongue seemed thick, unresponsive.

"Is the firemaster aboard?"

"I—I think not. There are three priests, one young, two older."

"Hanarith, Feltisith and Renkith then—the men who were aboard when my men went to warn them off touching shore. So we have only to deal with three lesser brothers and perhaps two dozen crewmen." Seeing the alarm in her eyes, he said, "No fear. We've taken many a vessel from more men than that." He frowned speculatively. "The firemaster is surely watching from somewhere ashore. If we approach the *Temple Star* from its seaward flank, where he cannot see that she's being boarded, then we will have no trouble from him. Not until later, at least."

Dara glanced past him at the handful of men he had gathered. Here was no crisply uniformed guard of restless young men. These were seasoned seamen, hard-faced, with scarred hands and ragged beards. They wore heavy blades at their belts.

"The core of my old crew. I've kept them in pay," Rinari explained. "And every one of them is worth ten ordinary seamen in a scuffle. Now, if you are coming with us—"

"I'm coming," she said. How could she remain here?

In fact, she remained with Rinari and his men scarcely long enough to climb into the boat he indicated and to take a seat between two heavily muscled crewmen. She noticed the guarded glance they shot at the flocks as they set the oars in place and propelled the boat from the pier. And then she was gone, flying across the water again on Ti-ri-ki's wings.

This time the flocks flew after her, the quirri and the seabirds screaming, the smaller birds of the woodland and the settlement beating the air furiously. They clouded the sky, her flocks, and threw a broad, rippling shadow across the water. Wheeling once, looking back, she saw that only a few quirri circled the boat, guarding her abandoned body.

It moved so slowly, Rinari's boat, although his men pulled at the oars with smooth, practiced power. And unless she imagined it, the sun had brightened in the sky. Drawing near the *Temple Star* again, she heard Tith's voice over the scream of the birds. His song wavered across the water, thin and high.

Which stanza did the priests sing now? Had they entered the second movement of the chant? The third? Why hadn't she asked Kentith how long the priests spent in song before their victims burned?

She circled the *Temple Star*. The men of the ship's crew were frozen at the rear rail of the ship. Briefly she saw Rinari's driver among them. The two older priests seemed as caught in trance as the younger man now. They stood with arched backs and upthrust fists, the glow of their eyes fierce. Tith's face writhed in swift, facile malice on their chests. He grimaced, he sneered, he gathered his thin lips into a mocking leer.

The beam was drawing tighter. Dara swooped across the deck of the *Temple Star,* and she saw that the circle of light that fell upon Kentith's heavily swathed chest was smaller, more intense.

Then, for a confused moment, she was crouched between Rinari's crewmen, peering frantically at the *Temple Star* from across the harbor. "Please, please . . ." she pleaded—and was gone again, torn back to the *Temple Star*.

For a moment, strangely, the sun dimmed. Momentarily her flocks clouded it, following her as she spiraled downward to the deck of the *Temple Star*.

Tith himself was present there now. She felt his heat and his arrogance as his strident voice rose and became thinner, more piercing. The priests' throats strained, glossy with perspiration, and their hair blew in fiery sheets. The apprentice continued to pull at the ropes, compensating for the rise and fall of the harbor water although he seemed entirely unaware of his surroundings. There was only one change.

Kentith had opened his eyes.

Dara swept near, stricken. He was pale, wrapped all in white, and there was blood at his hairline, as if he had been struck. It was dried to a thick crust. His pupils widened briefly at her stricken cry. He knew her. She was certain of it as she hovered there crying with Ti-ri-ki's voice.

He knew her, and the priests' voices had changed again. Suddenly the sun glared and their voices were as thin, as piercing as the beam of light that sprang from the lens.

It had narrowed again. It had become a rapier, its dancing blade so bright, so luminous, it seemed to quiver. And from the spot where it touched Kentith's shrouded chest, a single wisp of smoke rose.

No, she would not be torn back to Rinari's side. She would not vanish behind a protective curtain of quirri while Kentith burned. Grimly she clung to Ti-ri-ki's wings—and threw herself against Kentith's chest, impaling herself on the blade of light intended for him, pressing her breast feathers—no, Ti-ri-ki's breast feathers—to the germ of brightness that glowed among the shrouds.

The rapier of light pierced the glossy feathers of Ti-ri-ki's back. Feathers blackened and curled. He screamed—or was it she? Then, with the sharp sting of pain, the storm broke.

It was black and white and brown and all shades in between. It was feathered. It was furious. It brought with it a turbulence as great as the wind at hurricane stage. It screamed with hundreds of voices, hoarse and shrill at once.

The flocks descended upon the *Temple Star*. Quirri, seabirds, the smaller birds of woodland and town swarmed in fury. Dara pressed herself to Kentith's chest, staring back over Ti-ri-ki's spread wings as the birds fell upon Tith's priests, ripping at their bright hair, at their whipping gowns, at their exposed flesh. She glimpsed the priests only for an instant. Then they were lost among the swarming birds. But she heard their raw, dying voices as they were torn from their trance. Far overhead, the revenants circled on leathery wings.

Seamen froze in their places at the rail while others hurled themselves into the sea, screaming with a fear so harsh their voices were scarcely human. The apprentice crumpled to the deck, angry birds fluttering at him from every direction. His hand jerked at the ropes in a spastic gesture, jarring the lens. Then he too was lost among the screaming birds.

Dara shuddered. The rapier of light had withdrawn, leaving seared flesh and blackened feathers where it had touched Ti-ri-ki's back. There was no other heat, no second wisp of smoke from Kentith's shrouds. She had smothered the germ of flame. And the sun had lost its brief intensity.

But the storm continued to sweep across the *Temple Star*. Blood hung in the air like a summer mist. Fine droplets sprayed everywhere. Seamen were torn apart as they stood, as they cowered, as they scrambled for shelter below-decks. Others died struggling in the water below. Small boats rocked violently as their occupants jumped up in horror or tried to hide beneath narrow plank seats. A few moved briskly away, the men who pulled at their oars staring back in ashen horror at the *Temple Star*.

Then the men of the *Temple Star* were gone and the birds turned against the ship itself. They ripped at the furled wind-wings and shredded heavy ropes. They scarred decks and railings with angry beaks. Dara watched, pressing herself to Kentith's chest, and knew their fury could have only one origin: her own anger, her own fear.

She could not call them back. She tried, but they did not respond. She could not even regain her own body. She glimpsed it momentarily, sitting like a thing of stone in Rinari's boat, but she could not reach it. She had become fixed in Ti-ri-ki's body.

She huddled against Kentith's chest, sick and cold and lost. She did not know how much time passed before the flocks left the ship. It could have been minutes; it might have been hours. But eventually the frenzy passed and the flocks rose in silent clouds and spread themselves across the early afternoon sky.

The *Temple Star* stood alone in the rocking sea. Torn linen and flesh littered its decks. Here and there a larger bundle of matter lay at the center of a dark-spattered circle. Masts and timbers groaned like human souls.

There was no sanity in thought. Dara crouched on Kentith's chest, rising and falling with his breath, and let her mind fill with emptiness. Occasionally he opened his eyes and gazed at her, licking his lips. Several times he spoke to her, but she did not respond. Most of the time he lay with eyes closed, and only the steady beat of his heart assured her that he was not seriously injured.

Eventually she raised her head at the sound of footsteps and watched numbly as Kels Rinari picked a deliberate path toward them across the littered deck. He had discarded his cloak. He wore only a white shirt and dark trousers. Tall, silent, he was as stark, as grim as Dara had ever seen him.

His shadow fell across Kentith's chest. Before Dara

could struggle to her feet, he drew his blade and slashed the ropes that bound Kentith, then moved swiftly back. He stood for a moment, poised on the balls of his feet. Finally he stepped forward again and extended his hand to her.

"My men will not board. You must come with me."

Dara stared up at him, the numbness of shock still upon her.

"Will you permit me to free your friend? Will you come?" He licked his lips. "My men are good men, but they are superstitious. They will not wait long for us in these death-waters."

Shuddering, Dara let herself be lifted to his shoulder. She clung there as he pulled at the ropes that bound Kentith. "Wake up, man. Wake up." The words were soft, entreating.

Kentith revived finally and struggled free of the bindings and oil-soaked shrouds. He peered across the deck of the *Temple Star* with glazed eyes, as if he did not see what stood before him. Rinari had to support him to the rail, had to help him down the rope ladder.

There were things floating in the water—shattered things, torn things, unidentifiable things stained with scarlet foam. Dara saw that when they reached the boat and Rinari gently lifted the quirri from his shoulder. His shirt was stained with blood where Dara had unknowingly driven Ti-ri-ki's claws into his flesh. She shivered violently, then touched her face with a cold, uncertain hand and realized she had returned to her own body. Shrieking once, Ti-ri ki resumed his place on her shoulder.

Rinari's seamen stared at her grimly as they shoved away from the *Temple Star*. The two men at either side of her drew as far from her as they could, muttering under their breath. They hauled at the oars, grunting with effort.

Rinari glanced anxiously at the sun as the boat glided across the harbor. "He knows. By now it is entirely possible that he knows."

"What?" Dara said, not understanding.

"Narkith knows by now that his brothers from Chindora are dead. He knows it if he is anywhere among the crowds.

Or he knows it if he has just one man who reports to him while he hides himself. And he knows that you and I were the cause of it, one way or another.''

Dara glanced reluctantly toward the waterfront. No one there could have seen clearly what had happened aboard the *Temple Star*. The distance was too great. But the small boats that had ringed the *Temple Star* had already reached the piers. She imagined Narkith among the people who crowded around their occupants to hear the first hysterical reports of the carnage. Anxiously she glanced up at the sun.

But how could Narkith be among the people on the pier? How could a firemaster pass unnoticed in the crowds? Kentith had only to glance up from the seat across from hers and she saw the golden flash of his eyes. There was no way he could hide what he was. How, then, could the firemaster hide himself?

She frowned, remembering that moment the night before when some elusive memory had come almost within grasp.

Exposed, vulnerable, they made their way to shore. Avoiding the pier area, they went aground within a small cove to the south of the port. Rinari's men pulled the boat across a stretch of rocky sand and tied it to a twisted tree that stood above the tidemark. A rocky bluff rose steeply behind them.

Rinari paced back toward the water and peered in the direction of the *Temple Star*. He glanced up briefly at the wheeling flocks, then studied Kentith, who sat unsteadily on the side of the boat. "So now we find ourselves in the same position as this morning, except that I have lost a wagon and a driver, and the price on your head has gone beyond gold. And—'' He glanced toward his men, and his eyes narrowed. "And there may be some of you who prefer to dissociate yourselves from me now.''

Dara stood beside Kentith, clasping his hand with cold fingers. Rinari's seamen had gathered in a tight knot. She could not read any response to his words on their weathered faces, but two of them stared hard at their boots, refusing to meet his eyes.

Rinari seemed neither disappointed nor angry. "My best advice in that case is to go south immediately and ship out from New Faro or Port Salis at the first opportunity. If I'm still here when you make your way back to this shore, I will place you in pay again. Today was beyond duty or loyalty. And the profit is doubtful. Extremely doubtful." He turned back to Dara and Kentith. "The two of you must travel by the woodland this time. If you can find your way alone—"

Dara looked up at him in sharp surprise. "If you think I am going now—"

"You intend to stay here?"

"Yes, I intend to stay." After everything he had risked today—everything he still risked—how could she retreat to the safety of Wahonin?

He studied her closely, intently. "That was no pretty thing you did," he said finally. "It was you who did it, was it not? The birds did not simply act?"

"They—did not," she said. She had not intended what had happened. Nor had she been able to control it once it was begun. Yet the storm that had destroyed the *Temple Star* had sprung directly from her own anger, from her own fear.

Rinari nodded and stepped forward, frowning at the quirri on her shoulder. He extended one forearm. "Tell him to come to me."

Puzzled, Dara took the quirri from her shoulder and placed him on Rinari's extended arm. Rinari stepped back, peering so intently at the quirri that Ti-ri-ki uttered an uneasy cry. Finally Rinari looked back to Dara. "Is there any way you can make your hunter fly to my command instead of your own?"

"No," she said, startled. "He is blooded to me. He fought for my shoulder. I—I am an Ilijhari."

"And there is no way at all that you can instruct him that he is to fly for me? That he is to use his eyes for me?"

"If there is, I don't know of it," she said.

He nodded and set the quirri carefully back on her shoulder. "Then you are the one person here who can best search out the firemaster. And," he said with deliberate emphasis, "you are the one person who can best deal with him."

Dara clutched Kentith's hand and felt his fingers tighten in hers. "What do you mean?"

"What did I say? I have been slow to see the possibilities, but I see them clearly now, and you see them, too."

"I don't," Dara said. But she did. She had seen them as soon as he spoke. Who else could soar over the people gathered on the waterfront as she could? Who else could dart through the deserted streets of Port Calibe, looking into every secluded corner of the port settlement? Who else could find the man who should have been visible to everyone, the man whose sun-gold eyes—

—*whose sun-gold eyes were hidden behind the bandages of a blind man.* That was the teasing memory. She had seen the blind man on the streets twice, his eyes bound, his shaven head weeping with raw sores. He had been there the night her quirri had killed the runaway horse. She had seen him again yesterday, among the people gathering to watch the warehouses burn, and she had noticed that the bandages that covered his eyes were snowy white although his clothing was already streaked with ash.

Snowy white—as if he had drawn them over his eyes after the fires began, just before joining the gathering crowd.

"I know him," she said softly. She turned to Kentith. "I've seen him—Narkith. He—"

But Kentith did not hear. He had turned to stare fixedly at the sun, the fiercely burning sun, and his eyes had begun to burn just as fiercely.

CHAPTER SEVENTEEN

As Dara watched, dense clouds of fire swelled free of the sun's golden center and boiled into the afternoon sky. Spreading, thinning, the burning mist quickly filled half the sky. The light the roiling gases cast was intense, frightening. The vivid blue of the sky became a harsh indigo. Clouds vanished as if sucked into a void. Afternoon shadows dissolved, and every detail of earth and water stood out with blanched clarity. Rinari's seamen seemed caught, frozen, their staring faces rendered a sick, grainy white.

"The tides—" Kentith's voice was thick, painful. "His tides are rising. He—" His lips retracted in an involuntary grimace. Joints cracked as his back arched and his head jerked sharply backward. Dara caught at him, but he twisted convulsively away, his head striking the side of the boat. He fell to his side, his body stiffly arched. Tith's etched face leered through his torn shirt.

Rinari stared at the boiling sky. He did not see the seaman who lunged forward, blade drawn, and caught at the front of Kentith's shirt. Instinctively Dara threw herself against the man, deflecting the weapon. Unbalanced, they both fell to the sand. The seaman struggled to his feet, pushing her aside as she caught at his shirt. His face studded with perspiration, he raised the blade again.

Rinari wheeled at Ti-ri-ki's cry. "What is this?" Quickly he snatched the man back, twisting the blade from his hand. It rang loudly against an exposed rock and fell to the sand.

"The eyes—" the seaman gasped, frozen in Rinari's grasp. "He'll burn us all."

"He'll burn no one," Rinari said crisply, although his own face turned ashen when he glanced down into Kentith's burning eyes. "The firemaster is drawing power from him, but he can't find us through him. He can't touch us, not that way." He nodded to the quirri that settled indignantly on Dara's shoulder as she pushed herself up from the sand. "You're lucky you salvaged your own eyes from that bit of silliness, man." He turned back to Dara. "Can you do anything for him?"

Dara knelt at Kentith's side and took his hand. It quivered and jerked free. The motion seemed spasmodic, without will. She touched his face, but he did not respond. The glow of his eyes was blinding. If he knew her, if he was at all aware of his surroundings, she saw no sign of it.

"Nothing," she said. She glanced quickly up at Rinari. "The firemaster—" she said in alarm. "It's the blind man. He wears bandages on his eyes. You've seen him. And he surely knows where we came ashore."

Rinari's winged brows contracted sharply. He turned to his men. "Help me here. We must put distance between us and this spot. Percher, here— Manilo, put your shoulder into this. Don't drag him, carry him." He urged Dara to her feet and drew her across the narrow stretch of shoreline. "Up the bluff. There are tall weeds and rocks to hide us there."

Ti-ri-ki screamed and deserted Dara's shoulder as she scrambled up the steep bluff after Rinari. Slipping, fighting for a foothold, Dara glanced up and saw that twin bolts of fire had condensed from the burning mist that hung in the sky. They shimmered brilliantly against the fiery clouds, poised like swords of light. As she watched, the first reached down and struck casually at the *Temple Star*.

The priests' vessel burst into flame. Its masts became crosses of fire, its loosely furled wind-wings blazing brightly against the sullen indigo sky. Then the very waters of the harbor boiled up around the *Temple Star* and its blazing timbers were lost in clouds of steam. Staring back over her shoulder, Dara struggled ineffectually to find a stable footing. Rinari caught her hand, pulling her roughly up the slope.

By the time they reached the top, her trouser leg was torn, her knee bloody. She touched the raw flesh numbly, then straightened and looked back in confusion at the spot where the *Temple Star* had stood. There was only a slowly dissipating cloud of vapor.

Rinari helped his men haul themselves over the edge of the bluff, tugging Kentith's arched body with them. "My compound," he said without expression when the second shimmering bolt rippled from the sky and tasted at Port Calibe. He watched, every muscle still, until the first plume of grey smoke appeared. Then he turned deliberately away. "And you are right. It is the blind man. He has been in port since the rumors first began. He goes everywhere and hears everything. I've had him fed from my own gate." He glanced back toward Port Calibe, his face betraying nothing. "My warehouses will be next. But we'll save nothing by standing here and watching for them to go."

Dara hurried after him as he strode away across the irregular ground after his men. Could he really be as little moved as he seemed?

The third bolt of fire caught them bare minutes later. For a moment the entire sky rippled with light. Then a single shimmering finger formed from the moving gases, a long, curving claw at its tip. The air hissed and crackled loudly as the fiery claw touched earth.

Rinari's warehouses were not visible from their vantage point, but peering from behind her raised arm, Dara saw flames race along the protruding upper mast of one of the two vessels harbored behind his facilities. A strange, weeping light hung over the harbor, dissipating only as black smoke rose.

Dara glanced up and froze. This time it was not a finger that formed in the sky, sucking up the last glowing gases. It was a bright-scaled serpent. It rippled across the sky, its single fiery eye transfixing her. She could not breathe, nor could she move as its forked tongue licked the air.

Rinari snatched at her arm with an angry cry and pulled her away. Stumbling, half crying, she ran after him through tall grasses and thorny scrub. The soil was rocky and sandy at once, strewn with large, jagged rocks. Rinari's men ran heavily, swords drawn, as if they could defend themselves against the coiling serpent with steel blades.

The sky, strangely, was clear again, vividly blue, as it had been earlier. Dara saw that in the moment before the air sang shrilly around her and her hair stiffened and stood out rigidly from its roots. Then she was flat against the ground, sand in her mouth, and the air no longer sang. It screamed and burst, releasing a blast of dry heat.

She felt a brief scorching of her exposed forearms. A burning wind tugged at her hair. Ti-ri-ki screamed hoarsely. Rinari had thrown himself across her. His weight was heavy against her shoulders, upon her back.

"Don't breathe!" He pressed his face to her shoulder.

Dara lay with sand in her mouth, the hard bones of Rinari's cheek and jaw digging at her flesh, and waited with utter certainty for the moment when flames would take them both.

The moment did not come. Instead the hot wind tugged angrily at them and blew itself out. Slowly the air cooled.

Catching a long breath, Rinari rolled away. The exposed portions of his shirt were scorched a delicate shade of brown. One hand, one side of his face was brightly flushed, as if from overexposure to the midday sun.

Shakily Dara sat, touching the hot sand gingerly. Her forearms were hot and pink, the fine hair that grew there oddly withered. Numbly she rubbed at the flesh and brushed the singed hair away. Ti-ri-ki took her shoulder, the coarse feathers of his chest and neck ruffed. He glared around in ill-tempered confusion, complaining to himself.

Rinari's men stood and cursed volubly as they brushed themselves clean. Tensely Dara peered up. The sky was brightly blue, clear from horizon to horizon except for twin columns of smoke. The sun was no smaller, no paler than it had been earlier in the day. Yet it seemed so. It seemed fragile, wafer-thin.

Kentith lay in the tall grass, one hand flung limply over his eyes. Dara went quickly to his side and knelt, alarmed. The sun had not burned him as it had the others. He seemed untouched. Yet he did not respond when she took his hand, when she touched his face.

Rinari knelt and shook him, then pressed his head to his chest. "His heart is steady," he said, sinking back on his heels. "I think the firemaster has simply exhausted him. Or it may be that his own resistance has drained him."

"He slept yesterday," Dara said, trying to assure herself. "He slept afterward."

Rinari nodded, distracted. Then, without a word, he stood and strode away in the direction they had come.

Dara hesitated at Kentith's side, afraid to leave him.

A ruddy-faced seaman stepped forward, one of the two who had carried him from the cove. "Go with the master. No one will touch the priest." He weighed his blade in one thick hand.

Dara met his eyes and saw that he meant it. "Thank you," she said gratefully.

The coarser plants that caught at Dara's trousers as she ran after Rinari seemed undamaged, but the more delicate vegetation was withered and brown. As Dara neared the edge of the bluff, even the hardier vegetation was blackened. Entire plants, leaves and stems, fell away in ashes at the touch of her boots.

Rinari stood at the edge of the rise. Reaching his side, Dara caught a sharp breath and retreated a step. The cove where they had come ashore had been the focus of the fire-serpent's strike. What had been sand was now raw, fused glass. All that remained of the boat was ashes, those so white, so fine that the breeze had already begun to feather them away.

Quickly Dara followed the direction of Rinari's gaze. The columns of smoke that rose from the warehouse district, from Port Calibe itself, were thick and dark. "Perhaps—

perhaps it isn't your compound," Dara said. "Perhaps he set some other part of town afire."

Rinari shook his head. "It's my property. Yesterday he was concerned with creating a show, so he blew the powders. Today he has put his finger directly on me. And I was wrong."

"Wrong?" Dara said with quick dismay. Wrong in refusing to yield to Narkith? Wrong in helping her take Kentith from the priests? She glanced up and saw that her flocks had begun to gather again. They circled high overhead, their voices carrying faintly on the afternoon air.

Rinari turned. His gaze was long and concentrated. "I said you were the person to search him out and the person to deal with him. I was wrong. I will do it myself."

Dara stared up at him, disbelieving. "You can't do that." Could anyone, after what they had just seen?

The pupils of his eyes narrowed sharply. "Can I not?" he said, baring his teeth. "He has threatened me. He has intimidated me. He has destroyed my property and my reputation. He has taken everything I own—everything I've spent my lifetime assembling. Now I will have him."

Dara shook her head. "But how? Do you think—do you think he's exhausted himself?"

"As he's exhausted your friend? I doubt it. But it will be dark eventually. Then he will have no more fire than you have, than I have. And now we know his appearance; we know who he is. So I will hunt him out while he sleeps, and when he opens his eyes to the morning sun, I will be there. You will help me find him, of course."

So that was the demand she saw in his eyes; that she help him find the firemaster. But to wait until the sun rose to deal with him— She touched her forehead with a shaky hand. "I will help you find him—I will use my quirri to find him—if you will deal with him tonight."

"There's nothing to be gained from taking him that way."

"Gained?" Dara said incredulously. "He's destroyed your home. He's destroyed your business. He—"

"Yes, and at dawn, in those few minutes when he has the first full use of his fire, I will destroy him."

"Don't you mean he will destroy you?" How could he even speak of matching himself against Narkith when the sun shone?

Rinari raised one hand in an impatient gesture. "Let him do it if he can. I'll have surprise and a good blade on my side. He'll have fire, if he can call it up quickly enough. However it ends, I'll win back my name. What am I without that?"

"Alive! And he isn't a man. He—"

Rinari shook his head. "Whatever he is, I don't intend to take him in any way that won't gain me back my name. Will you use your quirri to find him?"

"I can use the quirri to kill him as well as to find him," Dara said in a low voice. Was that the only way to keep him from crossing his blade with the firemaster's bolt?

His winged brows rose skeptically. "Could you do that? Could you set your birds on a sleeping man?"

Dara gazed down at the ruined cove: at the water that lapped at the fused sand, at the ashes that scattered lightly in the breeze. "Yes. Yes, I could do it."

"Nice words, but I hear nothing behind them."

Dara drew a long breath. "If it was the only way I could keep you from killing yourself—" She broke off, surprised by the conviction she heard in her tone.

He frowned, waiting for her to go on. "Does it matter so much to you if I kill myself?" he demanded when she did not.

Flushing, she met his eyes, then glanced quickly away. "You are overmatched."

"Then you have very little faith in my ability with the blade."

"I have never seen you use it."

Rinari frowned and paced away, studying the twin columns of smoke that marked the sky. When he turned back, he spoke in a low voice. "You can do as you please. You can help me. You can refuse to help me. Or you can kill the firemaster yourself, with your hunters. There is no way

I can prevent you from doing that if you choose. But do it and I will never release you from the *damen-kest.*"

Startled, Dara studied his set face. "If I leave Narkith for you, you will release me?"

Rinari shrugged, an angry gesture. "Give me my prey and I will release you."

So if she denied him this suicidal confrontation, he would insist that she honor her pledge. But if she let him die— She shook her head. How could she expect to understand? His logic had never been hers. "I'll help you find him," she said finally. "For the rest—"

He waited, tense and still, his gaze unflinching.

"For the rest, I will leave him for you." Apparently she had persuaded him that she could direct her quirri against a sleeping man, if indeed Narkith slept tonight. She had not persuaded herself.

A momentary bleakness flickered in his eyes. He nodded stiffly and turned away, striding back toward the place where they had left the others.

His men had moved southward, following a footpath along the top of the bluff. Flying on Ti-ri-ki's wings, Dara found them huddled in a silent group against the weathered plank wall of a deserted fisher's hut.

Kentith sat a short distance from the seamen, the gold of his eyes tarnished, his face grey and drained. Rinari's men jumped to their feet at their approach, blades drawn. Dara ran directly to Kentith's side.

He stood, painfully, and met her anxious glance. "What has he done?" The words were tense, difficult.

She had to touch him. She had to reassure herself that he was unharmed. But he flinched as if even the slight pressure of her fingers brought pain. "We think he burned Rinari's compound—and his warehouses. But we know now who he is. He's been passing himself in Port Calibe as a blind man. I've seen him, and Rinari has seen him. He's been here since the rumors began. Kentith, if you don't resist him, if you just let him use you—"

"No. What does Rinari intend?"

"We'll go to Port Calibe and find him. We—"

"You're going back there?" he said in disbelief.

"We'll wait until dark," she assured him hastily. "I'll fly with Ti-ri-ki to find where he is spending the night. I'll—"

"No." His face, grey before, had taken a harsh, ashen tone. "He will have adherents by now. Even if he hasn't shown himself, there will be people there eager to do whatever they think might please him. After this afternoon, after the *Temple Star*—" He shook his head, releasing her. "I should never have brought you into this."

"But you didn't. I brought you. If I hadn't let you come back to Port Calibe with me—"

He shook his head impatiently. "I knew when I first saw you in the woodland that I should let you pass. But you were dressed just as my mother dressed, and you were alone, and so I followed you. I frightened you right into the path of those three animals. And now I've drawn you into Narkith's path. You can't go back to Port Calibe."

"She will go nowhere near the firemaster," Rinari said, joining them, placing a possessive hand on Dara's shoulder. "She will walk with me to the edge of town. Once there, she will fly ahead with her quirri and find him for me. And then she will do no more."

"You know that he can draw from the sun as soon as it crests the horizon?" Kentith demanded.

"I know that," Rinari said. "That is when I intend to take him, as the sun rises."

Kentith's eyes narrowed. He studied Rinari without expression. "The prize, of course," he said at last.

"The prize," Rinari affirmed. "It will be much greater if I take him when the power is in him. But Dara will remain behind, protected by her quirri, when I go to take him. No one will touch her. If Narkith is sleeping, she will have no further part in the matter at all. If he is awake, if he is moving around the settlement, then I will ask her to send this one to guide me to him." He indicated Ti-ri-ki, hunched protectively on Dara's other shoulder. The quirri winked back at him with intent yellow eyes.

Kentith passed a troubled hand over his face, turning

back to Dara. "Dara, if anything should happen to Ti-ri-ki while you wear his wings—" He studied Ti-ri-ki with a long, frowning glance. "Te-kia told me a story while you slept after your blooding."

"A story?" Dara demanded, puzzled, when he did not go on.

He met her eyes, his gaze reluctant, troubled. "He told me of a woman who found her mate's body in the forest, just as he had left it to go to the hunt the night before. She couldn't wake him. His flocks flew away in confusion when she tried, and his hunter was not among them. She took his body back to her hall and cared for it. A few days later, his kin found his hunter among the trees, its neck broken, apparently by some large predator. The woman cared for her mate's body until it died two year later, but he never returned to it."

Dara stared at his ashen face. Could it be true? If death caught Ti-ri-ki while she used his wings, would it catch her too, leaving her body waiting somewhere, vacant but alive? Ti-ri-ki uttered a low cry. Shaken, Dara reached to reassure him. Why hadn't Te-kia warned her?

When had she given him the opportunity? "Narkith knows I'm an Ilijhari," she said softly, thinking aloud. "He was in the crowd that gathered after my quirri killed the horse. He knows that the quirri are mine."

Rinari leveled a long, weighing glance at Kentith and withdrew his hand from Dara's shoulder. "Then you will go nowhere near him in the shape of a quirri once the sun rises," he said. "I will track him through the settlement by myself if I must. At that hour the streets are empty. And he will probably be safely asleep somewhere." He stepped back, turning to frown at the afternoon sun. "He may already have revealed himself. He may have shown himself when he set fire to my property."

Kentith nodded, studying Rinari as carefully as Rinari had studied him the moment before. "I think we must learn if he has," he said slowly. "I think we must learn if someone has offered him shelter, whether he will be guarded for the night, which of your associates have come openly to his side. Dara, if you were to take one of the lesser breeds, some breed people are accustomed to seeing in town—''

''I'll take a grey-dun,'' she said. And why wait until dark to learn what was happening in Port Calibe? She glanced up. The quirri, the small-flocks, the seabirds were wheeling restlessly overhead. ''I'll go now.''

''Not from here,'' Rinari said with a quick glance at his men. ''Let us walk farther along the path.''

Rinari tailored his pace to Kentith's. They retreated beyond the fisher's hut to a place where a circle of rocks stood silent guardian over a plot of bare soil. Sitting, Dara noticed how carefully the two men arranged themselves, Kentith to her right, Rinari to her left, neither claiming a closer position than the other. She noticed too the frankly evaluating glance they directed at each other again and she wondered distractedly what it meant.

She had only to raise one hand and the flocks came to her. They spun noisily from the sky and settled nearby, the quirri perching on the rocks, their yellow eyes vigilant, the smaller birds scattered in the grass and in the scrub. Glancing around, Dara found the leader of the grey-duns.

In the instant before she took wing, Rinari touched her arm. ''Wait, there is one thing. My—my woman. If you are near my compound, would you look to see that she escaped safely?''

The very diffidence of the request stayed Dara from correcting him. ''I'll look for her.'' And then she flew.

CHAPTER EIGHTEEN

Port Calibe was not far from the ruined cove by wing. Within minutes, Dara flew over the warehouse district. Spiraling down through the dense smoke, she knew at once which of the blazing buildings below were Rinari's. Those were the five southernmost structures—the structures no one attempted to save, although two of Rinari's uniformed men pounded up and down the street haranguing onlookers to take up buckets. Farther along the waterfront, the fire had spread to three smaller buildings as well. Bucket crews fought for those while small groups of men with sooted faces and sweat-stained shirts wet down adjoining facilities.

Dara winged low over the people who had gathered to watch the battle for the warehouses. Rough-bearded seamen, women in wigs and stained satins, an occasional child— Their eyes were watchful, wary, avid as they peered into the leaping flames.

Narkith hadn't shown himself. Dara was certain of it. Had he revealed himself, the mood of the crowd would be different. He, not the fires he had set, would be the focal point of attention.

Nor did Dara find any sign of him as she flew through the deserted streets beyond the waterfront.

No wet-lipped crowd attended the fire at Rinari's compound. Gliding low through the smoke, Dara saw that the perimeter wall still stood, blackened but intact, as did the exterior walls of the main house. Both were of quarried

stone. But flame ate hungrily at the smaller frame buildings of the compound, as it did at the interior of the house.

Men in stained uniforms struggled with screaming
horses, trying to evacuate the hysterical animals to the
safety of the street. As Dara watched, one of the animals
broke free and fled toward the burning stable, its fine-
boned legs striking gravel and earth in fluttering cadence.
Rinari's men stumbled after the shrilling animal, snatching
at its mane, at its tail, at its dragging lead rope, yelping
angrily.

Rinari's mother stood beyond the gate, fiercely silent.
A short distance away, a pair of uniformed men knelt over
a third man. A red hat lay in the street, trampled.

Dara fluttered near the unconscious man and recognized
the hard, narrow face of the young guard who had waited
at the first posthouse on the day she and Harmin had left
Wahonin. The whites of his eyes glared sightlessly against
his blackened face as his mates fought to revive him. There
was no sign of respiration. Dara remembered the bright,
hard sparkle of his eyes the last time she had seen him and
was sorry.

She was sorry too for the young fruit trees that stood
seared and withering in the orchard. Sorry for the grass
and white flowers, torn and trampled. Sorry for all the
quiet and order she remembered from the afternoon before.

She went then, seeking Narkith—seeking the blind man.
She darted through deserted streets, piercing drifting veils
of smoke, skirting occasional dark, rolling clouds. The
dun's respiratory passages stung as she searched the settlement for some sign of the man who bound his eyes.

Narkith was not among the boisterous men and women
who sat drinking under a broad-limbed tree near the place
where Dara's quirri had attacked the runaway horse. He
was not among the men who spoke in low voices around
a long, varnished table in the rear room of a deserted dry
goods store. Dara paused for a moment on the weathered
sill, listening as they detailed the demands they expected
the firemaster to make of them. They spoke dispassion-

ately, as if it were a foregone conclusion that they would yield in everything. And the firemaster was not among the half dozen people who grubbed through the ashes of the structures that had burned the day before, seeking booty.

Yet he must be near. Otherwise how had he known it was Rinari who had taken Kentith from the *Temple Star?* How had he known they had gone aground afterward at the cove? He had seen those things from some sheltered vantage point or he had mingled with the crowds, eyes bandaged, and heard of them.

Dara discovered another group of men closeted in the meeting room of an annex to the port prison. These men were neither quiet nor dispassionate, and it was not the firemaster they discussed. She listened briefly, then darted away, wondering if any of them had ever been Rinari's allies. If so, they were no longer.

To the north of the port prison, the broad, rutted thoroughfare that serviced the waterfront narrowed to a winding footpath. Dara followed it through an expanse of wind-sculpted trees to a place where a cluster of stone cottages stood a short distance above the tidemark. Their roofs were tumbled, their doors awry. Dara fluttered quickly from cottage to cottage and found nothing but spiderwebs, debris, and the damp smell of neglect.

But Narkith was near. She felt it more strongly than ever.

She flew northward along the shoreline, watching for movement among the rocks, among the occasional clumps of dwarfed trees. Once she found a place where a broad circle of tidal sand had been fused into glassy rubble. The water washed at it uneasily, spreading it with foam. Farther, she discovered a tree that had withered, as if from great heat, although there was no sign of fire. Beyond, she found an abandoned cookfire, ringed with rocks. The ashes were sunken, damp.

Instinctively she knew that Narkith did not keep himself so far from Port Calibe. She turned back, gliding along the water's edge. Seabirds swooped near, crying hoarsely in inquiry. Once she quivered with sharp alarm when a dark head reared from among the foaming rocks at the water's edge and peered at her with glistening eyes. Then she recognized the wet, dark pelt of a sea mammal, and her heart beat again.

In her first flight along the edge of the water, she had not seen the cottage at the other side of the footpath, half-lost among low-limbed trees. She saw it this time. It was shadowed and damp, its exterior walls heavily grown with velvet-black mosses, but its roof was intact and its door stood firmly on its hinges.

Her heart—the dun's heart—beat a little faster. As sedately as she could, she glided near and settled on a mossy sill.

The interior of the cottage was shadowed and stale, but the floor was swept clean and there was bedding piled in one corner. A large leather satchel stood near the rumpled blankets. Dara fluttered into the cottage and perched nervously on one worn corner of the satchel. If she could open the leather case, if she could glimpse its contents—

But she did not need golden robes or white bandages to convince her that she had found the firemaster's lair.

She retreated to the trees, waiting there for the firemaster to return. Strangely, as she settled to a sheltered branch, the dun began to sing and to call. Soon half a dozen duns flickered among the low-limbed trees, crying in nervous excitement. Dara found herself leaping weightlessly from branch to branch, joining in quick, darting games she didn't understand.

An hour passed, and the firemaster did not appear. Dara's companions grew tired and deserted her. She crouched alone in her leafy cavern and watched the sun through the leaves.

The first flicker of the sun was so slight that she thought it was simply the effect of shifting shadows. When it came again a few moments later, she knew it was not.

Her heart constricted. Late afternoon approached. Had Narkith other punishments to administer before the sun set? Feeling slight, feeling vulnerable, she abandoned her shelter and flew briefly along the footpath. She saw no one. In the distance, Port Calibe was no longer mantled with dark smoke, although a narrow column of smoke still rose from the warehouse district.

Had Narkith returned to Port Calibe? Dara flew aimlessly, avoiding a noisy flock of seabirds. The tide was rising. It foamed lazily at the shore. Glimpsing something dark in the water, Dara flew to investigate. Briefly, before the current took it under, she saw a charred timber from the *Temple Star*. For a moment she hung breathless in the air.

Recovering, she flew uncertainly to the north, searching again for some sign of the firemaster.

She found nothing. It was not until she turned back, leaving the water behind, following the rising curve of the land, that she saw the net of light. So faint, so gossamer it might have been an illusion, it streamed from the sun to dance above an isolated cluster of trees. Startled, Dara forgot for a moment what she did, and the dun's body faltered in the air.

Catching herself, she came to light on a thorny scrub. The net of light danced and spun above the treetops, first swirling into invisibility, then brightening, surging, falling finally into incandescent folds before it vanished again. The sun flickered in a corresponding cycle and Dara knew with a quick constriction of her throat where she would find the firemaster.

Her claws tightened on the branch where she perched. Her chest tightened, the dun's heart leaping so violently the rhythm jarred her. Forcing herself from the safety of her perch, she described a darting, indirect path toward the cluster of trees.

They grew at the top of a sharply sloping rise, tall and straight, their foliage brilliantly green. Rippling light fell across the glossy leaves, casting a series of swiftly changing shadows. Fluttering near, Dara saw that the trees grew in a ragged circle, as if set in place by an inexpert hand. And at the center of the circle—

The firemaster sat cross-legged on the rocky soil, staring into the sun. His bare scalp was raw. His face was lean, bony, the cheekbones standing sharply against the leathery flesh. His expression was chilling, vacant and cruel at once.

He had cast aside his loose-fitting shirt. He sat with his shoulders drawn sharply back, his hands clenched and up-raised. His back and torso were powerful, the skin un-marked, youthful. The muscles of his chest moved sleekly just beneath the supple surface, rippling and gliding, giv-ing life to Tith's etched face as the firemaster teased the weightless curtain of sunlight slowly toward him.

The vacancy of the priest's expression, the contrasting animation of the face that grimaced and scowled on his chest drew Dara. Fascinated and fearful at once, she flut-tered near. When the firemaster seemed not to notice, when indeed he seemed unaware of any presence but the sun's, Dara settled cautiously to a jutting rock that stood within the circle of trees. She crouched and drew in her head, making herself small.

Tith snarled. He leered. He smiled with twisted malice and slowly, as Dara watched, Narkith's eyes changed. The fiery golden pupils distended. Twin suns, they grew bright and heavy in his face, casting a light so fierce, so radiant it soon obscured his features.

His head fell back, slowly, as if it had grown heavy. The cartilage of his neck swelled into prominence. The chant, when it began, hardly seemed to stem from any human source. It rose like a stream of sound, high, thin, wordless—like a stream that welled up and overflowed its channel.

Dara shivered, wanting to flee, unable to find the power of her wings. Because the more fiercely the priest's eyes burned, the more shrilly he sang, the greater and the fiercer the animation of Tith's face. Finally it seemed that it was the etched face, not the priest, that lived, that called, that sang to the sun.

Fresh sheets of energy rained in the air, separating into trailing wisps that were quickly absorbed into the dancing net. Reinforced, the curtain of light began to descend. Dara stared up, transfixed, and experienced a crushing sense of a power great and uncaring, a power that did not recognize life, that did not recognize will, that knew nothing but its own silent magnitude.

Then she felt a rush of heat, the net touched the tree-tops, and the trees began to fall in ashes.

The dun shrilled and leaped from its perch, wings fluttering wildly. Instinctively Dara caught it, caught herself as the upper branches of the tall, straight trees sifted around her in fine white flakes.

There was no escape. Dara crouched against the rocky soil as the shimmering curtain ate relentlessly at the trees, and although the disintegration seemed slow, seemed stately, in reality it was not. Leaves, limbs, bark—all were swiftly consumed. Within moments, only stumps remained, and then those were gone as well. The curtain of light scoured brightly, hungrily at the bare soil. There was no smoke. Nor was ground or vegetation so much as scorched in any place the curtain had not touched.

Dara drew her wings near and tucked her head close to her chest. The beat of her heart was little more than a quiver. Her breath was a frightened rasp.

And then, confused, she became aware of several things at once. The priest had ceased to sing. The curtain of light had vanished. And Narkith's eyes had faded. He sat cross-legged on the ground gazing directly at her, and if he had been in trance before, he was not now. The pupils of his eyes were narrow and black, his lips were twisted. She thought at first that he grimaced. Reluctantly she recognized that instead he smiled. Terribly. And directly at her. The face on his chest had grown still.

"So you thought I did not see you," the firemaster said in a whispering voice. "You thought I could not distinguish a simple songbird from an Ilijhari witch, come to scout me out so that she can tell her friends where I am to be found.

"But why do your friends want to find me, little witch? Do they want so badly to die?

"I thought they had done that already. I thought I had already rendered them ashes on the wind. And you too, little bird. But I have failed, haven't I? So why do they wish now to give me a second chance, when there are so many things sweet in this world?

"Here, I know a song as dear as yours, witch-bird. Listen, and when I've sung it for you, you can fly away and sing it to your friends."

Horribly, he leaned forward, his staring eyes holding Dara's. His face was like a construct of bones sheathed in a leather mask too shrunken to properly contain it. The lesions on his scalp were fiery. They wept a yellow fluid that crusted on his skin. There seemed to be genuine pleasure in his smile as he began to sing.

His song held a soft, poisoned sweetness. Caught, held, Dara listened. She did not know the words he sang. They were of an old tongue, one not heard on this shore. But she knew nevertheless that he sang to her of things dear to him: of delicate flowers searing in the sun, of forest fragrances turning acrid and smoky, of small creatures whose fur burst into flames as they ran in play. She knew he sang of plain people working the summer soil, only to have it burst into flames and crumble beneath them; of sleek, fine-boned horses running in burning meadows; of proud men and strong women crying acid tears, tears that ate away their flesh, leaving the white bones shining free.

Narkith sang all those things, and Dara could not fly. She could only crouch and listen, caught in the terrible web of images he spun.

"I want to die in this lovely new land," he said softly, speaking again. "Yes, I came here to die. My eyes have burned too often, they have burned too brightly with Tith's clean flame. I have burned good men as they sat at table with their families because they spoke slightingly of their local priest. I have burned children who taunted an old blind man, not knowing that he was I. I have burned women who in the terror of childbirth cursed the man who seeded their precious child—the man who came to them from the blessed altar of Tith himself.

"My eyes have burned too often and too brilliantly. One

day I will waken as blind as I pretend now to be. Then I will huddle in the darkness of my mind, and I will go mad, and very soon after that I will die. A man of Tith must have light if he is to live. I am already half-mad from wearing my bandages. Yet the bandages are the only thing that have saved my vision for so long. I am old, you know. I am very old.

"Do you see the paradox, witch-bird? I must have light, yet it is the light that blinds me and destroys me. We always die so, half-mad, half-blind, those of us whom the sun chooses as his vassals.

"So I will die here. My brothers will come to this lovely new shore, this rich new shore—they will come when I have made ashes of your friends—and they will build for me an altar on a point of land overlooking the sea. And then I will call the sun to myself and I will burn.

"Tith will consume me. I will fly in ashes.

"They are beautiful, ashes. They are the refined essence of the man. Yet so few know that; so few understand the grace of Tith's cleansing fire. I do not destroy men and women. I refine them. I burn away the impurities that make them less than what they might be and then I turn them free on the wind. I burn away dissatisfaction and greed and cowardice and foolish will. And fear and venality and cupidity. I reduce them to the pure ash.

"It is so sweet, that burning, that purification. It will be sweet for me too when my altar is ready."

Stricken, Dara saw that it was not just the sores of his scalp that wept. Thick yellow fluid ran from his eyes too, draining down his leathery cheeks. And strangely, she pitied him, because she saw him clearly now for what he was: he was a man vicious and perverted and lonely; a man torn from his family as a child and given to the care of other men as vicious and perverted and lonely as he would one day be; a man born to a gift destined to destroy the very core of his humanity.

He was just what he said: an old man, half-mad, waiting for the release of a sweet, burning death.

At the same time that she saw those things, she saw that

his eyes had begun to brighten again, that the image on his chest had begun to writhe and grimace with a life of its own.

The dun, swifter than she was, leaped into the air just as the tiny bolt of fire bit at the soil. A second bright arrow darted after her as she swept away. She felt its heat. She heard its hissing passage through the air.

Then she was fleeing the circle of fallen trees, fleeing the vicious old man who launched his fiery darts after her. Her heart—the dun's heart—fluttered in her throat, struggling so violently she was convinced it knew the danger as well as she did.

She did not want to abandon the dun there, in midair. But Narkith knew now that Kentith and Rinari were alive, and she must warn them. With a wrench, she wrested herself free of the dun's senses.

Her eyes flew open to a sky that was already brightening unnaturally for the hour of day—and to two startled faces. Kentith and Rinari bent over her, hunched in protective postures. Black eyes and gold stared into hers, startled.

"He knows," she gasped. "He knows we are alive. The sun—"

They turned in unison and stared at the western sky. The late afternoon sun had distended. Billowing gases swelled from its bulging disk.

"He knows we're somewhere here, above the cove," Dara said. He had struck at the cove earlier, precisely and surely, but he had not caught them there. Now —

"The water," Rinari said, snatching at her arm, pulling her to her feet. "The water, man," he called over his shoulder to Kentith as he dragged Dara toward the edge of the long, curving bluff. Quirri and small-flocks rose from the ground and swarmed noisily around them. Dislodged from her shoulder, Ti-ri-ki swept after them screaming.

Then, abruptly, Rinari halted, his eyes stricken. "My men—" He stared back, paralyzed, toward the place where he had left his crew.

"There's no time." Catching them, Kentith propelled

them both across the bluff. "No time." But the second
warning was strangled. Kentith's back arched sharply, the
joints crackling, as his eyes took fire.

"No!" Dara cried as he fell. She tore free of Rinari's
grasp and threw herself beside Kentith's twisting body.
"Let him use you." Whatever fire Narkith could draw
from Kentith would make little difference. Narkith had so
much of his own. Surely he only drew Kentith into his
web because it pleased him to use him.

"He doesn't hear you. Here—" Rinari caught Kentith
beneath the armpits. Glancing up tensely, he tugged him
toward the edge of the bluff.

Sheets of fiery mist already swept across the exposed
ground, a burning rain that moved swiftly southward. Rinari's strength seemed superhuman as he fought Kentith's
convulsing body to the edge of the bluff and wrestled it
down the steep decline toward the water.

Dara stumbled after them. Once, glancing back up the
shoreline, she thought she saw a figure run across the narrow strip of sand and throw itself to the tide, its clothing
ablaze. But the rise and curve of the land did not permit
view of the fisher's hut or of the men they had left there.

She slid down the bluff after Kentith and Rinari, tearing
her trousers, lacerating her hands, and tumbled across the
sandy strip toward the tide. Rinari was already in the water. He caught Kentith beneath the chin and pulled him
under, leaving only his face exposed. Dara plunged after
them, her birds swirling over the water in screaming
clouds.

The land burned. Bright mist scoured it, setting fire to
every stalk of grass, to every leafy branch. Briefly a series
of spinning vortices formed from the burning mist. They
whirled along the tide line, whipping up the sand, leaving
behind trails of molten glass. Dipping, veering, they tasted
at the water. Steam rose in bursts. The flocks retreated in
confusion, crying indignantly.

Dara followed Rinari as deep into the water as she
dared. Following his shouted instructions, she submerged
herself, her breath held. She remained underwater until

her lungs screamed for air. Then she bobbed up, caught a gulping breath, and plunged beneath the surface again.

Her clothes clung to her, wet and heavy. Her hair streamed across her face. She shook it back each time she emerged for breath. When she reemerged, it blinded her again.

The scant vegetation on the bluff yielded little smoke. The breeze caught that, dispersing it. After a while, bobbing up for air, daring to glance around, Dara saw that the fiery mist had become little more than a wispy yellow fog. The breeze tore it away in patches. Turning, she saw that Kentith had ceased to writhe against Rinari's confining embrace. His eyes were shut, his face still, as if in unconsciousness.

The flocks returned, circling the water where they bobbed, crying querulously. Dara caught Rinari's eye. "Is it safe?"

"Wait," he said grimly.

They waited, poised to submerge themselves again. But the last vestiges of mist evaporated and the sun returned to its normal state in the western sky.

Finally, shivering so violently her teeth clashed, Dara accompanied Rinari from the water, taking as much of Kentith's weight as she could bear. Water streamed from them all. Rinari's hair was plastered to his skull and his face was set, implacable.

They fell together against the steep, protecting bank, the tide bare feet from where they huddled. Dara brushed the hair from Kentith's face and took his hands, trying to warm them with her own. His lips and nails were blue, his features cold and grey.

Rinari rested only a moment. Then he stood, looking down at them as if from a great distance. "I must find my men. If the fire returns, you will have to leave him here."

It took her a moment to understand what he meant: that if Narkith struck again before Rinari returned, she must go into the water alone. She could never hope to wrestle Kentith's convulsing body into the tide as Rinari had—or to keep him from drowning if she did.

"If you could wait—" she said desperately. She was so weak, so cold. She was not certain she could save even herself if Narkith struck again.

Rinari's brow creased faintly. He shook his head, more as if refusing himself than as if refusing her. "Those are good men, and they were caught out here because they followed me."

Dara sighed, understanding. "Of course," she said, and watched as he sprinted away. Shuddering with cold, she huddled close to Kentith.

After a while he responded and they sheltered in each other's arms, Dara's head buried against his shoulder, her eyes wet with more than seawater.

Because she saw now that she could not honor her promise to Rinari. She could not let Narkith live until the sun rose. She must go with her flocks as soon as it was fully dark. She must go and see that when Narkith slept tonight, he did not wake again. And she was afraid.

CHAPTER NINETEEN

Somehow she must have slept because for a time she was not aware of wind or water, or even of Kentith curled beside her. She stirred when he withdrew; but the dusk was sullen, the sky featureless and grey before she finally shivered fully awake. Her clothes were a cold weight against her back and legs. Her hair lay damp across one cheek. Her mouth tasted of salt.

She sat, brushing the hair off her cheek, and hugged herself briefly against the penetrating chill. Rinari had found his men but they were fewer than before. They were gathered a short distance away, Kentith among them, their heads bent in low-voiced discussion. One, she saw, had suffered blistering burns to his back and arms. He sat shivering and grey-faced among the others, the seared flesh stubbornly bare.

Their covert conversation ceased when they saw that she had awakened. Stiffly, she rose. The men made room for her within their circle, then stared silently at the ground, as if struck dumb. Not even Rinari spoke, although he studied her with a level, frowning gaze.

It struck Dara after a moment that they were waiting for her to say something, to make some declaration. She met Rinari's eyes and said in a low voice, "I won't wait for morning."

He nodded heavily. "There is no waiting," he concurred in a low, flat tone. "This is no longer a game. There is no longer a prize. This is a madman, and he must be exterminated. It has become as simple as that."

223

"Yes," Dara whispered, grateful that at last he understood. "Your—" She hesitated, aware of the four seamen listening intently to her every word. "Your woman is safe. She escaped the compound. And your men saved the horses—some of them at least. I saw only one person who was seriously injured." She could not bring herself to tell him that the careless young guard she had met on the road to Port Calibe was dead.

"How many did you see who were not seriously hurt?"

Dara frowned, reviewing the scene at the compound. "Eight. Perhaps nine. There were two others—two uniformed men—in the warehouse district, trying to organize a bucket gang."

"And having precious little luck, I'd guess."

She inclined her head silently and glanced at Kentith. His gaze was as level, as frowning as Rinari's. "He spoke to me," she said. "Narkith spoke to me. He's come here to die."

A quiver of expression touched Kentith's features. He leaned forward, briefly intent. "He would do that soon enough, using himself as he has today—if we could wait."

Rinari glanced impatiently from one to the other of them. "What do you mean? He would die soon enough?"

Kentith shrugged. "He is using himself too hard. A firemaster's eyes sustain damage every time he draws light from the sun. The more intense the light, the more prolonged his use of it, the greater the damage. At his age, Narkith is even more susceptible than a younger man. Let him use himself as hard as he did today for nine or ten days longer and he will blind himself—and his power will be gone."

"And then—and then he will die," Dara said.

"He will madden and starve himself. Or tear open the blood vessels in his wrists and bleed to death—unless he chooses to immolate himself with the last of his vision."

Rinari reflected for a moment, then shook his head impatiently. "We can't wait. After today, he'll never have to use himself so hard again. We are as good as beaten if we let him see the sun again. Where is he hiding?"

Licking her lips, swallowing back nausea and fear, Dara told him. Ti-ri-ki was hunched on a rock a short distance away. His yellow eyes winked at her through the gathering dusk. "I'll go for him when it's dark."

Rinari's brows rose sharply. "You will go? When you pledged him to me?"

Dara looked at him in surprise. "But that was earlier." Surely he did not intend her to keep her promise now, when they had both seen Narkith's power and his viciousness.

"Does it make some difference to you who kills him? So long as it is done tonight?"

Dara drew back. "No. But it must be done. It must be done tonight."

"And you don't trust me to do it?"

Dara shook her head helplessly. Why try to protect him? He had already guessed that his allies in Port Calibe would turn against him. "When I was searching Port Calibe, I found a group of men meeting in a small building attached to the prison. I stayed for a few minutes. I listened."

"Council was in session?"

"It was an emergency meeting, I think. They have placed a reward on you. And you need not be presented to them alive."

Rinari rose stiffly and paced toward the water's edge, his shoulders rigid. "So it's my body they want."

"Preferably."

"They said as much? Aloud? That they want my dead body?"

She glanced away, evading his fierce stare. "They said— they said it would be simpler that way."

He nodded, his features thunderous. "After this is done, you will identify for me the men who attended this meeting. You will identify the ones who spoke this way of me."

"And you—"

"Will I kill them?" He extended one hand and closed it into a hard fist. "The first one I find, perhaps I will, just for the pleasure of it. And then the others, if they care to live, can pay the reward directly into my hand from their own funds. I'll take the whole of it from each of them. I hope it was handsome enough to make it worth my while.''

"I didn't hear the amount," she said, uneasy at the dark relish he took in the betrayal. "But you cannot go anywhere near the settlement tonight."

"Can I stay here?" he demanded.

"Yes," she said. "Because I will go. With my flocks."

"You will go alone and kill the firemaster as he sleeps?" he said incredulously. "You spoke of that before, and you didn't convince me."

Nor had she convinced herself, earlier. But now— "I will do it with my quirri," she said. Because it had to be done, and because Rinari could not do it without placing his life at risk, no matter how well armed he went, no matter that he approached the firemaster only by dark.

"And the other part of the pledge?" he demanded. "The penalty you pay for snatching my prey? I have no intention of releasing you from that."

She stared at him, unable to believe what she heard. "You are obsessed. You are afraid to let anything go." She was trying to protect him from men who would kill him, and he insisted upon dickering over the *damen-kest*.

He grunted. "Grow up as I did. Live the life I've led. You learn never to let anything slip through your hands." But there was brief discomfort in his frown. He glanced at his men, at Kentith, then shrugged heavily. "We would do better resting than quarreling. There is a small field-stone cottage not so far south of here. I doubt the fire did it any essential damage. Let's turn in there until the moon rises."

Did he really intend to yield so easily? Or must they fight the entire matter again when the moon rose? Dara stood and swayed with a sudden, pulse-pounding weakness. She extended one hand involuntarily, but there was nothing to steady herself against. She glanced uncertainly at the circle of men. Slowly they took their feet.

"Do you think you can sleep again? So soon?" Rinari asked.

"I think I could sleep until next week," she answered honestly enough. She could not remember another day that had been so long, so terrifying, so grinding.

They straggled up the beach, climbing the steep embankment when the sandy strip narrowed into impassability. Burned vegetation crumbled under their feet as they made their way along the bluff. Occasionally a wisp of smoke rose from the ground. Once Dara disturbed a heap of dead ash and bared a worm's nest of bright embers. In places, the sand had fused to a crisp, fragile crust that crumbled underfoot. In others, they stumbled on lumps of raw glass.

The fieldstone cottage stood undamaged except for the seared moss that shrouded its exterior walls. Inside they found bounty: mildewed rags cast in a corner, untouched by fire. No one cared that they were soiled and stale-smelling. The men fell quickly to making a bed of them.

The men were stumbling-tired, all of them, even Rinari. Even so he stood in the doorway, silhouetted against the gathering night, for a long time after the rest had settled in their communal bed. Dara lay wedged between Kentith and a hard-breathing seaman and listened to the quieting cries of the flocks that had followed them. When finally Rinari joined the others, she slept.

She was aware several times of bodies shifting, of muttered words. Both the seaman and Kentith eventually moved away from her, and after a while she realized dimly that she slept alone. But there was no sign of moonlight at either window or door, and so she did not try to rouse herself.

She slept, but some portion of her mind remained wakeful, and after a while she began to dream: of men walking in a tight, wary clutch along a moonlit path; of starlight sparkling on crusted sand; of the imperfect stillness of settlement streets; of a shadowy group gathering near a blackened stone wall. Of dangers.

She started awake, her heart racing, and stared around

the dark room. No, there was no sign of the moon at window or door. Nor was there any sign of the stars, but some waking instinct told her they had surely risen.

Stumbling, she groped to the window. The darkness there was nothing more than a handful of loosely secured rags. The darkness at the doorway was of the same substance. Dara ripped it down and stared out at a startled seaman.

He half rose, the dark beard standing out against his pale flesh. He had covered his burned back and arms, wrapping himself loosely in soiled rags, but his heavy features were stamped with pain and cold.

Dara returned his stare, feeling the cold rise of fear. The moon stood high. Rinari had yielded to her and then he had slipped away with Kentith and his men, hanging makeshift curtains to ensure that moonlight would not wake her. Now half the night was gone.

Ti-ri-ki materialized from the roof of the cottage. He took his place on her shoulder, his eyes giddy yellow by moonlight.

The seaman licked his lips and stood, looking up as clouds of quirri suddenly stirred in the air, smaller birds rising among them. "The master set me to guard you," he said, his voice gruff and uncertain at once. "He wants you here safe while he goes to town for the firemaster."

"Was that what he told you?" That he wanted her safe while he went to claim the prize he did not wish to share? Was that why the low-toned conversation had stopped so suddenly when she woke earlier? Because Rinari and his men had been planning a foray that was not to include her?

And Kentith had joined them in their plans, saying nothing to her, betraying nothing. Ti-ri-ki cried angrily.

The seaman drew back, wincing as fabric tightened on burned flesh. "He said the firemaster must never take you on the wing. He won't permit that."

"And what is to prevent the men of Port Calibe from taking him? Everyone knows by now that there is a reward for him." And more compelling, whoever presented Nar-

kith with Rinari's body would surely win a much greater
prize in favor and influence.

The seaman glanced uneasily at the ground. "He took
the priest and three strong men. And there will be other
men at the compound, good men. They'll stand with
him."

Good men—as good as the wagon driver who had sold
Kentith to the priests? Dara shook her head angrily. If this
was the world Rinari lived in, why be surprised that he
was as he was? She stared up at the agitated flocks.

Sense told her to remain here, to let the seaman stand
vigil over her still body while she flew with Ti-ri-ki and
the quirri to the firemaster's hut. But her feet told her to
run after Rinari and Kentith, gathering small-flocks and
seabirds as she went.

Her feet spoke the most urgently. "When did they
leave?"

"They are in town by now. It isn't so far if you keep a
brisk pace. And it isn't so far beyond town to the place
where the firemaster hides himself, not from what you told
the master. They'll deal with him soon enough now." He
glanced up at the moon as if to reassure himself, then
looked quickly down again, his face draining.

Half a dozen revenants flew against the moon, their
beaks long and hooked, their heads crested. Their wingspan was many times that of a quirri. They were leather-
winged, entirely without plumage, their eyes small and
cold and white.

Dara stared up and felt the cold, hard chill of a fear she
did not understand.

She could stand here no longer. Ti-ri-ki cried loudly.
"Wait here," Dara instructed the seaman. And she ran.

The seaman cried after her in sharp surprise. Briefly she
heard the heavy fall of boots behind her. Then he abandoned the pursuit.

The flocks swooped overhead as she ran, casting a moving web of shadows on the scorched earth. Ti-ri-ki
launched himself from her shoulder with a hoarse cry and
gathered the quirri into a long, dark ribbon that coiled

after her, marking her passage. Her breath rasping, her heart pounding, Dara forgot after a while whether it was the birds who cried or whether it was she.

Sometimes when she glanced up, she saw those larger shapes, leathery wings spread, blotting the stars. They followed her effortlessly, never flexing their wings. Instead they glided on some secret air current. Occasionally Dara caught the cold, white glint of an eye or saw the ragged detail of a hooked beak.

Other times she glanced up and they were not there.

The seaman had been right. It was not so far to Port Calibe if the pace was brisk. Stumbling over rocks and lumps of fused glass, falling simply because she did not watch where she put her feet, Dara discovered a footpath that widened into a rutted, uneven track—which in turn became the pierside thoroughfare. Emerging at the edge of the warehouse district, she stood fighting for breath among charred shadows, the smell of smoke and ash choking-thick in her throat.

Catching her breath, she glanced down the unlit street. She saw no one. But she must have cover if she was to fly ahead on Ti-ri-ki's wings to find Rinari and Kentith. Retreating, she found a clump of trees growing on a piece of wasteland. She slipped into the shadow of the trees, calling her flocks after her. She bowed her head as they settled into the trees, quieting herself. Then she summoned Ti-ri-ki from among the others and took his wings.

They glided silently through the settlement, leaving the flocks to guard her body. The waterfront streets were strangely quiet. The bars and the brawlhouses were brightly lit; there were patrons within. But they did not spill noisily into the streets, and there was no merriment in their mood. Dara had only to glide past light-splashed windows to see that. Inside men and women gathered in tight, nervous groups, speaking in low voices, consuming their drinks and their dusts with hard purpose. Their wary peaked faces told her they were not finding the reassurance they sought.

Then she was flying through the darker streets beyond

the waterfront. Armed men lingered beneath shadowy trees, at the corners of darkened buildings, behind steps and walls. They were in every street, their eyes glinting from the imperfect darkness, their weapons drawn.

Dara's heart clutched, and when she glanced up, six dark forms shaped from the night, condensing from the very air. The revenants were larger than before. The gleam of their eyes was whiter, colder. Below she heard quick movement and choked exclamations of alarm. Chilled, Dara flew in the shadow of leathery wings.

The outer wall of Rinari's compound was blackened, as in her dream, but there was no shadowy group gathered nearby. There was no sign of Kentith, Rinari or any of Rinari's men anywhere in the grounds. The fire had burned itself out, except for occasional wisps and curls of smoke. The house was gutted. The stables, the work sheds, the men's quarters were in ashes.

Purified. Dara was surprised at her own bitterness.

Had Rinari and Kentith passed safely through the settlement then? She glided the length of the compound and saw that three men watched the gate from the shadows at the edge of the street.

The leather-winged hunters had vanished again. Dara settled for a moment on the soot-stained wall. If Kentith and Rinari had managed to pass through the settlement unnoticed, they had one advantage over the men who hunted them. They knew where they were bound.

Dara permitted Ti-ri-ki to clean his feathers and nibble at his clawed feet. When he had fluffed his feathers and stretched himself elaborately, they flew again.

She searched the town. She searched the trail that led northward from the port prison. She searched beyond, wondering if Rinari had passed the cottage in the dark without seeing it. There was no sign of Kentith, Rinari or Rinari's men.

Nor, she discovered with an unwelcome shock, was there any sign of the firemaster. Flying back toward Port Calibe, she settled on the sill of the cottage where he made his home and found it deserted. His satchel stood untouched. His blankets were as they had been that afternoon. He had not returned.

He was not to be found in the place to which she had directed Rinari.

Nor was Rinari.

CHAPTER TWENTY

Dara sat for a long time on the cottage sill. The night was not quiet. Overhanging branches groaned in the stiff breeze. The water spoke to the shore in an urging, intimate voice.

Narkith had guessed that she knew his hiding place, and so he had taken another. That much seemed clear. But where were Kentith and Rinari? Had they discovered the cottage standing empty and gone searching elsewhere? Or had they been caught as they passed through the settlement?

All those shadowy watchers—did they wait for prey that already had been taken?

Through overhanging branches, Dara saw the revenants gliding against the moon again and felt fear bite deep into her bones. Or had the fear come first, summoning the leather-winged hunters? A whispering voice seemed to speak at the edges of her consciousness. She listened for a moment but could not understand what it said. Perhaps it was only the wind.

One thing was clear. She must search out the firemaster again, and she must deal with him.

But if she did not discover Narkith's new hiding place before daybreak, if he caught her on the wing, with the sun in the sky—

Leathery wings glided nearer. She saw the cold fire of white eyes and knew she could not go and leave her body sitting vacant under the trees for any stranger to find—or any person who cared for her. Abandoning Ti-ri-ki with a bleak cry, she hovered briefly in some intervening darkness. Then she was sitting beneath the trees, near the pier-side road again.

She listened for a moment, then stood. The trees stirred restlessly with her flocks.

Then, strangely, the flocks fell still again. A dark shape glided beneath the trees. Dara extended her arm, surprised that Ti-ri-ki had reached her so quickly. She had left him far on the other side of Port Calibe only moments before.

But it was not Ti-ri-ki who settled to her wrist and blinked vivid yellow eyes at her. It was Ri-chi-ki, his chest rising and falling as if he had flown far and hard. He cocked his head, his eyes holding Dara's, and Dara had the sense again of a whispering voice. She licked her lips. "It is you, Te-kia?"

Ri-chi-ki stared at her with steady eyes, then ducked his head and spread his wings, making a low clucking in his throat. Frowning, Dara reached out for his senses.

She reeled with confusion. She sat upon her own wrist, staring into her own slack face, pale in the darkness beneath the trees. *Te-kia?*

Small-song, you have called up the revenants. I cannot leave you to remember for yourself the prohibitions on their use.

Te-kia, where are you? She had the vague sense of a dark shape standing upon a moonlit balcony, of Wahonin itself lying somewhere below and beyond, halls darkened with night.

I am in the tower at Wahonin. I came to speak with your father. Two of Rinari's men escorted him home, and he was about to leave again. He was about to return to Port Calibe.

No. Don't let him come back here. He can do nothing here. Nothing except increase her vulnerability.

I will not. Nor can I come myself, except on wings. Are you listening carefully for the instruction I gave you in the smoke?

I— She hesitated, confused. *I thought I heard someone speak.*

Did you hear the words? Did you understand what was said?

No.

He did not respond for moments. *Small-song, we should have taken smoke again before you left my hall. You came to me knowing nothing at all of our abilities and our ways. We had not enough time together. But for now . . . You are seeking your friends, I think, and I have seen them. They are aware that it is not safe to go afoot through the settlement, and so they have gone by water to the place where you directed them. I brushed near enough to learn that much. They will touch shore there soon.*

By water . . . She had not thought to search the harbor. Yet what better way to evade the men who watched the streets of the settlement? *I must meet them,* she said, preparing to withdraw.

He called her quickly back. *No. You are not ready. How do you intend to reach them?*

I'll go— Through those same streets, her birds screaming after her, alerting everyone to the direction she took? *Can you tell me how to make the flocks be still?*

Make yourself still. Make yourself still at the very center.

Make herself still when she was going to meet the firemaster? *Te-kia, I can't. I've tried.* All she had achieved was a brief lessening of the noisy agitation.

Again his response was moments in coming. *Small-song, Ri-chi-ki cannot contain us both for much longer. I will still the flocks for you while you slip through the settlement. It is the most I can do for you from here. As for the rest, you have summoned the revenants into the material plane. You have given them flesh, and so they are yours to use, as you use the quirri. But you must employ them far more carefully because their abilities are far different and much stranger. You must not immerse yourself too deeply in them. Nor must you fly too long upon their wings. There is danger there. And you must never permit them to taste blood.*

But I don't know how to use them!

Carefully. Dispassionately. Without anger. His voice had grown fainter.

What will happen if they draw blood? How could she keep them from it when she could not keep the quirri and the small-flocks from it?

Then they will not return to their proper plane. With the taste of blood, they become fully material. And in that state, there is no one who can command them and no one who can control them. Certainly you cannot. Nor can I, nor can any of my people now living.

Dara shuddered. *Then how can I send them back?*

If you cannot still the flocks while you make your way through the settlement, certainly you cannot send back the revenants. You haven't yet mastered the disciplines.

Can't you do it for me?

No. They have come to your call. You are the only one they will respond to. You must listen as well as you can for my voice from the smoke. If you can open yourself to my words . . .

But his voice had become little more than the wind. *Tekia, when the firemaster is dead, I'll come back to your hall and learn,* she promised, as if that would help her now.

Listen, small-song, and take care.

And then she no longer looked into her own still face. She looked into Ri-chi-ki's half-lidded eyes instead. He sat puffed and ruffled on her wrist, his head tucked close to his body. He blinked at her vacantly for a moment, then cautiously extended his neck and shook his feathers. He abandoned her with a low, hoarse cry.

Alone again, Dara glanced around. Her flocks sat in the trees. She could see their watching eyes, but they made not a sound.

Only the wind spoke. Carefully she stepped from beneath the trees. Still the birds did not cry. Choosing a dun, she sent it fluttering down the waterfront thoroughfare, then through the streets of the settlement.

There were not so many silent watchers as there had

been just a short time before. Instead men patrolled the streets now in small groups, sober and watchful. Dara had never seen so many sober men in Port Calibe as she saw as she chose her careful route.

Still she slipped through the settlement easily, her flocks dispersing themselves around her so loosely, so silently that no one noticed their passage. She made her way by quiet streets. She walked in shadow. Soon she stood at the far side of the settlement, the port prison behind her.

Ti-ri-ki rejoined her as she made her way down the narrowing path. Pausing, she took his wings and glided back to the cottage. Dark forms moved beneath the trees there now, speaking disjointedly among themselves. Dipping near, she recognized Rinari's voice, recognized the muted brightness of Kentith's hair when moonlight touched it. Relieved, Dara skimmed back toward her waiting body and slipped from Ti-ri-ki's wings.

She caught up with the men as they retreated along the shore north of the deserted cottage, Kentith and Rinari in the lead. They turned at her cry, but there was no welcome in their rigid stance as they waited for her to join them.

Shadow-grey eyes and black met, then frowned at her. Dara was so relieved to see them safe and together that she only laughed at Rinari's forbidding expression. "Thank you for the extra sleep!"

"My man?" Rinari demanded stiffly.

"There are men watching the streets, but I saw no one searching so far from the settlement," she assured him.

"It takes special fools to leave the company of men tonight," Rinari said bleakly. "Now that you've come, I suppose you've seen that the cottage is empty."

"Yes. Nothing has been disturbed since I saw Narkith this afternoon. He's taken a new hiding place. You said something to Kentith about caverns." She had caught only a few words of their disjointed conversation as they moved beneath the trees.

Again Rinari's eyes met Kentith's. Rinari measured out his answer deliberately. "There are no more than a dozen fisher's huts north of here, and they're in falling condition, all of them. But there are caverns all along this coastline, eaten out by the sea itself when it stood higher. I've used some of them for storage when I had cargo that I couldn't take directly to my warehouses.''

"Loot," Dara said.

"Exactly," he rejoined with a flash of annoyance. "There are a dozen large, dry caverns within an hour's walking distance of here. And the hillsides are honeycombed with smaller caverns. If he's gone to ground in one of those, we could search a dozen nights and miss him. Did you see any sign of him in Port Calibe?''

"No," Dara said thoughtfully, "although I suppose there are places where he could hide himself." Or places where a blind man could openly rent a room for the night, although it seemed unlikely that Narkith had done so.

"There are dozens of places there, so we must divide forces," Rinari said with crisp authority. "We have just a few hours until dawn. Kentith and I will take the men and search the most accessible of the caverns. You must station yourself in a sheltered spot and send one of your smaller birds back to Port Calibe. If the firemaster is there—''

"No." Dara shook her head emphatically, understanding him too well. He no more thought the firemaster was to be found in Port Calibe than she did. This was just another way of leaving her behind. "I'll go with you. I can search the caverns more quickly with my birds than you can on foot.''

Rinari's expression clouded. "And if we don't find him before sunrise?''

Dara glanced at Kentith and found him carefully neutral. "At least we will be together, won't we?''

"Do you prefer being together to being alive?" Rinari demanded sharply.

Dara turned on him, her voice brittle. "Do you prefer being dead to sharing your prize?''

Rinari's face darkened. "I told you—this is no longer a matter of a prize. This is a matter of a man who must not see the sun rise again. But perhaps he will. Perhaps we will not discover where he's hidden himself until he faces us with the sun in his eyes. And if I must worry about you, if I must worry about his catching your hunter on the wing and leaving you an empty shell—''

"If that happens, then you may withdraw the *damenkest*. My family will care for me.''

Rinari's eyes flashed with a quick, fierce anger. "Is that how little you think of me? My home is in ashes. My warehouses are destroyed. I've lost fully half my crew. I'm standing here on this forsaken shore in the middle of the night in wet boots, and you think I have nothing on my mind beyond a chestful of satins.''

"You were still thinking of the satins a few hours ago.''

"That was then. That was—'' He stepped forward, one fist raised in angry denial. "Let me tell you, I am just a little more a man than you seem to think. I am—''

Kentith placed a restraining hand on his arm. "She knows that. And she has as much right to die by Narkith's hand as we do, if it comes to that.'' He turned to Dara. "We were mistaken to leave you behind. Rinari was concerned because he holds himself responsible for your sister's death. I was concerned because—because I am concerned. So we elected to protect you even though we guessed, both of us, that you didn't want to be protected. You would have done as much for us, given the opportunity.''

Dara's eyes darted to Rinari. Could that be true? Were his motives—for once—so straightforward? She turned back to Kentith. "I would have,'' she said. "For you. For either of you.'' Strangely it was true. She had been as frightened for Rinari as for Kentith when she reached the cottage and found them missing.

Rinari shook his head impatiently. "You don't have to say more than you mean.''

"I seldom do.''

They stood frowning at each other, then glanced away at the same moment. Shrugging, Rinari paced restlessly along the tide line. "The caverns begin just north of here,'' he said finally. "There are some that can be reached best from the water, by boat. I doubt he's chosen any of those.

There are others set into the hillsides, well back from the shore, that require some climbing. I don't know if he's nimble enough to hide himself there.''

"I'll search the most accessible places first,'' Dara said. "If there is a place where I can sit while Ti-ri-ki flies—''

"We'd best get all of us from sight,'' one of the crew cautioned, with an anxious glance at Rinari.

"It's a night for care,'' Rinari agreed. He wheeled toward the small fisher's vessel they had dragged onto the shore. "Here,'' he said, offering Dara his hand. "There are places along the shore here that no one knows but us. We'll hide ourselves while you search.''

They were upon the water within minutes, Rinari and his men hauling at the oars. The vessel glided upon sheets of silver, but the moon's oblique position only touched Dara with fear. The night was passing so quickly. It was far more than half gone now.

She released Ti-ri-ki, gliding away upon his wings. Her flocks followed, but so quietly that the only sound was the beat of their wings. Even the seabirds were still, arching their wings in silent flight. And in the west, dark against the moon again—

The revenants soared nearer, casting their shadow across Dara's path as she swept northward along the coastline. She shivered, aware of the cold white of their eyes. If she had time to stop, if she had time to listen for the faint voice that seemed to whisper at the very perimeter of her mind again—

There was no time. Below, steep rock faces rose from the water, and even in the dark, she could see that they were riddled with chambers and cavities.

Narkith would not be there. Nor would he be in those lower caverns that the tide swept. But when she left the tidal zone, skimming along the series of bluffs and rises that fell back from the shore, there were other caverns, dozens of them. Some stood with black mouths open to the night. Others were half screened by coarse vegetation.

She soared toward the nearest, the most accessible, gliding into its wide, dark mouth—and was immediately lost in unrelieved darkness as the shaft narrowed and tunneled obliquely into the hillside. Ti-ri-ki's wing tips brushed unseen walls. Blinded, he screamed with fear and confusion. He wheeled in the dark and, before Dara could calm him, before she should orient herself, slammed head-first against an unseen wall.

Stunned, Dara raised her head and had a moment's glimpse of Kentith and Rinari staring at her in quick alarm.

Reaching out, she found Ti-ri-ki again as he struggled to his feet. He was lost in the stale, muffling darkness, and Dara felt his anger as keenly as if he spoke it. He was a hunter of the open spaces, of the forest and the forest floor. When he flew, no one snatched away the stars and raised invisible walls, black upon black, to stun him.

Carefully, Dara walked him from the cavern and left him sitting in bruised, angry silence as she chose a smaller bird.

Again, thick, muffling darkness defeated her. The tiny bird darted into the unfolding maze of the cavern and panicked. Dara fought briefly to master its fright, but the terrified bird carried her deeper into enveloping darkness, its fear a mindless scream. Finally she saw that it would surely dash itself against the walls—and not so harmlessly as Ti-ri-ki had done. Trembling, Dara broke free.

She shuddered back into her own body, and the revenants dipped near. They were larger than they had been just a few minutes before. The shadows of their wings were wide, sweeping.

Rinari caught her shoulder. "What is it?"

The voice had grown louder, the words more distinct. If only she knew how to listen. She strained, trying to understand, then shook her head. She glanced around. The boat had gone to shelter in a small inlet. They were safely hidden on three sides by rocky pillars. "It won't work," she said, her voice trembling. "Ti-ri-ki's eyes aren't made for that kind of darkness. I don't think any of the breeds can carry me into the caverns." She looked up in despair at the hundreds of birds that circled overhead so silently—so uselessly.

"Then we'll have to search the caverns ourselves," Rinari said grimly. "Although how we're to do it before dawn . . . If we could afford to wait another day—"

"We can't," Kentith said. "His tides are rising. One hint that we're still alive—"

"He'll get that as soon as my good friends on the Council think to send search crews for our bodies." He turned to his men. "Bigleri, Parr—"

Two of them bowed immediately to the oars, but the third glanced up anxiously, licking his lips. "Master, there's small birds that live in some of these caverns. You remember how they sweep out at us sometimes when we come here to check our stores."

Rinari stared at the man, then gazed keenly toward the mingled flocks. "They're not properly birds," he said slowly, turning back to Dara. "More like rats on the wing. We don't have them on the old shore. But there are mounds of droppings at the very back of these caves, so you know they have eyes for the dark. They feed in the woodland at night."

Dara met his narrowed gaze uncertainly. The whispering voice spoke more insistently now. She could almost understand what it said. It spoke—

"If you could find them, if you could use them—"

It spoke of the revenants. "I—I don't know," she said, pressing shaking fingers to her temples. "I think—"

She had called them up. Te-kia had told her that. Wherever they came from, whatever they were, they had answered the summons of her fear, and so they were hers to use when everything else had failed.

As it had failed now. Because dawn drew near, and the firemaster waited in some hidden place with rested body and restored powers. He waited to destroy them.

She shook her head again, but the voice persisted, louder now, the words not just distinct but insistent—the words not just of the smoke but of her own instinct, of her own judgment. The revenants were hers. They were the final guardian of her vulnerable flesh, of the vulnerable flesh of those for whom she cared. Their powers were strange and great. If she used them carelessly, she could bring great harm. But if she used them carefully, deliberately, as Tekia had taught her in the smoke—

But she remembered so little of that. Could she recall his words when she needed to, if she took those beckoning wings?

What other choice did she have? They must find Narkith, and they could not do it afoot.

Dara bowed her head. Then she looked up again and raised her arms to the revenants—and the world slowed and grew distant.

CHAPTER TWENTY-ONE

Dara floated on wings so old the flesh had grown tough and dry. She was armed with a beak that had first tasted blood long before any time she could imagine. Talons extended from her feet, talons that had closed on the living flesh of animals now long extinct. Her eyes were not made of living tissue but of light.

She knew these things without knowing how she knew them.

With a cool, drifting sense of detachment, she glided away from the small wooden vessel where she had left her body. It seemed to her, at first, that the shadow that flickered across the water below held as much life as the revenant that bore her. Still, there was a surviving kernel of life somewhere in the desiccated tissue. She felt it there, curled tight, waiting. It was dormant now, but if she roused it, it would burn with all the lust and anger of the ages.

And those were great. Those were consuming. Again, she knew without knowing how she knew.

She hung over the water, testing her unfamiliar new senses—seeing not the water's tossing surface but the thrash and shimmer of all the living organisms that inhabited it. Then she raised her head and, without any movement of her wings, glided toward the shore.

Rocks, sand, soil— Shadows teemed across the curiously porous land surfaces below. Gazing down, Dara recognized them as the shades of creatures that had walked and crawled and slithered upon this shore centuries before. Men had passed here and creatures that had been almost men—and others that had hardly been men at all. And long before any of those, in a time when this sea had been warm, when steaming jungles had grown upon the shore that was now rocky and cold—

No, she must not lose herself in the far past, although tonight it seemed almost as immediate, almost as real as the present. The jungles were gone. So were all the surging life-forms that had inhabited them. Tonight she searched for another kind of creature altogether.

Narkith had not hidden himself in the caverns. On the wings of the revenant, she glided through those dark cavities as easily as if it were daylight and looked with cold white eyes for him. She drifted through mazing chambers. She glided on wings that seemed to narrow with the narrowing of passages. She startled small animals and little screeching things that withdrew directly into the rock. Narkith was nowhere, although in places she found his scent. It held the flavor of vinegar and ashes.

Kentith and Rinari had come ashore. They followed the path of her search. Sometimes when she looked down, she saw their faces peering up at her, white and tense. Ti-ri-ki flew with them, leaving his flocks to guard her body.

She searched the larger caverns, the accessible caverns, and then she recognized that it was pointless to search longer among the bluffs and the hillsides. And so she carried her search northward along the shore, leaving Kentith and Rinari behind.

She explored her host as she flew. She reached deeper into its senses and its latent capabilities, and they were awesome. And in that dormant seed of life, there was such predator fury. It was bound up tightly now, but if she fed it, if she roused it—

Was the wind blowing? Had it taken a voice again? She disregarded it.

Narkith was not among the aeons of creatures she saw upon the northern stretches of the shore, and so she turned inland again, searching among clusters of trees and clumps of vegetation. As she grew accustomed to her host, her senses were taking an ever sharper edge. Her eyes were not hindered at all now by the retreating darkness. They penetrated shadows easily. Sometimes they penetrated the living tissue of trees and vegetation as well. Occasionally she looked down and peered directly into the soil. She saw beetles digging and rodents burrowing and old bones resting and rotting.

Kentith and Rinari had crossed her path again. They stumbled after her, their scurry frantic and somehow humorous. They looked up and shouted. At her? She gazed down loftily and did not heed.

Nor did she heed the wind, although it called to her in an ever louder voice, begging her to listen.

Twice she saw Narkith in places where he had paused the day before. Once, a pale shadow, he knelt to drink from a stream. Again he stood on a mossy boulder, his burning eyes raised to the sun, his angular limbs trailing away into the dense grey light of first dawn.

Something strange was happening to Kentith and Rinari. As they stumbled after her, they were becoming shadows among shadows. Pale creatures from other times interpenetrated them, while they in turn interpenetrated seemingly solid matter. Small animals darted between their legs and vanished. Lumbering seabirds flapped toward them and melted into their shadows, never to emerge. Kentith walked through trees, Rinari through rocks and boulders.

She was seeing sunrises now. The sun crested the watery horizon, and it was golden, it was crimson, it was cerise, it was shimmering yellow. As it slowly rose it was pale, it was bright, it was half-hidden by fog, it was totally lost in cloud. It rose into a sky that was clear, that was clouded, that surged with white mists and black storm. The water it rose above was smooth, was glassy, was windswept, was furious.

For the first time Dara felt torn. She cried out in confusion, and the revenant uttered a shriek that made the earth shake. Rinari threw himself to the ground, pulling Kentith down beside him. Dara dipped low, and for a moment she saw not two men she cared for but prey, waiting to be snatched. Terrified, she dragged at the revenant's wings and circled away.

What was happening to her? How, even with the revenant's cold white eyes, could she see the past as if it still lingered on the shore below? How could she see creatures long dead? How could she see Narkith in places where he had passed the day before? How could she see the sun rising above a hundred different seas on a hundred different days?

What was real? Were Kentith and Rinari real as they slowly, warily took their feet below? Was the sunrise real? Was the broad, rippling shadow of the revenant's wings real? When had the revenant grown so large?

She turned again, and then she was gliding over the place where a ragged circle of trees had stood until the afternoon before. They stood there again today, faint images. They stood there as seedlings, as saplings, as tall, sturdy young trees bowing to the wind. But the reality of their ashes was upon the ground at their feet. And as she looked upon those scattered grey piles, she saw a stirring that acted upon her like the shock of cold water.

As she watched, a lean grey figure rose from the ashes of the burned trees. Sweeping aside banks of loose material, scattering grey flakes from every limb, Narkith took his feet. His loose shirt, his trousers were stained. His face was crusted and smeared. But his eyes found the first risen rim of the sun and wielded narrow swords of light from its dawning rays.

The revenant's shadow shriveled, the creature swiftly becoming as small as a grey-dun. Stimulated, the tiny, dormant seed it contained throbbed with sudden, aching intensity.

Dara listened for the wind then. She listened in cold terror, straining to understand. *Do not immerse yourself too deeply in the revenant. Do not fly too long upon its wings. Never permit it to taste blood.* So Te-kia had warned her. But she had already disregarded the first of his commandments, however unintentionally. She had lost herself in the revenant. And now—

She hung in the air, her eyes no more than pinpoints of light, and she saw that Kentith and Rinari had reached the bottom of the incline. The firemaster stood above them wielding his supple blades of light much as if he performed a morning exercise, a limbering. They had only to take a few steps, he had only to glance down, and he would see them. And she—

She was hungry. It was long since she had fed. How many ages had passed? How many species had come and gone? How many sunsets? If she were to dart at the firemaster's glowing eyes, if she were to blind him with her sharp, hooked beak—

Dara shuddered with the hungry intensity of the impulse. Instinctively she gazed down at the revenant's fluttering shadow and imagined it wide again, imagined the leathery wings growing, reaching—

The hunger lessened as the creature took size. Somehow she had known that it would, and she thought about that. Had Te-kia taught her that in the smoke? Perhaps if she listened hard enough for the other things he had taught her—

No, if she had learned one thing about the disciplines of the Ilijhari, it was that she must not strain for the sound of his voice. Instead she must open herself to it.

If there was time. If she hadn't immersed herself too deeply in the revenant. If she could let its hunger go crying.

The creature caught scent of her betrayal and screamed. Narkith glanced up. "Witch!" His ash-crusted features twisted. Swiftly he reached out with twin swords of light.

Seeing, Rinari shouted in angry alarm and charged at the slope, his own blade in hand. Kentith struggled after him.

Dara learned two things then. The revenant felt pain. Perhaps the firemaster's blades only called up the memory of pain it had experienced when its body tissues still lived. But remembered or real, the pain was fierce as the burning blades touched the tough flesh.

The second thing: the firemaster's blades could not harm

a creature that was already dead, a creature of desiccated tissues, memory and cold white light. He stabbed at its wings, he burned at the toughened flesh of its body, he slashed at the vacancy of its eyes, and his light passed through harmlessly. Only if he struck directly at the deep place where the tiny kernel of its life lay hidden—

But Kentith and Rinari did not know that. They saw the revenant impaled on blades of light. They heard its enraged screams, and they scrambled up the sloping hillside, shouting.

Startled, Narkith briefly drew back his swords. His lips retracted as he recognized the two men. Forgetting the revenant, he reached out again, almost joyously, slashing toward them.

Dara hung stunned in the air, watching the fiery light lance at Kentith, at Rinari. Narkith struck at their feet, at their legs. He grazed fabric and leather, making them smoke—laughing when the men slipped and stumbled.

He was playing with them, playing with them like a cat with prey. Playing before he killed, and Dara's instinct as Kentith and Rinari struggled for their footing on the slope was to dive, to drive her hooked beak deep into the flesh of Narkith's throat, to tear at his limbs.

But that was anger and pain and fear speaking. And she must act with care and dispassion instead.

She hung for a moment longer, drawing carefully back from the revenant's anger, drawing back from her own anger as a lancing sword of light caught Rinari's sword arm, setting his shirt sleeve afire. He faltered, slapping at the flames with his bare hand, his feet slipping.

She waited until the moment when she felt no anger at all. And then, as Narkith lashed out again, she dropped from the air. Talons carefully curled, beak thrust against her chest, she slammed against the firemaster's back, knocking him to his knees. He shouted, throwing out his arms, and crumpled to the ashes.

Te-kia's voice spoke clearly from the smoke then, naming for her the powers she held. He spoke not in words but in knowledge that flowed into her awareness, knowledge that had the power of memory and instinct.

Distancing herself from the firemaster's struggles, from the vinegar scent of his fear, from the deeper, more provocative scent of the blood pounding just beneath the surface of his skin, Dara took weight and size. Flexing her leathery wings in a way she had not guessed she could, she embraced the firemaster. Covering his eyes, holding him close, she smothered his flame as she might smother the flame in a firepot by setting the lid upon it.

Narkith struggled against the tough leather of her wings. He shouted angrily, shouted things she could not understand. He managed to struggle to his feet and stagger a short distance. But she clung, her wings wrapped around him like darkness. He fell back to the ground, sobbing.

"Witch-bird, you will burn! I will make ash of you!" The words were muffled, half-coherent.

But he could not burn her, she realized, so long as she kept the sun from his eyes. He could not burn anything. Some of her tension easing, she drew her wings more snugly around him and glanced up. The sky was empty. Yet when she called to her ancient flock, her five flying mates materialized and swept down, taking a size commensurate with her own. Bobbing their crested heads, flapping their leathery wings, they grouped themselves behind her.

Their company reassured her. Yet she sensed their impatience to share her prey. They were as hungry as she.

If only Narkith's blood did not smell so strong, so hot. Uneasily, Dara curled her talons more tightly against themselves so they could not accidentally pierce his flesh— and remembered Te-kia's injunction against wearing the revenant's wings for too long.

How long would it take the firemaster to go mad, blinded as he was? How long would it take for him to lose his fire?

The question was like a second dash of cold water. He was half-mad now in his panic and his fury, but it might require days of darkness to completely quench his power.

She did not have days.

And she did not know what to do next. It was as simple as that. Narkith was helpless in her grasp, yet she dared not touch him with beak or claws. She could make herself large enough to fly with him to the water, to drown him there, but if he struggled against her clutching talons, tearing his flesh—

She gazed in mute appeal at Kentith, at Rinari. They glanced tensely at each other, and Rinari stepped forward, his blade poised. Briefly Dara saw the total concentration of the predator in his dark eyes. Sensing some change, Narkith ceased to struggle. He hung limp in her embrace.

All she had to do, she saw with relief, was release him for the barest instant, and Rinari would slip the blade between his ribs.

And the blood would spill out, salty and strong. The flock would feed. They were already stirring with anticipation, arching their necks, gathering their wings close to their sides.

Dara screamed—screamed with such raw, anguished force that Rinari jumped back as if flung. He landed in a half-crouch, his eyes blazing so angrily that for a moment Dara was afraid he would lunge forward again without thinking. Quickly, the firemaster still clutched in her leathery wings, she made herself large. She took all the size she could find and loomed over the two men, crying her warning.

Rinari lowered his blade and said to Kentith in baffled anger, "If she intends to behave like one of the simple folk now, afraid to take blood—"

Kentith shook his head, his expression troubled, distracted. "No. This is no way to deal with a firemaster. There is an alternative due him, no matter how little you respect his calling." He stepped forward. "Narkith, do you hear my voice?"

The firemaster stiffened in Dara's embrace. For a moment she expected some venomous response. Instead he sighed and said, "I hear you, and if I had my fire, I would burn you. You have stolen the flame from your temple."

"And I intend to bury it in the inland, where it will never harm anyone again. Just as you will never harm anyone again."

"I have only fulfilled the proper duties of my office," Narkith responded. "I have never called down the fire upon any man or woman who did not require cleansing."

"I know that by the laws of the temples that is true. But now you have come to the end of your office. I tell you that now, as Tith rises on the horizon. And I tell you that although it is not required of us, we will permit you the death you have earned."

As Dara stared at Kentith in confusion, the firemaster sighed again and seemed to shrink. She felt the beat of his pulse. She felt the contours of his body and the heat it gave. Yet it seemed he had grown as small as a child in the embrace of her wings. Carefully she released some of her own size and clasped her wings more securely around him. Her flock shifted impatiently.

"We grant you this, that you die by your own flame, but listen closely to me, Narkith," Kentith said. "If you betray us, you will die anyway, either by Rinari's blade or by Dara's talons. You cannot burn us quickly enough, all of us, to escape that. And I promise you that if you do betray us and if it is necessary that we take your life ourselves, we will leave your body where it falls.

"There will be no pyre. No one will sing over your ashes because there will be no ashes. Your body will lie here, just as it falls, and turn to earth. You will be impure—forever impure."

Dara felt Narkith shudder violently, and for a moment she thought he was about to struggle again. Instead he relaxed within her grip, as if he suddenly entrusted himself to her. His voice, when he spoke again, was low and strangely childlike. "If I call Tith to myself, will you sing with me?"

"Yes, I will sing with you."

"Will you lend me your fire?"

Kentith drew a long, harsh breath. He had become very

pale. Perspiration stood on his brow, on his upper lip. "I will lend it, and then it will never burn again."

"And the song of ashes—"

Rinari had stepped forward. He caught Kentith's arm, his face disbelieving. "Man—"

Kentith seemed not to notice. "I will sing the song of ashes for you, and I will remain with you until the wind comes to carry you away. The things you have done are unforgivable in my eyes, but I know you did them because it was required."

"I have always done what was required," Narkith said, and Dara heard the pride in his voice. "Tith is my father. He gifted me lavishly, and so much has been required of me. And I have given it. I have always given it."

"This is what is required now. By me. By Tith. By your own ashes, if they are to be." Kentith met Dara's eyes— the revenant's eyes—and said in a low voice, "Release him."

Dara stiffened. Did he really expect her to do that? Did he really expect Narkith to take his life and not theirs if she let him see the sun?

Rinari was no more assured than Dara was. He caught Kentith's arm again. "Man, why don't you just ask me to run us all through with my blade and let him go? You'll get the same result."

"I will get the result I want if he doesn't want his body to rot."

"Bodies rot all over this world."

"Then tell him that. Tell him that if he calls the fire upon anyone but himself, you will fell him—and leave him where he falls."

"If Dara is fool enough to let him free, I'll put him to the blade and I'll never touch the filth of his body!"

"No, not if Dara lets him free. If she lets him free and he fails in his promise to me. You have promised me, have you not, Narkith, to draw your fire only to yourself?"

The firemaster had grown tense again. His muffled voice wavered, and Dara recognized fear in the choked syllables of his response. "I pledge you no one will burn but me."

Was he really so afraid they would simply leave his body to rot? Dara remembered how eloquently he had spoken the day before of the grace of Tith's cleansing fire. She glanced to Rinari.

He and Kentith stared at each other, Kentith's eyes blazing with challenge and something very like anger. "Do you truly believe what he tells you?" Rinari demanded finally.

"Yes. And I believe he is entitled to die as a priest. He no more chose his priesthood than I chose mine. It chose him, and it cost him all the things mine cost me."

Family. Warmth. Freedom. But Narkith had embraced the power of fire instead of rejecting it, and so it had cost him sanity as well. And humanity.

Still Dara did not feel the same passion for his final rights that Kentith seemed to feel. Nor the same trust in his word.

"Release him," Kentith said.

Rinari hesitated a moment longer, then nodded almost imperceptibly. "Release him and I will hold my blade to his back while he burns," he said with grim conviction. "And if one lick of fire touches me, then he will die by steel instead."

Kentith sighed deeply. "You are entitled."

"I am as entitled as he is."

And Dara could not even tell Rinari, as he circled warily, why there must be no thrust of the blade—and no blood. She waited until he reached her side, his approach a slow, taut dance, in his eyes the concentration she had seen before, the narrow attention a predator gives prey. Then she unfolded her wings and stepped back, setting the firemaster free.

Narkith staggered and glanced around, blinking. Briefly he looked back at the dark flock that crouched behind him and there was bafflement in his golden eyes. He licked his lips. "Here?" he demanded finally, turning back to Kentith.

"Here."

He was afraid. Afraid of the flock of revenants that

watched in dark silence. Afraid of the blade that touched his back now. Afraid of the pale young priest who stood before him, chest bare, Tith's face scowling upon the exposed flesh.

Then he gazed past Kentith at the rising sun, and his eyes widened with fierce joy. "Yes, you are right. My father has come for me," he said in a hoarse, impassioned voice. "And none of you will forget this. None of you will ever forget." For a moment his eyes glittered with spite. Then they began to blaze.

The image on Kentith's chest leaped to life, grimacing with the same ferocious pleasure that twisted Narkith's lips as he commenced his chant. The firemaster's voice was thin, high. Kentith's eyes burned in answer, but Kentith did not arch and buckle to the ground. Instead he threw back his head and joined his voice to Narkith's.

Dara saw the trees again as they chanted. They stood tall and straight, framing the scene. The ground was briefly carpeted with flowers, and for a moment Dara thought she saw a child bending to pick them, the curve of his neck tender, reverent. When the child raised his head, his eyes blazed with sunlight and the flowers withered in his hand.

The sword of light reached through the trees then. It burned through their phantom trunks with surgical care, touching brightly at the firemaster's chest. Briefly his chant became a high, whining cry. Then he stood before them at the center of a column of fire.

Dara cried out in raw fear and Rinari jumped back. But only for a moment. His face grim, he moved forward again, his blade extended. Its tip glowed blue as it pierced the column of fire.

Within the column, the firemaster did a strange, mute dance. He no longer chanted. His voice was gone. But he stood with head thrown back and mouth open. His body jerked and twisted and finally became a black husk that drifted slowly to the ground as if it had no weight at all.

Kentith continued to chant, no longer aware of Dara, of Rinari. He continued to chant in a high, thin voice, the face on his chest twisting with anger and grief, until the charred shell that had been Narkith crumbled to ash.

Kentith's voice fell an octave then and slowly the sword of light drew back. The sun brightened and grew larger. Eventually it rose and hung entirely above the horizon. By then the breeze had come to tug at the ashes that lay at their feet.

Only then did Kentith's voice die entirely, releasing them all from the spell of the chant.

Only then did Rinari drop to his knees, the blade falling from the seared and blistered hand he had thrust too near the flames.

Only then did Dara know that Narkith had been right. They would never forget.

EPILOGUE

It was two hours before dawn when Kentith slipped away from Te-kia's hall. Dara woke as he left the hall and lay with heavy heart, listening to his receding footsteps. She knew he did not want her to run after him, to cry, to do anything to make his going harder. And so she did not. She simply lay with tears staining her cheeks until the sun came through the high narrow windows. Then she sent Ti-ri-ki winging after him. It was the tenth day since Narkith's death.

Accompanying Kentith on Ti-ri-ki's wings, Dara hunted for him and she scouted his path as he made his way through the mountains, finding ways to warn him of obstacles and dangers. Sometimes she rode upon his shoulder or perched on a nearby branch when he stopped to rest. She saw all the things he saw, all the bright, sunlit clearings, all the tree-shadowed passages, all the icy streams. Sometimes at the end of day, when he had pushed himself hard, her legs ached in sympathy with his. Occasionally, hovering near as he slept, she almost felt she shared his dreams. But she could speak with no voice but Ti-ri-ki's, and there were many times when the quirri did not carry her upon his wings at all. She had other duties, other concerns. And so the bond between them grew tenuous.

It almost seemed, as Kentith descended the mountains and began his long journey into the broad, empty lands beyond, that he forgot that his traveling companion was anything more than a quirri. He spoke to the hunter absently as he walked, almost as if he spoke to himself. He spoke of the weather, of the terrain, of the occasional herds of game they saw. Dara could respond with nothing more than a plaintive cry.

Perhaps it was simpler that way. Perhaps the pain of parting was less, spread as it was over a long period of days. But finally one morning Kentith rose and looked back, and the mountains were little more than misty shadows in the distance. Dara looked back too and knew their paths would part that day.

They would part, and they would not meet again. And Dara had no voice to tell him all the last things she wanted to say, the things he had refused to hear when he left Tekia's hall, the things that had threatened her control and his. If he simply walked from her sight with no farewell, with no sign that he was aware of her hovering presence—

But he was aware of her today. She saw that as he rolled his bedding and drew his pack to his back. There was a small taut frown between his brows that had not been there before, and he walked away from the place where he had slept without taking his morning meal, although his pack was full. And when he paused beside a running stream a short time later to wash, he sat back on his heels for a very long time, staring at the fading mountains. Then, sighing, he took his feet and began to walk, Dara gliding ahead of him on Ti-ri-ki's wings.

She flew to the point where she could no longer see with Ti-ri-ki's eyes, and she found no danger there. She found no predators, and she found no sign of human habitation. Instead she found only a bright, sunlit land, broad and gently rolling and beckoning.

Had she been able to walk into that land beside him . . .

But the smoke had shown them both that her path did not lead there.

She flew back to him, crying silently, begging him to speak to her before he walked beyond her vision.

He walked without a word, frowning and distracted, until midmorning. Then, reaching a place where the stream widened briefly into a pool, he paused. The sun touched the surface of the pool brightly, as brightly as it touched Kentith's hair. Fish swam in the water. Dara saw the glint of their silver scales. There was an innocence in the land here, and the sun shared that innocence. Dara guessed that if there were people living here, they gave the sun some name that recognized its light and not its fire.

Kentith stood for a moment gazing back toward the vanishing mountains, then raised one arm, summoning the quirri that glided restlessly over the pool.

Relieved, Dara settled to his arm, pulling in her claws.

"So we part now," he said softly. "I'll never know the rest of your story, and you'll never know the rest of mine. But I'll tell myself tales about you sometimes, and you'll tell yourself tales about me. For you, I'll imagine—" His voice broke and he turned his head sharply away, the sun glittering on tears. "I'll imagine adventure and love and someday a daughter with grey eyes," he continued finally. "And perhaps one day your great-grandchild will come to explore the inland, and he will hear stories of a fugitive priest who grew very wise and full of years and never regretted being alone because he didn't feel alone at all, not so long as he could hear the birds sing."

Dara uttered a low cry, and Kentith laughed sharply. "He will probably hear, too, that sometimes the priest became maudlin," he said, mocking himself. He hesitated for a moment, frowning, then lifted his arm. "Thank you for coming into my life. Now leave me—and be well."

Leave him? Dara only crouched lower on his arm, stricken by the unfairness of the moment. He had spoken. Why couldn't she? Why couldn't she say the things she wanted to say? The things she had bitten back the first time they had parted?

That she would always carry his light in her heart. That no one else would ever know as many of her secrets as he did. That, yes, she would tell herself tales. She would tell herself many tales.

"Leave me," he pleaded.

And she had no voice for the things she wanted to say, so she did. She left him before Ti-ri-ki could utter the anguished cry she felt, before Kentith's trembling smile could turn to something far more painful. She spread her wings and flew, and she did not look back until he reached the point where her sight faded. Then she floated on the bright air and watched as he vanished into the broad, sun-lit land.

She floated there for an hour, for two, and nothing stirred but the wind. Finally, returning to her own body, she hid herself in the trees and cried until dusk. The small birds of the forest cried with her, and the quirri circled restlessly. Ti-ri-ki winged his way back to her slowly, as if he came bearing news of defeat.

Rinari did not reach Te-kia's hall until three days later, and Dara was glad for that. She could not have spoken to him sooner.

Still she was glad to see him when he came. She glimpsed him as he climbed the mountainside, and something in his grim determination touched her. He had not asked her if he could come to her here, nor had he asked Te-kia, and he was afraid. She saw that clearly in his pallor, in his nervous, darting glance as he climbed. Still he made the journey and came striding stark and tall across Te-kia's plaza late on the third afternoon after Dara had parted from Kentith.

Dara stepped from the hall to meet him and saw his shoulders relax slightly. He was dressed as always, in dark trousers and spotless white shirt. He had changed from his soiled shirt not an hour before, when he washed in the stream. She had seen him do it. His blade hung at his waist. On one hand he wore a black leather glove.

He halted, studying her. Then he glanced up at the quirri that glided lazily among the trees, gathering for the evening hunt. "The birds permitted me to come this far, so I suppose I am welcome."

"You are," she said. She was surprised at the small clutch she felt at her heart as he faced her across the paving stones.

"And you are well?" he demanded formally.

"I'm very well." Te-kia had taught her much since she

had returned to Hendarra. Under his tutelage, she had begun to understand her gifts and to grow into them. It no longer disturbed her that she could call herself neither an Ilijhari nor one of the simple folk. She was simply herself, with a path of her own, and that was enough.

"I have thought of you," Rinari said.

"I have thought of you," she responded, and it was true. He had come walking through her dreams more and more often recently, even as she grieved for Kentith. "Your hand— Have you much use of it?"

Rinari raised the black glove and closed the fingers. The exercise was slow and obviously painful. "The scar tissue binds despite the ointment Te-kia sent me to use. I doubt I'll ever have full use of it again. But it has its value. You are now addressing Lord Blackhand of the Autonomous Coastal District of Calibe."

Dara's brows rose. "So you've taken a title after all." She thought he had disavowed all that when he withdrew the *damen-kest*.

"No, it has been conferred upon me. By the people in the street. My colleagues on the District Council use it, too, but not to my face. They are afraid to be quite so loose with me just yet."

"And your home?"

"My warehouse facilities have been entirely restored and my house rebuilt. Refurnished too, in a much grander style than I would have chosen for myself." His smile was quick, white, wolfish.

"Your colleagues on the Council are grateful," she said dryly.

"Exceedingly," he said with satisfaction. "Especially those who offered a reward for me. They still have their heads and the greater part of their fortunes. While I have the chairmanship of the Council and the ownership of certain pieces of land and certain shares of business that I intended to acquire anyway over the next few years. It is surprising how quickly the balance of power can shift in a small community like Port Calibe. And how profitably."

"So your plans haven't changed at all."

"Of course not. My colleagues are like weather vanes. They turn in the wind. I do not, and I don't intend to trust the development of this coastline to the whim of men who do. We've seen the first priest from the old shore—but not the last."

Dara shivered. No, surely they had not seen the last. And he was right about his colleagues as well. It surprised her, in fact, when she thought about it, how often he was right. Somehow it didn't seem fitting that a person who was so cocksure should also be right. "You've walked a long distance today. Can I prepare you a meal?"

Rinari hesitated, glancing past her at the hall. "When we have settled this, yes, I would like a meal."

"Settled—this?"

His eyes narrowed. "Do you think I've blistered my feet and worn out my boots just to take dinner with you? I've withdrawn the *damen-kest*. I've released you entirely from any obligation to me. But that doesn't mean I've disavowed interest."

Dara drew a long breath. "No, I didn't think it did." And apparently he didn't intend to approach the matter obliquely or with any particular ceremony.

Rinari's brows drew together. He studied her closely, then shrugged, not entirely satisfied with her initial response. "So it has become a voluntary matter, one I think we should speak of. I have certain things to offer you. You have certain things to offer me. Together we will be richer and stronger than either of us could ever be separately. Perhaps you think it isn't important to be rich and strong, but I don't share your opinion."

Dara shook her head. "I have no objection so long as you use your money and your strength well."

"Then we will surely disagree about what constitutes using it well. And about any number of other things. Because I have changed no more than you have with all this. I am the same person I always was, just as you are."

Dara shook her head. "No, we have both changed a great deal." She had learned the disciplines of the Ilijhari. She had found confidence and strength and control. And he had at least learned that everything could not be taken. She thought probably he had learned more.

He frowned, then shrugged the contradiction aside. "If you see it so. I don't. But in either case, I am interested in your answer, not in a long argument. I've walked too far today for that."

"And what if the only answer I can give you is that I will think about it?"

His eyes flashed. "Are you telling me no?"

"No," she said softly. "I'm telling you that I must think about it a while longer." If she chose to make her home with him—and she thought that eventually she would—she would not have a serene life or an easy one. There would always be ambitions and schemes and contradictions—and enemies too. That was his nature. And it would never be her nature to accede blindly to him. But there would be good things too, and together they would balance each other and influence the shape of the future along their coastline. She thought that was important.

Had she wanted quiet and peace, after all, she could have remained in the library at Wahonin. "If you will come to Wahonin for the harvest festival, I will give you an answer then."

Rinari's brows arched. "Ah," he said with quick, pleased comprehension. "You were thinking about your answer well before I came with my question."

"Yes," she admitted. She had thought about it even before Kentith left for the inland. It had been obvious to her that the question would be asked.

Rinari's pleasure lasted for a moment, then evaporated as quickly as it had come. He paced away from her to the edge of the plaza and gazed up at the gathering quirri. His face was guarded when he turned back, his eyes intent. "And do you see anything in this alliance beyond mutual comfort and convenience?"

Dara almost laughed aloud at that. Comfort and convenience were the last things she expected from any alliance with Lord Blackhand of the Autonomous Coastal

District of Calibe. "I told you just a moment ago, Rinari. I have been thinking of you."

His expression remained guarded for several moments longer. Then his eyes glinted, first with relief and then with something like fervor. "And I have been thinking of you."

His embarrassment at the utterance was immediate. Flushing, he averted his eyes, scowling down at the perfectly groomed nails of his undamaged hand. He cleared his throat. "Very well. If we've settled that, how long do you intend to keep me standing here hungry?"

Dara did laugh then, and after a moment Rinari was able to laugh, too, although the scarlet refused to leave his face. Then they went into the hall to share a meal and argue plans.

When SYDNEY J. VAN SCYOC graduated from high school in 1957, she discovered that being at the top of her class in math and science was not a plus for a young woman: several colleges refused to send her application forms when they learned she wanted to study in their engineering and technical writing programs. Realizing that she wasn't going to get a scholarship for science or math, she married and the next year acquired a venerable Underwood typewriter and started writing fiction. Early on she decided to submit her work under her first name, Sydney, because "Joyce was the individual who was refused college application forms." *Galaxy* published her first short story.

Currently Ms. Van Scyoc and her husband live in Hayward, California, on the one-acre remnant of a dairy farm. She converted the milk processing shed into an office and reports, "There is a drain in one corner of the floor so I can hose away excess verbiage. I store old manuscripts in the odd construction we call the refrigerator-bump. The barn stands ten feet from my desk. If I forget to feed the pony before sitting down to work, she loudly reminds me."

Sydney J. Van Scyoc is the author of nine science fiction novels, among them *Darkchild, Bluesong,* and *Starsilk.* FEATHER STROKE, her tenth published novel, is her very first fantasy.